Reserve

# THE MURDER AT
# THE VICARAGE

## This is the Story

IN the peaceful village of St. Mary Mead nothing ever happens. So it seems almost incredible when Colonel Protheroe, the churchwarden, is discovered, shot through the head, in the Vicarage study.

Everybody thinks they know who has done it—including Miss Marple, the real old maid of the village who knows everything and sees everything and hears everything! She declares that at least *seven* people have reasons for wishing Colonel Protheroe out of the way!

Excitement dies down when somebody confesses to having committed the crime. But that is not the end, for almost immediately somebody quite different also confesses! And there is a third confession through the telephone!

But who *really* killed Colonel Protheroe?

### By the Same Author

THE MURDER OF ROGER ACKROYD      THE BIG FOUR

THE MYSTERY OF THE BLUE TRAIN      PARTNERS IN CRIME

THE SEVEN DIALS MYSTERY    THE MYSTERIOUS MR. QUIN

# THE MURDER AT THE VICARAGE
## AGATHA CHRISTIE

*Published for*

# THE CRIME CLUB LTD.

*by*

W. COLLINS SONS & CO LTD

LONDON

HarperCollins*Publishers*
77–85 Fulham Palace Road,
Hammersmith, London W6 8JB
www.harpercollins.co.uk

This facsimile edition published by HarperCollins*Publishers* 2005

1

First published in Great Britain by
Collins, The Crime Club 1930

ISBN 0 00 720842 1

Printed and bound in Great Britain by
Clays Ltd, St Ives plc

To
ROSALIND

# CHAPTER I

It is difficult to know quite where to begin this story, but I have fixed my choice on a certain Wednesday at luncheon at the Vicarage. The conversation, though in the main irrelevant to the matter in hand, yet contained one or two suggestive incidents which influenced later developments.

I had just finished carving some boiled beef (remarkably tough by the way) and on resuming my seat I remarked, in a spirit most unbecoming to my cloth, that any one who murdered Colonel Protheroe would be doing the world at large a service.

My young nephew, Dennis, said instantly:

"That'll be remembered against you when the old boy is found bathed in blood. Mary will give evidence, won't you, Mary? And describe how you brandished the carving knife in a vindictive manner."

Mary, who is in service at the Vicarage as a stepping-stone to better things and higher wages, merely said in a loud, business-like voice, "Greens," and thrust a cracked dish at him in a truculent manner.

My wife said in a sympathetic voice: "Has he been *very* trying?"

I did not reply at once, for Mary, setting the greens on the table with a bang, proceeded to thrust a dish of singularly moist and unpleasant dumplings under my nose. I said, "No, thank you," and she deposited the dish with a clatter on the table and left the room.

"It is a pity that I am such a shocking housekeeper," said my wife, with a tinge of genuine regret in her voice.

I was inclined to agree with her. My wife's name is Griselda—a highly suitable name for a parson's wife. But there the suitability ends. She is not in the least meek.

7

I have always been of the opinion that a clergyman should be unmarried. Why I should have urged Griselda to marry me at the end of twenty-four hours' acquaintance is a mystery to me. Marriage, I have always held, is a serious affair, to be entered into only after long deliberation and forethought, and suitability of tastes and inclinations is the most important consideration.

Griselda is nearly twenty years younger than myself. She is most distractingly pretty and quite incapable of taking anything seriously. She is incompetent in every way, and extremely trying to live with. She treats the parish as a kind of huge joke arranged for her amusement. I have endeavoured to form her mind and failed. I am more than ever convinced that celibacy is desirable for the clergy. I have frequently hinted as much to Griselda, but she has only laughed.

" My dear," I said, " if you would only exercise a little care——"

" I do sometimes," said Griselda. " But, on the whole, I think things go worse when I'm trying. I'm evidently *not* a housekeeper by nature. I find it better to leave things to Mary and just make up my mind to be uncomfortable and have nasty things to eat."

" And what about your husband, my dear ? " I said reproachfully, and proceeding to follow the example of the devil in quoting Scripture for his own ends I added : " She looketh to the ways of her household . . ."

" Think how lucky you are not to be torn to pieces by lions," said Griselda, quickly interrupting. " Or burnt at the stake. Bad food and lots of dust and dead wasps is really nothing to make a fuss about. Tell me more about Colonel Protheroe. At anyrate the early Christians were lucky enough not to have churchwardens."

" Pompous old brute," said Dennis. " No wonder his first wife ran away from him."

" I don't see what else she could do," said my wife.

" Griselda," I said sharply. " I will not have you speaking in that way."

"Darling," said my wife affectionately. "Tell me about him. What was the trouble ? Was it Mr. Hawes's becking and nodding and crossing himself every other minute ? "

Hawes is our new curate. He has been with us just over three weeks. He has High Church views and fasts on Fridays. Colonel Protheroe is a great opposer of ritual in any form.

"Not this time. He did touch on it in passing. No, the whole trouble arose out of Mrs. Price Ridley's wretched pound note."

Mrs. Price Ridley is a devout member of my congregation. Attending early service on the anniversary of her son's death, she put a pound note into the offertory bag. Later, reading the amount of the collection posted up, she was pained to observe that one ten-shilling note was the highest item mentioned.

She complained to me about it, and I pointed out, very reasonably, that she must have made a mistake.

"We're none of us so young as we were," I said, trying to turn it off tactfully. "And we must pay the penalty of advancing years."

Strangely enough, my words only seemed to incense her further. She said that things had a very odd look and that she was surprised I didn't think so also. And she flounced away and, I gather, took her troubles to Colonel Protheroe. Protheroe is the kind of man who enjoys making a fuss on every conceivable occasion. He made a fuss. It is a pity he made it on a Wednesday. I teach in the Church Day School on Wednesday mornings, a proceeding that causes me acute nervousness and leaves me unsettled for the rest of the day.

"Well, I suppose he must have some fun," said my wife, with the air of trying to sum up the position impartially. "Nobody flutters round him and calls him the dear vicar, and embroiders awful slippers for him, and gives him bed-socks for Christmas. Both his wife and his daughter are fed to the teeth with him. I suppose it makes him happy to feel important somewhere."

" He needn't be offensive about it," I said with some heat. " I don't think he quite realised the implications of what he was saying. He wants to go over all the Church accounts—in case of defalcations—that was the word he used. Defalcations ! Does he suspect me of embezzling the Church funds ? "

" Nobody would suspect you of anything, darling," said Griselda. " You're so transparently above sus-picion that really it would be a marvellous opportunity. I wish you'd embezzle the S.P.G. funds. I hate missionaries—I always have."

I would have reproved her for that sentiment, but Mary entered at that moment with a partially cooked rice pudding. I made a mild protest, but Griselda said that the Japanese always ate half-cooked rice and had marvellous brains in consequence.

" I dare say," she said, " that if you had a rice pudding like this every day till Sunday, you'd preach the most marvellous sermon."

" Heaven forbid," I said with a shudder.

" Protheroe's coming over to-morrow evening and we're going over the accounts together," I went on. " I must finish preparing my talk for the C.E.M.S. to-day. Looking up a reference, I became so engrossed in Canon Shirley's *Reality* that I haven't got on as well as I should. What are you doing this afternoon, Griselda ? "

" My duty," said Griselda. " My duty as the Vicaress. Tea and scandal at four-thirty."

" Who is coming ? "

Griselda ticked them off on her fingers with a glow of virtue on her face.

" Mrs. Price Ridley, Miss Wetherby, Miss Hartnell, and that terrible Miss Marple."

" I rather like Miss Marple," I said. " She has, at least, a sense of humour."

" She's the worst cat in the village," said Griselda. " And she always knows every single thing that happens —and draws the worst inferences from it."

Griselda, as I have said, is much younger than I am. At my time of life, one knows that the worst is usually true.

"Well, don't expect *me* in for tea, Griselda," said Dennis.

"Beast!" said Griselda.

"Yes, but look here, the Protheroes really *did* ask me for tennis to-day."

"Beast!" said Griselda again.

Dennis beat a prudent retreat and Griselda and I went together into my study.

"I wonder what we shall have for tea," said Griselda, seating herself on my writing table. "Dr. Stone and Miss Cram, I suppose, and perhaps Mrs. Lestrange. By the way, I called on her yesterday, but she was out. Yes, I'm sure we shall have Mrs. Lestrange for tea. It's so mysterious, isn't it, her arriving like this and taking a house down here, and hardly ever going outside it? Makes one think of detective stories. You know—"*Who was she, the mysterious woman with the pale, beautiful face? What was her past history? Nobody knew. There was something faintly sinister about her.*" I believe Dr. Haydock knows something about her."

"You read too many detective stories, Griselda," I observed mildly.

"What about you?" she retorted. "I was looking everywhere for *The Stain on the Stairs* the other day when you were in here writing a sermon. And at last I came in to ask you if you'd seen it anywhere, and what did I find?"

I had the grace to blush.

"I picked it up at random. A chance sentence caught my eye and——"

"I know those chance sentences," said Griselda. She quoted impressively, "*And then a very curious thing happened—Griselda rose, crossed the room and kissed her elderly husband affectionately.*"

She suited the action to the word.

"Is that a very curious thing?" I inquired.

" Of course it is," said Griselda. " Do you realise, Len, that I might have married a Cabinet Minister, a Baronet, a rich Company Promoter, three subalterns and a ne'er-do-weel with attractive manners, and that instead I chose you ? Didn't it astonish you very much ? "

" At the time it did," I replied. " I have often wondered why you did it."

Griselda laughed.

" It made me feel so powerful," she murmured. " The others thought me simply wonderful and of course it would have been very nice for *them* to have *me*. But I'm everything you most dislike and disapprove of, and yet you couldn't withstand me ! My vanity couldn't hold out against that. It's so much nicer to be a secret and delightful sin to anybody than to be a feather in their cap. I make you frightfully uncomfortable and stir you up the wrong way the whole time, and yet you adore me madly. You do adore me madly, don't you ? "

" Naturally I am very fond of you, my dear."

" Oh ! Len, you adore me. Do you remember that day when I stayed up in town and sent you a wire you never got because the postmistress's sister was having twins and she forgot to send it round ? The state you got into and you telephoned Scotland Yard and made the most frightful fuss."

There are things one hates being reminded of. I had really been strangely foolish on the occasion in question. I said :

" If you don't mind, dear, I want to get on with the C.E.M.S."

Griselda gave a sigh of intense irritation, ruffled my hair up on end, smoothed it down again, said :

" You don't deserve me. You really don't. I'll have an affair with the artist. I will—really and truly. And then think of the scandal in the parish."

" There's a good deal already," I said mildly.

Griselda laughed, blew me a kiss, and departed through the window.

# CHAPTER II.

GRISELDA is a very irritating woman. On leaving the luncheon table, I had felt myself to be in a good mood for preparing a really forceful address for the Church of England Men's Society. Now I felt restless and disturbed.

Just when I was really settling down to it, Lettice Protheroe drifted in.

I use the word drifted advisedly. I have read novels in which young people are described as bursting with energy—*joie de vivre*, the magnificent vitality of youth. . . . Personally, all the young people I come across have the air of amiable wraiths.

Lettice was particularly wraith-like this afternoon. She is a pretty girl, very tall and fair and completely vague. She drifted through the French window, absently pulled off the yellow beret she was wearing and murmured vaguely with a kind of far-away surprise :

" Oh ! it's you."

There is a path from Old Hall through the woods which comes out by our garden gate, so that most people coming from there come in at that gate and up to the study window instead of going a long way round by the road and coming to the front door. I was not surprised at Lettice coming in this way, but I did a little resent her attitude.

If you come to a Vicarage, you ought to be prepared to find a Vicar.

She came in and collapsed in a crumpled heap in one of my big arm-chairs. She plucked aimlessly at her hair, staring at the ceiling.

" Is Dennis anywhere about ? "

" I haven't seen him since lunch. I understood he was going to play tennis at your place."

" Oh ! " said Lettice. " I hope he isn't. He won't find anybody there."

13

"He said you asked him."

"I believe I did. Only that was Friday. And to-day's Tuesday."

"It's Wednesday," I said.

"Oh! how dreadful," said Lettice. "That means that I've forgotten to go to lunch with some people for the third time."

Fortunately it didn't seem to worry her much.

"Is Griselda anywhere about?"

"I expect you'll find her in the studio in the garden —sitting to Lawrence Redding."

"There's been quite a shemozzle about him," said Lettice. "With father, you know. Father's dreadful."

"What was the she—whatever it was about?" I inquired.

"About his painting me. Father found out about it. Why shouldn't I be painted in my bathing dress? If I go on a beach in it, why shouldn't I be painted in it?"

Lettice paused and then went on.

"It's really absurd—father forbidding a young man the house. Of course, Lawrence and I simply shriek about it. I shall come and be done here in your studio."

"No, my dear," I said. "Not if your father forbids it."

"Oh! dear," said Lettice, sighing. "How tiresome every one is. I feel shattered. Definitely. If only I had some money I'd go away, but without it I can't. If only father would be decent and die, I should be all right."

"You must not say things like that, Lettice."

"Well, if he doesn't want me to want him to die, he shouldn't be so horrible over money. I don't wonder mother left him. Do you know, for years I believed she was dead. What sort of a young man did she run away with? Was he nice?"

"It was before your father came to live here."

"I wonder what's become of her. I expect Anne will have an affair with some one soon. Anne hates me—she's quite decent to me, but she hates me. She's getting old and she doesn't like it. That's the age you break out, you know."

I wondered if Lettice was going to spend the entire afternoon in my study.

"You haven't seen my gramophone records, have you?" she asked.

"No."

"How tiresome. I know I've left them somewhere. And I've lost the dog. And my wrist watch is somewhere, only it doesn't much matter because it won't go. Oh! dear, I am so sleepy. I can't think why, because I didn't get up till eleven. But life's very shattering, don't you think? Oh! dear, I must go. I'm going to see Dr. Stone's barrow at three o'clock."

I glanced at the clock and remarked that it was now five-and-twenty to four.

"Oh! is it? How dreadful. I wonder if they've waited or if they've gone without me. I suppose I'd better go down and do something about it."

She got up and drifted out again, murmuring over her shoulder :

"You'll tell Dennis, won't you?"

I said "Yes" mechanically, only realising too late that I had no idea what it was I was to tell Dennis. But I reflected that in all probability it did not matter. I fell to cogitating on the subject of Dr. Stone, a well-known archæologist who had recently come to stay at the Blue Boar, whilst he superintended the excavation of a barrow situated on Colonel Protheroe's property. There had already been several disputes between him and the colonel. I was amused at his appointment to take Lettice to see the operations.

It occurred to me that Lettice Protheroe was something of a minx. I wondered how she would get on with the archæologist's secretary, Miss Cram. Miss Cram is a healthy young woman of twenty-five, noisy in manner, with a high colour, fine animal spirits and a mouth that always seems to have more than its full share of teeth.

Village opinion is divided as to whether she is no better than she should be, or else a young woman of iron virtue who purposes to become Mrs. Stone at an early opportunity. She is in every way a great contrast to Lettice.

I could imagine that the state of things at Old Hall might not be too happy. Colonel Protheroe had married again some five years previously. The second Mrs. Protheroe was a remarkably handsome woman in a rather unusual style. I had always guessed that the relations between her and her stepdaughter were not too happy.

I had one more interruption. This time, it was my curate, Hawes. He wanted to know the details of my interview with Protheroe. I told him that the colonel had deplored his " Romish tendencies " but that the real purpose of his visit had been on quite another matter. At the same time, I entered a protest of my own, and told him plainly that he must conform to my ruling. On the whole, he took my remarks very well.

I felt rather remorseful when he had gone for not liking him better. These irrational likes and dislikes that one takes to people are, I am sure, very un-Christian.

With a sigh, I realised that the hands of the clock on my writing-table pointed to a quarter to five, a sign that it was really half-past four, and I made my way to the drawing-room.

Four of my parishioners were assembled there with teacups. Griselda sat behind the tea table trying to look natural in her environment, but only succeeding in looking more out of place than usual.

I shook hands all round and sat down between Miss Marple and Miss Wetherby.

Miss Marple is a white-haired old lady with a gentle, appealing manner—Miss Wetherby is a mixture of vinegar and gush. Of the two Miss Marple is much the more dangerous.

"We were just talking," said Griselda in a honey-sweet voice, "about Dr. Stone and Miss Cram."

A ribald rhyme concocted by Dennis shot through my head.

"Miss Cram doesn't give a damn."

I had a sudden yearning to say it out loud and observe the effect, but fortunately I refrained.

Miss Wetherby said tersely:

"No nice girl would do it," and shut her thin lips disapprovingly.

"Do what?" I inquired.

"Be a secretary to an unmarried man," said Miss Wetherby in a horrified tone.

"Oh! my dear," said Miss Marple, "*I* think married ones are the worst. Remember poor Mollie Carter."

"Married men living apart from their wives are, of course, notorious," said Miss Wetherby.

"And even some of the ones living with their wives," murmured Miss Marple. "I remember——"

I interrupted these unsavoury reminiscences.

"But surely," I said, "in these days a girl can take a post in just the same way as a man does."

"To come away to the country? And stay at the same hotel?" said Mrs. Price Ridley in a severe voice.

Miss Wetherby murmured to Miss Marple in a low voice.

"And all the bedrooms on the same floor. . . ."

They exchanged glances.

Miss Hartnell, who is weather-beaten and jolly and much dreaded by the poor, observed in a loud, hearty voice:

"The poor man will be caught before he knows where he is. He's as innocent as a babe unborn, you can see that."

Curious what turns of phrase we employ. None of the ladies present would have dreamed of alluding to an actual baby till it was safely in the cradle, visible to all.

"Disgusting, I call it," continued Miss Hartnell, with

B

her usual tactlessness. "The man must be at least twenty-five years older than she is."

Three female voices rose at once making disconnected remarks about the Choir Boys' Outing, the regrettable incident at the last Mothers' Meeting, and the draughts in the church. Miss Marple twinkled at Griselda.

"Don't you think," said my wife, "that Miss Cram may just like having an interesting job ? And that she considers Dr. Stone just as an employer."

There was a silence. Evidently none of the four ladies agreed. Miss Marple broke the silence by patting Griselda on the arm.

"My dear," she said, "you are very young. The young have such innocent minds."

Griselda said indignantly that she hadn't got at all an innocent mind.

"Naturally," said Miss Marple, unheeding of the protest, "you think the best of every one."

"Do you really think she wants to marry that bald-headed dull man ? "

"I understand he is quite well off," said Miss Marple. "Rather a violent temper, I'm afraid. He had quite a serious quarrel with Colonel Protheroe the other day."

Every one leaned forward interestedly.

"Colonel Protheroe accused him of being an ignoramus."

"How like Colonel Protheroe, and how absurd," said Mrs. Price Ridley.

"Very like Colonel Protheroe, but I don't know about it being absurd," said Miss Marple. "You remember the woman who came down here and said she represented Welfare, and after taking subscriptions she was never heard of again and proved to have nothing whatever to do with Welfare. One is so inclined to be trusting and take people at their own valuation."

I should never have dreamed of describing Miss Marple as trusting.

"There's been some fuss about that young artist, Mr. Redding, hasn't there ? " asked Miss Wetherby.

Miss Marple nodded.

" Colonel Protheroe turned him out of the house. It appears he was painting Lettice in her bathing dress."

Suitable sensation !

" I always *thought* there was something between them," said Mrs. Price Ridley. " That young fellow is always mouching off up there. Pity the girl hasn't got a mother. A stepmother is never the same thing."

" I dare say Mrs. Protheroe does her best," said Miss Hartnell.

" Girls are so sly," deplored Mrs. Price Ridley.

" Quite a romance, isn't it ? " said the softer-hearted Miss Wetherby. " He's a very good-looking young fellow."

" But loose," said Miss Hartnell. " Bound to be. An artist ! Paris ! Models ! The Altogether ! "

" Painting her in her bathing dress," said Mrs. Price Ridley. " Not quite nice."

" He's painting me too," said Griselda.

" But not in your bathing dress, dear," said Miss Marple.

" It might be worse," said Griselda solemnly.

" Naughty girl," said Miss Hartnell, taking the joke broad-mindedly. Everybody else looked slightly shocked.

" Did dear Lettice tell you of the trouble ? " asked Miss Marple of me.

" Tell me ? "

" Yes. I saw her pass through the garden and go round to the study window."

Miss Marple always sees everything. Gardening is as good as a smoke screen, and the habit of observing birds through powerful glasses can always be turned to account.

" She mentioned it, yes," I admitted.

" Mr. Hawes looked worried," said Miss Marple. " I hope he hasn't been working too hard."

" Oh ! " cried Miss Wetherby excitedly. " I quite

forgot. I knew I had some news for you. I saw Dr. Haydock coming out of Mrs. Lestrange's cottage."

Every one looked at each other.

" Perhaps she's ill," suggested Mrs. Price Ridley.

" It must have been very sudden, if so," said Miss Hartnell. " For I saw her walking round her garden at three o'clock this afternoon, and she seemed in perfect health."

" She and Dr. Haydock must be old acquaintances," said Mrs. Price Ridley. " He's been very quiet about it."

" It's curious," said Miss Wetherby, " that he's never *mentioned* it."

" As a matter of fact——" said Griselda in a low, mysterious voice, and stopped.

Every one leaned forward excitedly.

" I happen to *know*," said Griselda impressively. " Her husband was a missionary. Terrible story. *He was eaten*, you know. Actually eaten. And she was forced to become the chief's head wife. Dr. Haydock was with an expedition and rescued her."

For a moment excitement was rife, then Miss Marple said reproachfully, but with a smile :

" Naughty girl ! "

She tapped Griselda reprovingly on the arm.

" Very unwise thing to do, my dear. If you make up these things, people are quite likely to believe them. And sometimes that leads to complications."

A distinct frost had come over the assembly. Two of the ladies rose to take their departure.

" I wonder if there *is* anything between young Lawrence Redding and Lettice Protheroe," said Miss Wetherby. " It certainly looks like it. What do you think, Miss Marple ? "

Miss Marple seemed thoughtful.

" I shouldn't have said so myself. Not *Lettice*. *Quite* another person I should have said."

" But Colonel Protheroe must have thought——"

" He has always struck me as rather a stupid man," said Miss Marple. " The kind of man who gets the wrong idea into his head and is obstinate about it. Do you remember Joe Bucknell who used to keep the Blue Boar? Such a to-do about his daughter carrying on with young Bailey. And all the time it was that minx of a wife of his."

She was looking full at Griselda as she spoke, and I suddenly felt a wild surge of anger.

"Don't you think, Miss Marple," I said, "that we're all inclined to let our tongues run away with us too much. Charity thinketh no evil, you know. Inestimable harm may be done by the foolish wagging of tongues in ill-natured gossip."

"Dear Vicar," said Miss Marple, "you are so un-worldly. I'm afraid that observing human nature for as long as I have done, one gets not to expect very much from it. I dare say idle tittle-tattle is very wrong and unkind, but it is so often true, isn't it?"

That last Parthian shot went home.

# CHAPTER III

" NASTY old cat," said Griselda, as soon as the door was closed.

She made a face in the direction of the departing visitors and then looked at me and laughed.

" Len, do you really suspect me of having an affair with Lawrence Redding ? "

" My dear, of course not."

" But you thought Miss Marple was hinting at it. And you rose to my defence simply beautifully. Like —like an angry tiger."

A momentary uneasiness assailed me. A clergyman of the Church of England ought never to put himself in the position of being described as an angry tiger. However, I trusted that Griselda exaggerated.

" I felt the occasion could not pass without a protest," I said. " But Griselda, I wish you would be a little more careful in what you say."

" Do you mean the cannibal story ? " she asked. " Or the suggestion that Lawrence was painting me in the nude ! If they only knew that he was painting me in a thick cloak with a very high fur collar—the sort of thing that you could go quite purely to see the Pope in—not a bit of sinful flesh showing anywhere ! In fact, it's all marvellously pure. Lawrence never even attempts to make love to me—I can't think why."

" Surely, knowing that you're a married woman——"

" Don't pretend to come out of the ark, Len. You know very well that an attractive young woman with an elderly husband is a kind of gift from heaven to a young man. There must be some other reason—it's not that I'm unattractive—I'm not."

" Surely you don't want him to make love to you ? "

" N-n-o," said Griselda, with more hesitation than I thought becoming.

22

" If he's in love with Lettice Protheroe——"

" Miss Marple didn't seem to think he was."

" Miss Marple may be mistaken."

" She never is. That kind of old cat is always right."
She paused a minute and then said, with a quick side-
long glance at me : " You do believe me, don't you ?
I mean, that there's nothing between Lawrence and
me."

" My dear Griselda," I said, surprised. " Of course."
My wife came across and kissed me.

" I wish you weren't so terribly easy to deceive, Len.
You'd believe me whatever I said."

" I should hope so. But, my dear, I do beg of you
to guard your tongue and be careful what you say.
These women are singularly deficient in humour,
remember, and take everything seriously."

" What they need," said Griselda, " is a little im-
morality in their lives. Then they wouldn't be so busy
looking for it in other people's."

And on this she left the room, and glancing at my
watch I hurried out to pay some visits that ought to
have been made earlier in the day.

The Wednesday evening service was sparsely attended
as usual, but when I came out through the church, after
disrobing in the vestry, it was empty save for a woman
who stood staring up at one of our windows. We have
some rather fine old stained glass, and indeed the church
itself is well worth looking at. She turned at my footsteps, and I saw that it was Mrs. Lestrange.

We both hesitated a moment, and then I said :

" I hope you like our little church."

" I've been admiring the screen," she said.

Her voice was pleasant, low, yet very distinct, with a
clear-cut enunciation. She added :

" I'm so sorry to have missed your wife yesterday."

We talked a few minutes longer about the church.
She was evidently a cultured woman who knew something of Church history and architecture. We left the
building together and walked down the road, since one

way to the Vicarage led past her house. As we arrived at the gate, she said pleasantly :

" Come in, won't you ? And tell me what you think of what I have done."

I accepted the invitation. Little Gates had formerly belonged to an Anglo-Indian colonel, and I could not help feeling relieved by the disappearance of the brass tables and the Burmese idols. It was furnished now very simply, but in exquisite taste. There was a sense of harmony and rest about it.

Yet I wondered more and more what had brought such a woman as Mrs. Lestrange to St. Mary Mead. She was so very clearly a woman of the world that it seemed a strange taste to bury herself in a country village.

In the clear light of her drawing-room I had an opportunity of observing her closely for the first time.

She was a very tall woman. Her hair was gold with a tinge of red in it. Her eyebrows and eyelashes were dark, whether by art or by nature I could not decide. If she was, as I thought, made up, it was done very artistically. There was something Sphinxlike about her face when it was in repose and she had the most curious eyes I have ever seen—they were almost golden in shade.

Her clothes were perfect and she had all the ease of manner of a well-bred woman, and yet there was something about her that was incongruous and baffling. You felt that she was a mystery. The word Griselda had used occurred to me—*sinister*. Absurd, of course, and yet—was it so absurd ? The thought sprang un-bidden into my mind : " This woman would stick at nothing."

Our talk was on most normal lines—pictures, books, old churches. Yet somehow I got very strongly the impression that there was something else—something of quite a different nature that Mrs. Lestrange wanted to say to me.

I caught her eyes on me once or twice, looking at me

with a curious hesitancy, as though she were unable to make up her mind. She kept the talk, I noticed, strictly to impersonal subjects. She made no mention of a husband, or of friends or relations.

But all the time there was that strange urgent appeal in her glance. It seemed to say : " Shall I tell you ? I want to. Can't you help me ? "

Yet in the end it died away—or perhaps it had all been my fancy. I had the feeling that I was being dismissed. I rose and took my leave. As I went out of the room, I glanced back and saw her staring after me with a puzzled, doubtful expression. On an impulse I came back :

" If there is anything I can do——"

She said doubtfully : " It's very kind of you——"

We were both silent. Then she said :

" I wish I knew. It's very difficult. No, I don't think any one can help me. But thank you for offering to do so."

That seemed final, so I went. But as I did so, I wondered. We are not used to mysteries in St. Mary Mead.

So much is this the case that as I emerged from the gate I was pounced upon. Miss Hartnell is very good at pouncing in a heavy and cumbrous way.

" *I* saw you ! " she exclaimed with ponderous humour. " And I *was* so excited. Now can you tell us all about it."

" About what ? "

" The mysterious lady ! Is she a widow or has she a husband somewhere ? "

" I really couldn't say. She didn't tell me."

" How very peculiar. One would think she would be certain to mention something casually. It almost looks, doesn't it, as though she had a reason for not speaking ? "

" I really don't see that."

" Ah ! but as dear Miss Marple says, you are so unworldly, dear vicar. Tell me, has she known Dr. Haydock long ? "

" She didn't mention him, so I don't know."

" Really ?  But what did you talk about then ? "

" Pictures, music, books," I said truthfully.

Miss Hartnell, whose only topics of conversation are the purely personal, looked suspicious and unbelieving. Taking advantage of a momentary hesitation on her part as to how to proceed next, I bade her good-night and walked rapidly away.

I called in at a house farther down the village and returned to the Vicarage by the garden gate, passing, as I did so, the danger point of Miss Marple's garden. However, I did not see how it was humanly possible for the news of my visit to Mrs. Lestrange to have yet reached her ears, so I felt reasonably safe.

As I latched the gate, it occurred to me that I would just step down to the shed in the garden which young Lawrence Redding was using as a studio, and see for myself how Griselda's portrait was progressing.

I append a rough sketch here which will be useful in the light of after happenings, only sketching in such details as are necessary.

I had no idea there was any one in the studio. There had been no voices from within to warn me, and I suppose that my own footsteps made no noise upon the grass.

I opened the door and then stopped awkwardly on the threshold. For there were two people in the studio, and the man's arms were round the woman and he was kissing her passionately.

The two people were the artist, Lawrence Redding, and Mrs. Protheroe.

I backed out precipitately and beat a retreat to my study. There I sat down in a chair, took out my pipe, and thought things over. The discovery had come as a great shock to me. Especially since my conversation with Lettice that afternoon, I had felt fairly certain that there was some kind of understanding growing up between her and the young man. Moreover, I was convinced that she herself thought so. I felt positive

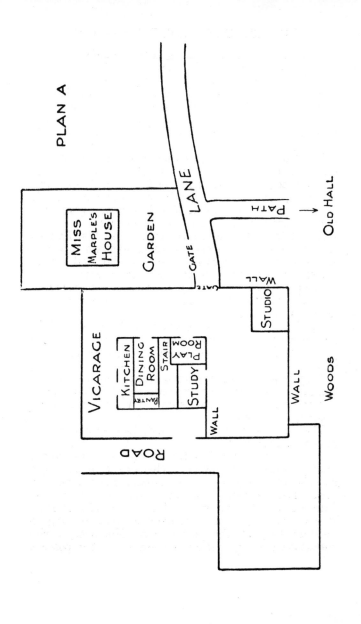

that she had no idea of the artist's feelings for her stepmother.

A nasty tangle. I paid a grudging tribute to Miss Marple. She had not been deceived but had evidently suspected the true state of things with a fair amount of accuracy. I had entirely misread her meaning glance at Griselda.

I had never dreamed of considering Mrs. Protheroe in the matter. There has always been rather a suggestion of Cæsar's wife about Mrs. Protheroe—a quiet, self-contained woman whom one would not suspect of any great depths of feeling.

I had got to this point in my meditations when a tap on my study window aroused me. I got up and went to it. Mrs. Protheroe was standing outside. I opened the window and she came in, not waiting for an invitation on my part. She crossed the room in a breathless sort of way and dropped down on the sofa.

I had the feeling that I had never really seen her before. The quiet self-contained woman that I knew had vanished. In her place was a quick-breathing, desperate creature. For the first time I realised that Anne Protheroe was beautiful.

She was a brown-haired woman with a pale face and very deep set grey eyes. She was flushed now and her breast heaved. It was as though a statue had suddenly come to life. I blinked my eyes at the transformation.

" I thought it best to come," she said. " You—you saw just now ? "

I bowed my head.

She said very quietly : " We love each other. . . ."

And even in the middle of her evident distress and agitation she could not keep a little smile from her lips. The smile of a woman who sees something very beautiful and wonderful.

I still said nothing, and she added presently :

" I suppose to you that seems very wrong ? "

" Can you expect me to say anything else, Mrs. Protheroe ? "

" No—no, I suppose not."

I went on, trying to make my voice as gentle as possible :

" You are a married woman———"

She interrupted me.

" Oh ! I know—I know. Do you think I haven't gone over all that again and again ? I'm not a bad woman really—I'm not. And things aren't—aren't—as you might think they are."

I said gravely : " I'm glad of that."

She asked rather timorously :

" Are you going to tell my husband ? "

I said rather dryly :

" There seems to be a general idea that a clergyman is incapable of behaving like a gentleman. That is not true."

She threw me a grateful glance.

" I'm so unhappy. Oh ! I'm so dreadfully unhappy. I can't go on. I simply can't go on. And I don't know what to do." Her voice rose with a slightly hysterical note in it. " You don't know what my life is like. I've been miserable with Lucius from the beginning. No woman could be happy with him. I wish he were dead. . . . It's awful, but I do . . . I'm desperate. I tell you, I'm desperate."

She started and looked over at the window.

" What was that ? I thought I heard some one ? Perhaps it's Lawrence."

I went over to the window which I had not closed as I had thought. I stepped out and looked down the garden, but there was no one in sight. Yet I was almost convinced that I, too, had heard some one. Or perhaps it was her certainty that had convinced me.

When I re-entered the room she was leaning forward, drooping her head down. She looked the picture of despair. She said again :

" I don't know what to do. I don't know what to do."

I came and sat down beside her. I said the things I thought it was my duty to say, and tried to say them

with the necessary conviction, uneasily conscious all
the time that that same morning I had given voice to
the sentiment that a world without Colonel Protheroe
in it would be improved for the better.

Above all, I begged her to do nothing rash. To leave
her home and her husband was a very serious step.

I don't suppose I convinced her. I have lived long
enough in the world to know that arguing with any one
in love is next door to useless, but I do think my words
brought to her some measure of comfort.

When she rose to go, she thanked me, and promised
to think over what I had said.

Nevertheless, when she had gone, I felt very uneasy.
I felt that hitherto I had misjudged Anne Protheroe's
character. She impressed me now as a very desperate
woman, the kind of woman who would stick at nothing
once her emotions were aroused. And she was desperately, wildly, madly in love with Lawrence Redding,
a man several years younger than herself.

I didn't like it.

# CHAPTER IV

I HAD entirely forgotten that we had asked Lawrence Redding to dinner that night. When Griselda burst in and scolded me, pointing out that it lacked two minutes to dinner time, I was quite taken aback.

" I hope everything will be all right," Griselda called up the stairs after me. " I've thought over what you said at lunch, and I've really thought of some quite good things to eat."

I may say, in passing, that our evening meal amply bore out Griselda's assertion that things went much worse when she tried than when she didn't. The menu was ambitious in conception, and Mary seemed to have taken a perverse pleasure in seeing how best she could alternate undercooking and overcooking. Some oysters which Griselda had ordered, and which would seem to be beyond the reach of incompetence, we were, unfortunately, not able to sample as we had nothing in the house to open them with—an omission which was discovered only when the moment for eating them arrived.

I had rather doubted whether Lawrence Redding would put in an appearance. He might very easily have sent an excuse.

However, he arrived punctually enough, and the four of us went in to dinner.

Lawrence Redding has an undeniably attractive personality. He is, I suppose, about thirty years of age. He has dark hair, but his eyes are of a brilliant, almost startling blue. He is the kind of young man who does everything well. He is good at games, an excellent shot, a good amateur actor, and can tell a first-rate story. He is capable of making any party go. He has, I think, Irish blood in his veins. He is not, at all, one's idea of the typical artist. Yet I believe he is a clever painter in

31

the modern style. I know very little of painting myself.

It was only natural that on this particular evening
he should appear a shade *distrait*. On the whole, he
carried off things very well. I don't think Griselda or
Dennis noticed anything wrong. Probably I should not
have noticed anything myself if I had not known
beforehand.

Griselda and Dennis were particularly gay—full of
jokes about Dr. Stone and Miss Cram—the Local
Scandal! It suddenly came home to me with something
of a pang that Dennis is nearer Griselda's age than I
am. He calls me Uncle Len, but her Griselda. It gave
me, somehow, a lonely feeling.

I must, I think, have been upset by Mrs. Protheroe.
I'm not usually given to such unprofitable reflections.

Griselda and Dennis went rather far now and then,
but I hadn't the heart to check them. I have always
thought it a pity that the mere presence of a clergyman
should have a damping effect.

Lawrence took a gay part in the conversation.
Nevertheless I was aware of his eyes continually straying
to where I sat, and I was not surprised when after dinner
he manœuvred to get me into the study.

As soon as we were alone his manner changed. His
face became grave and anxious. He looked almost
haggard.

" You've surprised our secret, sir," he said. " What
are you going to do about it ? "

I could speak far more plainly to Redding than I
could to Mrs. Protheroe, and I did so. He took it very well.

" Of course," he said, when I had finished, " you're
bound to say all this. You're a parson. I don't mean
that in any way offensively. As a matter of fact, I think
you're probably right. But this isn't the usual sort of
thing between Anne and me."

I told him that people had been saying that particular
phrase since the dawn of time, and a queer little smile
creased his lips.

" You mean every one thinks their case is unique ? Perhaps so. But one thing you must believe."

He assured me that so far—" there was nothing wrong in it." Anne, he said, was one of the truest and most loyal women that ever lived. What was going to happen he didn't know.

" If this were only a book," he said gloomily, " the old man would die—and a good riddance to everybody."

I reproved him.

" Oh ! I didn't mean I was going to stick him in the back with a knife, though I'd offer my best thanks to any one else who did so. There's not a soul in the world who's got a good word to say for him. I rather wonder the first Mrs. Protheroe didn't do him in. I met her once, years ago, and she looked quite capable of it. One of those calm dangerous women. He goes blustering along, stirring up trouble everywhere, mean as the devil, and with a particularly nasty temper. You don't know what Anne has had to stand from him. If I had a penny in the world I'd take her away without any more ado."

Then I spoke to him very earnestly. I begged him to leave St. Mary Mead. By remaining there, he could only bring greater unhappiness on Anne Protheroe than was already her lot. People would talk, the matter would get to Colonel Protheroe's ears—and things would be made infinitely worse for her.

Lawrence protested.

" Nobody knows a thing about it except you, padre."

" My dear young man, you underestimate the detective instinct of village life. In St. Mary Mead every one knows your most intimate affairs. There is no detective in England equal to a spinster lady of uncertain age with plenty of time on her hands."

He said easily that that was all right. Every one thought it was Lettice.

" Has it occurred to you," I asked, " that possibly Lettice might think so herself."

He seemed quite surprised by the idea. Lettice, he

C

said, didn't care a hang about him. He was sure of that.

" She's a queer sort of girl," he said. " Always seems in a kind of dream, and yet underneath I believe she's really rather practical. I believe all that vague stuff is a pose. Lettice knows jolly well what she's doing. And there's a funny vindictive streak in her. The queer thing is that she hates Anne. Simply loathes her. And yet Anne's been a perfect angel to her always."

I did not, of course, take his word for this last. To infatuated young men, their inamorata always behaves like an angel. Still, to the best of my observation, Anne had always behaved to her stepdaughter with kindness and fairness. I had been surprised myself that afternoon at the bitterness of Lettice's tone.

We had to leave the conversation there, because Griselda and Dennis burst in upon us and said I was not to make Lawrence behave like an old fogy.

" Oh ! dear," said Griselda, throwing herself into an arm-chair. " How I would like a thrill of some kind. A murder—or even a burglary.

" I don't suppose there's any one much worth burgling," said Lawrence, trying to enter into her mood. " Unless we stole Miss Hartnell's false teeth."

" They do click horribly," said Griselda. " But you're wrong about there being no one worth while. There's some marvellous old silver at Old Hall. Trencher salts and a Charles II. Tazza—all kinds of things like that. Worth thousands of pounds, I believe."

" The old man would probably shoot you with an army revolver," said Dennis. " Just the sort of thing he'd enjoy doing."

" Oh ! we'd get in first and hold him up," said Griselda. " Who's got a revolver ? "

" I've got a Mauser pistol," said Lawrence.

" Have you ? How exciting ! Why do you have it ! "

" Souvenir of the war," said Lawrence briefly.

" Old Protheroe was showing the silver to Stone

to-day," volunteered Dennis. "Old Stone was pretending to be no end interested in it."

"I thought they'd quarrelled about the barrow," said Griselda.

"Oh! they've made that up," said Dennis. "I can't think what people want to grub about in barrows for, anyway."

"That man Stone puzzles me," said Lawrence. "I think he must be very absent-minded. You'd swear sometimes he knew nothing about his own subject."

"That's love," said Dennis. "Sweet Gladys Cram, you are no sham. Your teeth are white and fill me with delight. Come, fly with me, my bride to be. And at the Blue Boar, on the bedroom floor——"

"That's enough, Dennis," I said.

"Well," said Lawrence Redding, "I must be off. Thank you very much, Mrs. Clement, for a very pleasant evening."

Griselda and Dennis saw him off. Dennis returned to the study alone. Something had happened to ruffle the boy. He wandered about the room aimlessly, frowning and kicking the furniture.

Our furniture is so shabby already that it can hardly be damaged further, but I felt impelled to utter a mild protest.

"Sorry," said Dennis.

He was silent for a moment and then burst out:

"What an absolutely rotten thing gossip is!"

I was a little surprised. Dennis does not usually take that attitude.

"What's the matter?' I asked.

"I don't know whether I ought to tell you."

I was more and more surprised.

"It's such an absolutely rotten thing," Dennis said again. "Going round and saying things. Not even saying them. Hinting them. No, I'm damned—sorry—if I'll tell you! It's too absolutely rotten."

I looked at him curiously but I did not press him

further. I wondered very much, though. It is very
unlike Dennis to take anything to heart.

Griselda came in at that moment.

" Miss Wetherby's just rung up," she said.  " Mrs.
Lestrange went out at a quarter-past eight and hasn't
come in yet. Nobody knows where she's gone."

" Why should they know ? "

" But it isn't to Dr. Haydock's. Miss Wetherby does
know that, because she telephoned to Miss Hartnell
who lives next door to him and who would have been
sure to see her."

" It is a mystery to me," I said, " how any one ever
gets any nourishment in this place. They must eat their
meals standing up by the window so as to be sure of
not missing anything."

" And that's not all," said Griselda, bubbling with
pleasure. " They've found out about the Blue Boar.
Dr. Stone and Miss Cram have got rooms next door to
each other, BUT "—she waved an impressive forefinger
—" *no communicating door !* "

" That," I said, " must be very disappointing to
everybody."

At which Griselda laughed.

Thursday started badly. Two of the ladies of my parish
elected to quarrel about the church decorations. I was
called in to adjudicate between two middle-aged ladies,
each of whom was literally trembling with rage.    If it
had not been so painful, it would have been quite an
interesting physical phenomenon.

Then I had to reprove two of our choir boys for
persistent sweet sucking during the hours of divine
service, and I had an uneasy feeling that I was not
doing the job as whole-heartedly as I should have done.

Then our organist, who is distinctly " touchy," had
taken offence and had to be smoothed down.

And four of my poorer parishioners declared open
rebellion against Miss Hartnell, who came to me bursting
with rage about it.

I was just going home when I met Colonel Protheroe.

He was in high good-humour, having sentenced three poachers, in his capacity as magistrate.

" Firmness," he shouted in his stentorian voice. He is slightly deaf and raises his voice accordingly as deaf people often do. " That's what's needed nowadays— firmness ! Make an example. That rogue Archer came out yesterday and is vowing vengeance against me, I hear. Impudent scoundrel. Threatened men live long, as the saying goes. I'll show him what his vengeance is worth next time I catch him taking my pheasants. Lax ! We're too lax nowadays ! I believe in showing a man up for what he is. You're always being asked to consider a man's wife and children. Damned nonsense. Fiddlesticks. Why should a man escape the conse-quences of his acts just because he whines about his wife and children ? It's all the same to me—no matter what a man is—doctor, lawyer, clergyman, poacher, drunken wastrel—if you catch him on the wrong side of the law, let the law punish him. You agree with me, I'm sure."

" You forget," I said. " My calling obliges me to respect one quality above all others—the quality of mercy."

" Well, I'm a just man. No one can deny that."

I did not speak, and he said sharply :

" Why don't you answer ? A penny for your thoughts, man."

I hesitated, then I decided to speak.

" I was thinking," I said, " that when my time comes, I should be sorry if the only plea I had to offer was that of justice. Because it might mean that only justice would be meted out to me. . . ."

" Pah ! What we need is a little militant Christianity. I've always done my duty, I hope. Well, no more of that. I'll be along this evening, as I said. We'll make it a quarter-past six instead of six, if you don't mind. I've got to see a man in the village."

" That will suit me quite well."

He flourished his stick and strode away. Turning,

I ran into Hawes. I thought he looked distinctly ill this morning. I had meant to upbraid him mildly for various matters in his province which had been muddled or shelved, but seeing his white strained face, I felt that the man was ill.

I said as much, and he denied it, but not very vehemently. Finally he confessed that he was not feeling too fit, and appeared ready to accept my advice of going home to bed.

I had a hurried lunch and went out to do some visits. Griselda had gone to London by the cheap Thursday train.

I came in about a quarter to four with the intention of sketching the outline of my Sunday sermon, but Mary told me that Mr. Redding was waiting for me in the study.

I found him pacing up and down with a worried face. He looked white and haggard.

He turned abruptly at my entrance.

" Look here, sir. I've been thinking over what you said yesterday. I've had a sleepless night thinking about it. You're right. I've got to cut and run."

" My dear boy," I said.

" You were right in what you said about Anne. I'll only bring trouble on her by staying here. She's—she's too good for anything else. I see I've got to go. I've made things hard enough for her as it is, Heaven help me."

" I think you have made the only decision possible," I said. " I know that it is a hard one, but believe me, it will be for the best in the end."

I could see that he thought that that was the kind of thing easily said by some one who didn't know what he was talking about.

" You'll look after Anne ? She needs a friend."

" You can rest assured that I will do everything in my power."

" Thank you, sir." He wrung my hand. " You're a good sort, Padre. I shall see her to say good-bye this evening, and I shall probably pack up and go to-morrow. No good prolonging the agony. Thanks for letting me have the shed to paint in. I'm sorry not to have finished Mrs. Clement's portrait."

" Don't worry about that, my dear boy. Good-bye, and God bless you."

When he had gone I tried to settle down to my sermon, but with very poor success. I kept thinking of Lawrence and Anne Protheroe.

I had rather an unpalatable cup of tea, cold and black, and at half-past five the telephone rang. I was informed that Mr. Abbott of Lower Farm was dying and would I please come at once.

I rang up Old Hall immediately, for Lower Farm was nearly two miles away and I could not possibly get back by six fifteen. I have never succeeded in learning to ride a bicycle.

I was told, however, that Colonel Protheroe had just started out in the car, so I departed, leaving word with Mary that I had been called away, but would try to be back by six-thirty or soon after.

# CHAPTER V

It was nearer seven than half-past six when I approached the Vicarage gate on my return. Before I reached it, it swung open and Lawrence Redding came out. He stopped dead on seeing me, and I was immediately struck by his appearance. He looked like a man who was on the point of going mad. His eyes stared in a peculiar manner, he was deathly white, and he was shaking and twitching all over.

I wondered for a moment whether he could have been drinking, but repudiated the idea immediately.

"Hullo," I said, "have you been to see me again? Sorry I was out. Come back now. I've got to see Protheroe about some accounts—but I dare say we shan't be long."

"Protheroe," he said. He began to laugh. "Protheroe? You're going to see Protheroe? Oh! you'll see Protheroe all right. Oh! my God—yes."

I stared. Instinctively I stretched out a hand towards him. He drew sharply aside.

"No," he almost cried out. "I've got to get away —to think. I've got to think. I must think."

He broke into a run and vanished rapidly down the road towards the village, leaving me staring after him, my first idea of drunkenness recurring.

Finally I shook my head, and went on to the Vicarage. The front door is always left open, but nevertheless I rang the bell. Mary came, wiping her hands on her apron.

"So you're back at last," she observed.

"Is Colonel Protheroe here?" I asked.

"In the study. Been here since a quarter past six."

"And Mr. Redding's been here?"

"Come a few minutes ago. Asked for you. I told him you'd be back any minute and that Colonel Protheroe was waiting in the study, and he said he'd wait too, and went there. He's there now."

"No, he isn't," I said. "I've just met him going down the road."

"Well, I didn't hear him leave. He can't have stayed more than a couple of minutes. The mistress isn't back from town yet."

I nodded absent-mindedly. Mary beat a retreat to the kitchen quarters and I went down the passage and opened the study door.

After the dusk of the passage, the evening sunshine that was pouring into the room made my eyes blink. I took a step or two across the floor and then stopped dead.

For a moment I could hardly take in the meaning of the scene before me.

Colonel Protheroe was lying sprawled across my writing table in a horrible unnatural position. There was a pool of some dark fluid on the desk by his head, and it was slowly dripping on to the floor with a horrible drip, drip, drip.

I pulled myself together and went across to him. His skin was cold to the touch. The hand that I raised fell back lifeless. The man was dead—shot through the head.

I went to the door and called Mary. When she came I ordered her to run as fast as she could and fetch Dr. Haydock who lives just at the corner of the road. I told her there had been an accident.

Then I went back and closed the door to await the doctor's coming.

Fortunately, Mary found him at home. Haydock is a good fellow, a big, fine, strapping man with an honest, rugged face.

His eyebrows went up when I pointed silently across the room. But, like a true doctor, he showed no signs of emotion. He bent over the dead man, examining him rapidly. Then he straightened himself and looked across at me.

" Well ? " I asked.

" He's dead right enough—been dead half an hour, I should say."

" Suicide ? "

" Out of the question, man. Look at the position of the wound. Besides, if he shot himself, where's the weapon ? "

True enough, there was no sign of any such thing."

" We'd better not mess around with anything," said Haydock. " I'd better ring up the police."

He picked up the receiver and spoke into it. He gave the facts as curtly as possible and then replaced the telephone and came across to where I was sitting.

" This is a rotten business. How did you come to find him ? "

I explained.

" A rotten business," he repeated.

" Is—is it murder ? " I asked rather faintly.

" Looks like it. Mean to say, what else can it be ? Extraordinary business. Wonder who had a down on the poor old fellow. Of course I know he wasn't popular, but one isn't often murdered for that reason—worse luck."

" There's one rather curious thing," I said. " I was telephoned for this afternoon to go to a dying parishioner. When I got there every one was very surprised to see me. The sick man was very much better than he had been for some days, and his wife flatly denied telephoning for me at all."

Haydock drew his brows together.

" That's suggestive—very. You were being got out of the way. Where's your wife ? "

" Gone up to London for the day."

" And the maid ? "

" In the kitchen—right at the other side of the house."

" Where she wouldn't be likely to hear anything that went on in here. It's a nasty business. Who knew that Protheroe was coming here this evening ? "

" He referred to the fact this morning in the village street at the top of his voice as usual."

" Meaning that the whole village knew it ! Which they always do in any case. Know of any one who had a grudge against him ? "

The thought of Lawrence Redding's white face and staring eyes came to my mind. I was spared answering by a noise of shuffling feet in the passage outside.

" The police," said my friend, and rose to his feet.

Our police force was represented by Constable Hurst, looking very important but slightly worried.

" Good-evening, gentlemen," he greeted us. " The Inspector will be here any minute. In the meantime I'll follow out his instructions. I understand Colonel Protheroe's been found shot—in the Vicarage."

He paused and directed a look of cold suspicion at me, which I tried to meet with a suitable bearing of conscious innocence.

He moved over to the writing table and announced :

" Nothing to be touched till the Inspector comes."

For the convenience of my readers, I append a sketch plan of the room.

He got out his notebook, moistened his pencil and looked expectantly at both of us.

I repeated my story of discovering the body. When he had got it all down, which took some time, he turned to the doctor.

" In your opinion, Dr. Haydock, what was the cause of death ? "

" Shot through the head at close quarters."

" And the weapon ? "

" I can't say with certainty until we get the bullet out. But I should say in all probability the bullet was fired from a pistol of small calibre—say a Mauser .25."

I started, remembering our conversation of the night before, and Lawrence Redding's admission. The police constable brought his cold, fish-like eye round on me.

" Did you speak, sir ? "

I shook my head. Whatever suspicions I might have,

Bookshelf

Writing Table

Chair

Tallboy

Chair

Table

Chair

Tall Stand with Pot on it

Window

Table with Lamp

Armchair

Armchair

Sofa

Door

Fireplace

PLAN B

they were no more than suspicions, and as such to be kept to myself.

" When, in your opinion, did the tragedy occur ? "

The doctor hesitated for a minute before he answered. Then he said :

" The man has been dead just over half an hour, I should say. Certainly not longer. "

Hurst turned to me.

" Did the girl hear anything ? "

" As far as I know she heard nothing," I said. " But you had better ask her."

But at this moment Inspector Slack arrived, having come by car from Much Benham, two miles away.

All that I can say of Inspector Slack is that never did a man more determinedly strive to contradict his name. He was a dark man, restless and energetic in manner, with black eyes that snapped ceaselessly. His manner was rude and overbearing in the extreme.

He acknowledged our greetings with a curt nod, seized his subordinate's notebook, perused it, exchanged a few curt words with him in an undertone, then strode over to the body.

" Everything's been messed up and pulled about, I suppose," he said.

" I've touched nothing," said Haydock.

" No more have I," I said.

The Inspector busied himself for some time peering at the things on the table and examining the pool of blood.

" Ah ! " he said in a tone of triumph. " Here's what we want. Clock overturned when he fell forward. That'll give us the time of the crime. Twenty-two minutes past six. What time did you say death occurred, doctor ? "

" I said about half an hour, but——"

The Inspector consulted his watch.

" Five minutes past seven. I got word about ten minutes ago, at five minutes to seven. Discovery of the body was at about a quarter to seven. I understand you were fetched immediately. Say you examined it at ten minutes to—— Why, that brings it to the identical second almost ! "

" I don't guarantee the time absolutely," said Haydock. " That is an approximate estimate."

" Good enough, sir, good enough."

I had been trying to get a word in.

" About that clock——"

" If you'll excuse me, sir, I'll ask you any questions I want to know. Time's short. What I want is absolute silence."

" Yes, but I'd like to tell you——"

" Absolute silence," said the Inspector, glaring at me ferociously.

I gave him what he asked for.

He was still peering about the writing table.

" What was he sitting here for," he grunted. " Did he want to write a note—— Hullo—what's this ? "

He held up a piece of notepaper triumphantly. So pleased was he with his find that he permitted us to come to his side and examine it with him.

It was a piece of Vicarage notepaper, and it was headed at the top 6.20.

" DEAR CLEMENT "—it began—" Sorry I cannot wait any longer, but I must . . ."

Here the writing tailed off in a scrawl.

" Plain as a pikestaff," said Inspector Slack triumphantly. " He sits down here to write this, an enemy comes softly in through the window and shoots him as he writes. What more do you want ? "

" I'd just like to say——" I began.

" Out of the way, if you please, sir. I want to see if there are footprints."

He went down on his hands and knees, moving towards the open window.

" I think you ought to know——" I said obstinately.

The Inspector rose. He spoke without heat, but firmly.

" We'll go into all that later. I'd be obliged if you gentlemen will clear out of here. Right out, if you please."

We permitted ourselves to be shooed out like children.

Hours seemed to have passed—yet it was only a quarter-past seven.

" Well," said Haydock. " That's that. When that conceited ass wants me, you can send him over to the surgery. So long."

" The mistress is back," said Mary, making a brief appearance from the kitchen. Her eyes were round and agog with excitement. " Come in about five minutes ago."

I found Griselda in the drawing-room. She looked frightened, but excited.

I told her everything and she listened attentively.

" The letter is headed 6.20," I ended. " And the clock fell over and has stopped at 6.22."

" Yes," said Griselda. " But that clock, didn't you tell him that it was always kept a quarter of an hour fast ? "

" No," I said. " I didn't. He wouldn't let me. I tried my best."

Griselda was frowning in a puzzled manner.

" But, Len," she said, " that makes the whole thing perfectly extraordinary. Because when that clock said twenty past six it was really only five minutes past, and at five minutes past I don't suppose Colonel Protheroe had even arrived at the house."

# CHAPTER VI

WE puzzled over the business of the clock for some time, but we could make nothing of it. Griselda said I ought to make another effort to tell Inspector Slack about it, but on that point I was feeling what I can only describe as " mulish."

Inspector Slack had been abominably and most unnecessarily rude. I was looking forward to a moment when I could produce my valuable contribution and effect his discomfiture. I would then say in a tone of mild reproach :

" If you had only listened to me, Inspector Slack——"

I expected that he would at least speak to me before he left the house, but to our surprise we learned from Mary that he had departed, having locked up the study door and issued orders that no one was to attempt to enter the room.

Griselda suggested going up to Old Hall.

" It will be so awful for Anne Protheroe—with the police and everything," she said. " Perhaps I might be able to do something for her."

I cordially approved of this plan, and Griselda set off with instructions that she was to telephone to me if she thought that I could be of any use or comfort to either of the ladies.

I now proceeded to ring up the Sunday School teachers who were coming at 7.45 for their weekly preparation class. I thought that under the circumstances it would be better to put them off.

Dennis was the next person to arrive on the scene, having just returned from a tennis party. The fact that murder had taken place at the Vicarage seemed to afford him acute satisfaction.

" Fancy being right on the spot in a murder case," he exclaimed. " I've always wanted to be right in the

48

midst of one. Why have the police locked up the study ? Wouldn't one of the other door keys fit it ? "

I refused to allow anything of the sort to be attempted. Dennis gave in with a bad grace. After extracting every possible detail from me he went out into the garden to look for footprints, remarking cheerfully that it was lucky it was only old Protheroe, whom every one disliked.

His cheerful callousness rather grated on me, but I reflected that I was perhaps being hard on the boy. At Dennis's age a detective story is one of the best things in life, and to find a real detective story, complete with corpse, waiting on one's own front doorstep, so to speak, is bound to send a healthy-minded boy into the seventh heaven of enjoyment. Death means very little to a boy of sixteen.

Griselda came back in about an hour's time. She had seen Anne Protheroe, having arrived just after the Inspector had broken the news to her.

On hearing that Mrs. Protheroe had last seen her husband in the village about a quarter to six, and that she had no light of any kind to throw upon the matter, he had taken his departure, explaining that he would return on the morrow for a fuller interview.

" He was quite decent in his way," said Griselda grudgingly.

" How did Mrs. Protheroe take it ? " I asked.

" Well—she was very quiet—but then she always is."

" Yes," I said. " I can't imagine Anne Protheroe going into hysterics."

" Of course it was a great shock. You could see that. She thanked me for coming and said she was very grateful but that there was nothing I could do."

" What about Lettice ? "

" She was out playing tennis somewhere. She hadn't got home yet."

There was a pause, and then Griselda said :

" You know, Len, she was really very queer—very queer indeed."

D

" The shock," I suggested.

" Yes—I suppose so. And yet——" Griselda furrowed her brows perplexedly. " It wasn't like that, somehow. She didn't seem so much bowled over as —well—terrified."

" Terrified ? "

" Yes—not showing it, you know. At least not meaning to show it. But a queer, watchful look in her eyes. I wonder if she has a sort of idea who did kill him. She asked again and again if any one were suspected."

" Did she ? " I said thoughtfully.

" Yes. Of course Anne's got marvellous self-control, but one could see that she was terribly upset. More so than I would have thought, for after all it wasn't as though she were so devoted to him. I should have said she rather disliked him, if anything."

" Death alters one's feelings sometimes," I said.

" Yes, I suppose so."

Dennis came in and was full of excitement over a footprint he had found in one of the flower beds. He was sure that the police had overlooked it and that it would turn out to be the turning point of the mystery.

I spent a troubled night. Dennis was up and about and out of the house long before breakfast to " study the latest developments," as he said.

Nevertheless it was not he, but Mary, who brought us the morning's sensational bit of news.

We had just sat down to breakfast when she burst into the room, her cheeks red and her eyes shining, and addressed us with her customary lack of ceremony.

" Would you believe it ? The baker's just told me. They've arrested young Mr. Redding."

" Arrested Lawrence," cried Griselda incredulously. " Impossible. It must be some stupid mistake."

" No mistake about it, mum," said Mary with a kind of gloating exultation. " Mr. Redding, he went there himself and gave himself up. Last night, last thing.

Went right in, threw down the pistol on the table, and
' I did it,' he says.  Just like that."

She looked at us both, nodded her head vigorously,
and withdrew satisfied with the effect she had produced.
Griselda and I stared at each other.

"Oh!  it isn't true," said Griselda.  "It *can't* be
true."

She noticed my silence, and said :  "Len, *you* don't
think it's true ? "

I found it hard to answer her.  I sat silent, thoughts
whirling through my head.

"He must be mad," said Griselda.  "Absolutely
mad.  Or do you think they were looking at the pistol
together and it suddenly went off."

"That doesn't sound at all a likely thing to happen."

"But it must have been an accident of some kind.
Because there's not a shadow of a motive.  What
earthly reason could Lawrence have for killing Colonel
Protheroe ? "

I could have answered that question very decidedly,
but I wished to spare Anne Protheroe as far as possible.
There might still be a chance of keeping her name out
of it.

"Remember they had had a quarrel," I said.

"About Lettice and her bathing dress.  Yes, but
that's absurd. and even if he and Lettice were engaged
secretly—well, that's not a reason for killing her father."

"We don't know what the true facts of the case
may be, Griselda."

"You *do* believe it, Len !  Oh !  how can you !  I tell
you, I'm *sure* Lawrence never touched a hair of his head."

"Remember, I met him just outside the gate.  He
looked like a madman."

"Yes, but—oh !  it's impossible."

"There's the clock, too," I said.  "This explains the
clock.  Lawrence must have put it back to 6.20 with
the idea of making an alibi for himself.  Look how
Inspector Slack fell into the trap."

"You're wrong, Len.  Lawrence knew about that

clock being fast. 'Keeping the vicar up to time!' he used to say. Lawrence would never have made the mistake of putting it back to 6.22. He'd have put the hands somewhere possible—like a quarter to seven."

"He mayn't have known what time Protheroe got here. Or he may have simply forgotten about the clock being fast."

Griselda disagreed.

"No, if you were committing a murder, you'd be awfully careful about things like that."

"You don't know, my dear," I said mildly. "You've never done one."

Before Griselda could reply, a shadow fell across the breakfast table, and a very gentle voice said:

"I hope I am not intruding. You must forgive me. But in the sad circumstances—the very sad circumstances——"

It was our neighbour, Miss Marple. Accepting our polite disclaimers, she stepped in through the window, and I drew up a chair for her. She looked faintly flushed and quite excited.

"Very terrible, is it not? Poor Colonel Protheroe. Not a very pleasant man, perhaps, and not exactly popular, but it's none the less sad for that. And actually shot in the Vicarage study, I understand?"

I said that that had indeed been the case.

"But the dear vicar was not here at the time?" Miss Marple questioned of Griselda.

I explained where I had been.

"Mr. Dennis is not with you this morning?" said Miss Marple, glancing round.

"Dennis," said Griselda, "fancies himself as an amateur detective. He is very excited about a footprint he found in one of the flower beds, and I fancy has gone off to tell the police about it."

"Dear, dear," said Miss Marple. "Such a to-do, is it not? And Mr. Dennis thinks he knows who committed the crime. Well, I suppose we all think we know."

"You mean it is obvious?" said Griselda.

"No, dear, I didn't mean that at all. I dare say every one thinks it is somebody different. That is why it is so important to have *proofs*. I, for instance, am quite *convinced* I know who did it. But I must admit I haven't one shadow of proof. One must, I know, be very careful of what one says at a time like this—criminal libel, don't they call it? I had made up my mind to be *most* careful with Inspector Slack. He sent word he would come and see me this morning, but now he has just phoned up to say it won't be necessary after all."

"I suppose, since the arrest, it isn't necessary," I said.

"The arrest?" Miss Marple leaned forward, her cheeks pink with excitement. "I didn't know there had been an arrest."

It is so seldom that Miss Marple is worse informed than we are that I had taken it for granted that she would know the latest developments.

"It seems we have been talking at cross purposes," I said. "Yes, there has been an arrest—Lawrence Redding."

"Lawrence Redding?" Miss Marple seemed very surprised. "Now I should not have thought——"

Griselda interrupted vehemently.

"I can't believe it even now. No, not though he has actually confessed."

"Confessed?" said Miss Marple. "You say he has confessed? Oh! dear, I see I have been sadly at sea—yes, sadly at sea."

"I can't help feeling it must have been some kind of an accident," said Griselda. "Don't you think so, Len? I mean his coming forward to give himself up looks like that."

Miss Marple leant forward eagerly.

"He gave himself up, you say?"

"Yes."

"Oh!" said Miss Marple, with a deep sigh. "I am so glad—so very glad."

I looked at her in some surprise.

" It shows a true state of remorse, I suppose," I said.

" Remorse ? " Miss Marple looked very surprised. " Oh ! but surely dear, dear vicar, you don't think that he is guilty ? "

It was my turn to stare.

" But since he has confessed——"

" Yes, but that just proves it, doesn't it ? I mean that he had nothing to do with it."

" No," I said. " I may be dense, but I can't see that it does. If you have not committed a murder, I cannot see the object of pretending you have."

" Oh ! of course, there's a reason," said Miss Marple. " Naturally. There's always a reason, isn't there ? And young men are so hot-headed and often prone to believe the worst."

She turned to Griselda.

" Don't you agree with me, my dear ? "

" I—I don't know," said Griselda. " It's difficult to know what to think. I can't see any reason for Lawrence behaving like a perfect idiot."

" If you had seen his face last night——" I began.

" Tell me," said Miss Marple.

I described my homecoming while she listened attentively.

When I had finished she said :

" I know that I am very often rather foolish and don't take in things as I should, but I really do not see your point.

" It seems to me that if a young man had made up his mind to the great wickedness of taking a fellow creature's life, he would not appear distraught about it afterwards. It would be a premeditated and cold-blooded action and though the murderer might be a little flurried and possibly might make some small mistake, I do not think it likely he would fall into a state of agitation such as you describe. It is difficult to put oneself in such a position, but I cannot imagine getting into a state like that myself."

" We don't know the circumstances," I argued. " If

there was a quarrel, the shot may have been fired in a sudden gust of passion, and Lawrence might afterwards have been appalled at what he had done. Indeed, I prefer to think that that is what did actually occur."

"I know, dear Mr. Clement, that there are many ways we prefer to look at things. But one must actually take facts as they are, must one not? And it does not seem to me that the facts bear the interpretation you put upon them. Your maid distinctly stated that Mr. Redding was only in the house a couple of minutes, not long enough, surely, for a quarrel such as you describe. And then again, I understand the colonel was shot through the back of the head while he was writing a letter—at least that is what my maid told me."

"Quite true," said Griselda. "He seems to have been writing a note to say he couldn't wait any longer. The note was dated 6.20, and the clock on the table was overturned and had stopped at 6.22, and that's just what has been puzzling Len and myself so frightfully."

She explained our custom of keeping the clock a quarter of an hour fast.

"Very curious," said Miss Marple. "Very curious indeed. But the note seems to me even more curious still. I mean——"

She stopped and looked round. Lettice Protheroe was standing outside the window. She came in, nodding to us and murmuring "Morning."

She dropped into a chair and said, with rather more animation than usual:

"They've arrested Lawrence, I hear."

"Yes," said Griselda. "It's been a great shock to us."

"I never really thought any one would murder father," said Lettice. She was obviously taking a pride in letting no hint of distress or emotion escape her. "Lots of people wanted to, I'm sure. There are times when I'd have liked to do it myself."

"Won't you have something to eat or drink, Lettice?' asked Griselda.

"No, thank you. I just drifted round to see if you'd got my beret here—a queer little yellow one. I think I left it in the study the other day."

"If you did, it's there still," said Griselda. "Mary never tidies anything."

"I'll go and see," said Lettice, rising. "Sorry to be such a bother, but I seem to have lost everything else in the hat line."

"I'm afraid you can't get it now," I said. "Inspector Slack has locked the room up."

"Oh! what a bore. Can't we get in through the window?"

"I'm afraid not. It is latched on the inside. Surely, Lettice, a yellow beret won't be much good to you at present?"

"You mean mourning and all that? I shan't bother about mourning. I think it's an awfully archaic idea. It's a nuisance about Lawrence—yes, it's a nuisance."

She got up and stood frowning abstractedly.

"I suppose it's all on account of me and my bathing dress. So silly, the whole thing. . . ."

Griselda opened her mouth to say something, but for some unexplained reason shut it again.

A curious smile came to Lettice's lips.

"I think," she said softly, "I'll go home and tell Anne about Lawrence being arrested."

She went out of the window again. Griselda turned to Miss Marple.

"Why did you step on my foot?"

The old lady was smiling.

"I thought you were going to say something, my dear. And it is often so much better to let things develop on their own lines. I don't think, you know, that that child is half so vague as she pretends to be. She's got a very definite idea in her head and she's acting upon it."

Mary gave a loud knock on the dining-room door and entered hard upon it.

"What is it?" said Griselda. "And Mary, you must

remember not to knock on doors. I've told you about it before."

"Thought you might be busy," said Mary. "Colonel Melchett's here. Wants to see the master."

Colonel Melchett is Chief Constable of the county. I rose at once.

"I thought you wouldn't like my leaving him in the hall, so I put him in the drawing-room," went on Mary. "Shall I clear ?"

"Not yet," said Griselda. "I'll ring."

She turned to Miss Marple and I left the room.

# CHAPTER VII

COLONEL MELCHETT is a dapper little man with a habit of snorting suddenly and unexpectedly. He has red hair and rather keen bright blue eyes.

"Good-morning, vicar," he said. "Nasty business, eh? Poor old Protheroe. Not that I liked him. I didn't. Nobody did, for that matter. Nasty bit of work for you, too. Hope it hasn't upset your missus?"

I said Griselda had taken it very well.

"That's lucky. Rotten thing to happen in one's house. I must say I'm surprised at young Redding—doing it the way he did. No sort of consideration for any one's feelings."

A wild desire to laugh came over me, but Colonel Melchett evidently saw nothing odd in the idea of a murderer being considerate, so I held my peace.

"I must say I was rather taken aback when I heard the fellow had marched in and given himself up," continued Colonel Melchett, dropping on to a chair.

"How did it happen exactly?"

"Last night. About ten o'clock. Fellow rolls in, throws down a pistol, and says: 'Here I am. I did it.' Just like that."

"What account does he give of the business?"

"Precious little. He was warned, of course, about making a statement. But he merely laughed. Said he came here to see you—found Protheroe here. They had words and he shot him. Won't say what the quarrel was about. Look here, Clement—just between you and me, do you know anything about it? I've heard rumours—about his being forbidden the house and all that. What was it—did he seduce the daughter, or what? We don't want to bring the girl into it more than we can help for everybody's sake. Was that the trouble?"

"No," I said. "You can take it from me that it was something quite different, but I can't say more at the present juncture."

He nodded and rose.

"I'm glad to know. There's a lot of talk. Too many women in this part of the world. Well, I must get along. I've got to see Haydock. He was called out to some case or other, but he ought to be back by now. I don't mind telling you I'm sorry about Redding. He always struck me as a decent young chap. Perhaps they'll think out some kind of defence for him. After-effects of war, shell shock, or something. Especially if no very adequate motive turns up. I must be off. Like to come along?"

I said I would like to very much, and we went out together.

Haydock's house is next door to mine. His servant said the doctor had just come in and showed us into the dining-room, where Haydock was sitting down to a steaming plate of eggs and bacon.

He greeted me with an amiable nod.

"Sorry I had to go out. Confinement case. I've been up most of the night, over your business. I've got the bullet for you."

He shoved a little box along the table. Melchett examined it.

"Point two five?"

Haydock nodded.

"I'll keep the technical details for the inquest," he said. "All you want to know is that death was practically instantaneous. Silly young fool, what did he want to do it for? Amazing, by the way, that nobody heard the shot."

"Yes," said Melchett, "that surprises me."

"The kitchen window gives on the other side of the house," I said. "With the study door, the pantry door, and the kitchen door all shut, I doubt if you would hear anything, and there was no one but the maid in the house."

" H'm," said Melchett. " It's odd, all the same. I wonder the old lady—what's her name—Marple, didn't hear it. The study window was open."

" Perhaps she did," said Haydock.

" I don't think she did," said I. " She was over at the Vicarage just now and she didn't mention anything of the kind which I'm certain she would have done if there had been anything to tell."

" May have heard it and paid no attention to it—thought it was a car backfiring."

It struck me that Haydock was looking much more jovial and good-humoured this morning. He seemed like a man who was decorously trying to subdue unusually good spirits.

" Or what about a silencer ? " he added. " That's quite likely. Nobody would hear anything then."

Melchett shook his head.

" Slack didn't find anything of the kind, and he asked Redding, and Redding didn't seem to know what he was talking about at first and then denied point blank using anything of the kind. And I suppose one can take his word for it."

" Yes, indeed, poor devil."

" Damned young fool," said Colonel Melchett. " Sorry, Clement. But he really is ! Somehow one can't get used to thinking of him as a murderer."

" Any motive ? " asked Haydock, taking a final draught of coffee and pushing back his chair.

" He says they quarrelled and he lost his temper and shot him."

" Hoping for manslaughter, eh ? " The doctor shook his head. " That story doesn't hold water. He stole up behind him as he was writing and shot him through the head. Precious little ' quarrel ' about that."

" Anyway, there wouldn't have been time for a quarrel," I said, remembering Miss Marple's words. " To creep up, shoot him, alter the clock hands back to 6.20, and leave again would have taken him all his time. I shall never forget his face when I met him outside

the gate, or the way he said, ' You want to see Protheroe
—oh ! you'll see him all right ! ' That in itself ought
to have made me suspicious of what had just taken
place a few minutes before. "

Haydock stared at me.

" What do you mean—what had just taken place ?
When do you think Redding shot him ? "

" A few minutes before I got to the house."

The doctor shook his head.

" Impossible. Plumb impossible. He'd been dead
much longer than that."

" But, my dear man," cried Colonel Melchett, " you
said yourself that half an hour was only an approximate
estimate."

" Half an hour, thirty-five minutes, twenty-five
minutes, twenty minutes—possibly, but less, no. Why,
the body would have been warm when I got to it."

We stared at each other. Haydock's face had changed.
It had gone suddenly grey and old. I wondered at the
change in him.

" But, look here, Haydock." The colonel found his
voice. " If Redding admits shooting him at a quarter
to seven——"

Haydock sprang to his feet.

" I tell you it's impossible," he roared. " If Redding
says he killed Protheroe at a quarter to seven, then
Redding lies. Hang it all, I tell you I'm a doctor, and
I know. The blood had begun to congeal."

" If Redding is lying," began Melchett. He stopped,
shook his head.

" We'd better go down to the police station and see
him," he said.

# CHAPTER VIII

WE were rather silent on our way down to the police station. Haydock drew behind a little and murmured to me :

" You know I don't like the look of this. I don't like it. There's something here we don't understand."

He looked thoroughly worried and upset.

Inspector Slack was at the police station and presently we found ourselves face to face with Lawrence Redding.

He looked pale and strained but quite composed— marvellously so, I thought, considering the circumstances. Melchett snorted and hummed, obviously nervous.

" Look here, Redding," he said, " I understand you made a statement to Inspector Slack here. You state you went to the Vicarage at approximately a quarter to seven, found Protheroe there, quarrelled with him, shot him, and came away. I'm not reading it over to you, but that's the gist of it."

" Yes."

" I'm going to ask you a few questions. You've already been told that you needn't answer them unless you choose. Your solicitor——"

Lawrence interrupted.

" I've nothing to hide. I killed Protheroe."

" Ah ! well——" Melchett snorted. " How did you happen to have a pistol with you ? "

Lawrence hesitated.

" It was in my pocket."

" You took it with you to the Vicarage ? "

" Yes."

" Why ? "

" I always take it."

He had hesitated again before answering, and I was absolutely sure that he was not speaking the truth.

" Why did you put the clock back ? "

" The clock ? "

He seemed puzzled.

" Yes, the hands pointed to 6.22."

A look of fear sprang up in his face.

" Oh ! that—yes. I—I altered it."

Haydock spoke suddenly.

" Where did you shoot Colonel Protheroe ? "

" In the study at the Vicarage."

" I mean in what part of the body ? "

" Oh !—I—through the head, I think. Yes, through the head."

" Aren't you sure ? "

" Since you know, I can't see why it is necessary to ask me."

It was a feeble kind of bluster. There was some commotion outside. A constable without a helmet brought in a note.

" For the vicar. It says very urgent on it."

I tore it open and read :

" Please—please—come to me. I don't know what to do. It is all too awful. I want to tell some one. Please come immediately, and bring any one you like with you.—ANNE PROTHEROE."

I gave Melchett a meaning glance. He took the hint. We all went out together. Glancing over my shoulder, I had a glimpse of Lawrence Redding's face. His eyes were rivetted on the paper in my hand, and I have hardly ever seen such a terrible look of anguish and despair in any human being's face.

I remembered Anne Protheroe sitting on my sofa and saying :

" I'm a desperate woman," and my heart grew heavy within me. I saw now the possible reason for Lawrence Redding's heroic self-accusation.

Melchett was speaking to Slack.

" Have you got any line on Redding's movements earlier in the day ? There's some reason to think he shot Protheroe earlier than he says. Get on to it, will you ? "

He turned to me and without a word I handed him Anne Protheroe's letter. He read it and pursed up his lips in astonishment. Then he looked at me inquiringly.

" Is this what you were hinting at this morning ? "

" Yes. I was not sure then if it was my duty to speak. I am quite sure now." And I told him of what I had seen that night in the studio.

The colonel had a few words with the inspector and then we set off for Old Hall. Dr. Haydock came with us.

A very correct butler opened the door, with just the right amount of gloom in his bearing.

" Good-morning," said Melchett.    " Will you ask Mrs. Protheroe's maid to tell her we are here and would like to see her, and then return here and answer a few questions."

The butler hurried away and presently returned with the news that he had despatched the message.

" Now let's hear something about yesterday," said Colonel Melchett.  " Your master was in to lunch ? "

" Yes, sir."

" And in his usual spirits ? "

" As far as I could see, yes, sir."

" What happened after that ? "

" After luncheon Mrs. Protheroe went to lie down and the colonel went to his study.  Miss Lettice went out to a tennis party in the two-seater.  Colonel and Mrs. Protheroe had tea at four-thirty, in the drawing-room.  The car was ordered for five-thirty to take them to the village.  Immediately after they had left Mr. Clement rang up "—he bowed to me—" I told him they had started."

" H'm," said Colonel Melchett.  " When was Mr. Redding last here ? "

" On Tuesday afternoon, sir."

" I understand that there was a disagreement between them ? "

" I believe so, sir.  The colonel gave me orders that Mr. Redding was not to be admitted in future."

" Did you overhear the quarrel at all ? " asked Colonel Melchett bluntly.

" Colonel Protheroe, sir, had a very loud voice, especially when it was raised in anger. I was unable to help overhearing a few words here and there."

" Enough to tell you the cause of the dispute ? "

" I understood, sir, that it had to do with a portrait Mr. Redding had been painting—a portrait of Miss Lettice."

Melchett grunted.

" Did you see Mr. Redding when he left ? "

" Yes, sir, I let him out."

" Did he seem angry ? "

" No, sir ; if I may say so, he seemed rather amused."

" Ah ! He didn't come to the house yesterday ? "

" No, sir."

" Any one else come ? "

" Not yesterday, sir."

" Well, the day before ? "

" Mr. Dennis Clement came in the afternoon. And Dr. Stone was here for some time. And there was a lady in the evening."

" A lady ? " Melchett was surprised. " Who was she ? "

The butler couldn't remember her name. It was a lady he had not seen before. Yes, she had given her name, and when he told her that the family were at dinner, she had said that she would wait. So he had shown her into the little morning room.

She had asked for Colonel Protheroe, not Mrs. Protheroe. He had told the colonel and the colonel had gone to the morning room directly dinner was over.

How long had the lady stayed ? He thought about half an hour. The colonel himself had let her out. Ah ! yes, he remembered her name now. The lady had been a Mrs. Lestrange.

This was a surprise.

E

" Curious," said Melchett. " Really very curious."

But we pursued the matter no further, for at that moment a message came that Mrs. Protheroe would see us.

Anne was in bed. Her face was pale and her eyes very bright. There was a look on her face that puzzled me—a kind of grim determination.

She spoke to me.

" Thank you for coming so promptly," she said. " I see you've understood what I meant by bringing any one you liked with you."

She paused.

" It's best to get it over quickly, isn't it ? " she said. She gave a queer, half-pathetic little smile. " I suppose you're the person I ought to say it to, Colonel Melchett. You see, it was I who killed my husband."

Colonel Melchett said gently :

" My dear Mrs. Protheroe——"

" Oh ! it's quite true. I suppose I've said it rather bluntly, but I never can go into hysterics over anything. I've hated him for a long time, and yesterday I shot him."

She lay back on the pillows and closed her eyes.

" That's all. I suppose you'll arrest me and take me away. I'll get up and dress as soon as I can. At the moment I am feeling rather sick."

" Are you aware, Mrs. Protheroe, that Mr. Lawrence Redding has already accused himself of committing the crime."

Anne opened her eyes and nodded brightly.

" I know. Silly boy. He's very much in love with me, you know. It was frightfully noble of him—but very silly."

" He knew that it was you who had committed the crime ? "

" Yes."

" How did he know ? "

She hesitated.

" Did you tell him ? "

Still she hesitated. Then at last she seemed to make up her mind.

"Yes—I told him . . ."

She twitched her shoulders with a movement of irritation.

"Can't you go away now? I've told you. I don't want to talk about it any more."

"Where did you get the pistol, Mrs. Protheroe?"

"The pistol! Oh! it was my husband's. I got it out of the drawer of his dressing-table."

"I see. And you took it with you to the Vicarage?"

"Yes. I knew he would be there——"

"What time was this?"

"It must have been after six—quarter—twenty past —something like that."

"You took the pistol meaning to shoot your husband?"

"No—I—I meant it for myself."

"I see. But you went to the Vicarage?"

"Yes. I went along to the window. There were no voices. I looked in. I saw my husband. Something came over me—and I fired."

"And then?"

"Then? Oh! then I went away."

"And told Mr. Redding what you had done?"

Again I noticed the hesitation in her voice before she said "Yes."

"Did anybody see you entering or leaving the Vicarage?"

"No—at least, yes. Old Miss Marple. I talked to her a few minutes. She was in her garden."

She moved restlessly on the pillows.

"Isn't that enough? I've told you. Why do you want to go on bothering me?"

Dr. Haydock moved to her side and felt her pulse.

He beckoned to Melchett.

"I'll stay with her," he said in a whisper, "whilst you make the necessary arrangements. She oughtn't to be left. Might do herself a mischief."

Melchett nodded.

We left the room and descended the stairs. I saw a thin, cadaverous-looking man come out of the adjoining room and on impulse I remounted the stairs.

" Are you Colonel Protheroe's valet ? "

The man looked surprised.

" Yes, sir."

" Do you know whether your late master kept a pistol anywhere ? "

" Not that I know of, sir."

" Not in one of the drawers of his dressing-table ? Think, man."

The valet shook his head decisively.

" I'm quite sure he didn't, sir. I'd have seen it if so. Bound to."

I hurried down the stairs after the others.

Mrs. Protheroe had lied about the pistol.

Why ?

# CHAPTER IX

AFTER leaving a message at the police station, the Chief Constable announced his intention of paying a visit to Miss Marple.

"You'd better come with me, vicar," he said. "I don't want to give a member of your flock hysterics. So lend the weight of your soothing presence."

I smiled. For all her fragile appearance, Miss Marple is capable of holding her own with any policeman or Chief Constable in existence.

"What's she like?" asked the colonel, as we rang the bell. "Anything she says to be depended upon or otherwise?"

I considered the matter.

"I think she is quite dependable," I said cautiously. "That is, in so far as she is talking of what she has actually seen. Beyond that, of course, when you get on to what she thinks—well, that is another matter. She has a powerful imagination and systematically thinks the worst of every one."

"The typical elderly spinster, in fact," said Melchett, with a laugh. "Well, I ought to know the breed by now. Gad, the tea parties down here!"

We were admitted by a very diminutive maid and shown into a small drawing-room.

"A bit crowded," said Colonel Melchett, looking round. "But plenty of good stuff. A lady's room, eh, Clement?"

I agreed, and at that moment the door opened and Miss Marple made her appearance.

"Very sorry to bother you, Miss Marple," said the colonel, when I had introduced him, putting on his bluff military manner which he had an idea was attractive to elderly ladies. "Got to do my duty, you know."

"Of course, of course," said Miss Marple. "I quite

understand. Won't you sit down ? And might I offer you a little glass of cherry brandy ? My own making. A receipt of my grandmother's."

" Thank you very much, Miss Marple. Very kind of you. But I think I won't. Nothing till lunch time, that's my motto. Now, I want to talk to you about this sad business—very sad business indeed. Upset us all, I'm sure. Well, it seems possible that owing to the position of your house and garden, you may have been able to tell us something we want to know about yesterday evening."

" As a matter of fact, I *was* in my little garden from five o'clock onwards yesterday, and, of course, from there—well, one simply cannot help seeing anything that is going on next door."

" I understand, Miss Marple, that Mrs. Protheroe passed this way yesterday evening ? "

" Yes, she did. I called out to her, and she admired my roses."

" Could you tell us about what time that was ? "

" I should say it was just a minute or two after a quarter past six. Yes, that's right. The church clock had just chimed the quarter."

" Very good. What happened next ? "

" Well, Mrs. Protheroe said she was calling for her husband at the Vicarage so that they could go home together. She had come along the lane, you understand, and she went into the Vicarage by the back gate and across the garden."

" She came from the lane ? "

" Yes, I'll show you."

Full of eagerness, Mis Marple led us out into the garden and pointed out the lane that ran along by the bottom of her garden.

" The path opposite with the stile leads to the Hall," she explained. " That was the way they were going home together. Mrs. Protheroe came from the village."

" Perfectly, perfectly," said Colonel Melchett. " And she went across to the Vicarage, you say ? "

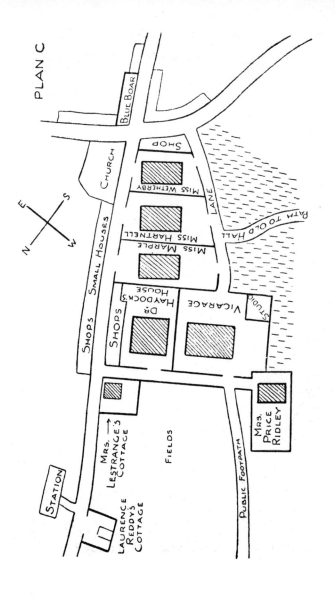

" Yes. I saw her turn the corner of the house. I suppose the colonel wasn't there yet, because she came back almost immediately, and went down the lawn to the studio—that building there. The one the vicar lets Mr. Redding use as a studio."

" I see. And—you didn't happen to hear a shot, Miss Marple ? "

" I didn't hear a shot then," said Miss Marple.

" But did you hear one sometime ? "

" Yes, I think there was a shot somewhere in the woods. But quite five or ten minutes afterwards—and, as I say, out in the woods. At least, I think so. It couldn't have been—surely it couldn't have been——"

She stopped, pale with excitement.

" Yes, yes, we'll come to all that presently," said Colonel Melchett. " Please go on with your story. Mrs. Protheroe went down to the studio ? "

" Yes, she went inside and waited. Presently Mr. Redding came along the lane from the village. He came to the Vicarage gate, looked all round——"

" And saw you, Miss Marple."

" As a matter of fact, he didn't see me," said Miss Marple, flushing slightly. " Because, you see, just at that minute I was bending right over—trying to get up one of those nasty dandelions, you know. So difficult. And then he went through the gate and down to the studio."

" He didn't go near the house ? "

" Oh, no ! he went straight to the studio. Mrs. Protheroe came to the door to meet him, and then they both went inside."

Here Miss Marple contributed a singularly eloquent pause.

" Perhaps she was sitting to him ? " I suggested.

" Perhaps," said Miss Marple.

" And they came out—when ? "

" About ten minutes later."

" That was roughly ? "

" The church clock had chimed the half-hour. They

strolled out through the garden gate and along the lane, and just at that minute, Dr. Stone came down the path leading to the Hall, and climbed over the stile and joined them. They all walked towards the village together. At the end of the lane, I think, but I can't be quite sure, they were joined by Miss Cram. I think it must have been Miss Cram because her skirts were so short."

"You must have very good eyesight, Miss Marple, if you can observe as far as that."

"I was observing a bird," said Miss Marple. "A golden crested wren, I think he was. A sweet little fellow. I had my glasses out, and that's how I happened to see Miss Cram (if it was Miss Cram, and I think so), join them."

"Ah! well, that may be so," said Colonel Melchett. "Now, since you seem very good at observing, did you happen to notice, Miss Marple, what sort of expression Mrs. Protheroe and Mr. Redding had as they passed along the lane ? "

"They were smiling and talking," said Miss Marple. "They seemed very happy to be together, if you know what I mean."

"They didn't seem upset or disturbed in any way ? "

"Oh, no ! Just the opposite."

"Deuced odd," said the colonel. "There's something deuced odd about the whole thing."

Miss Marple suddenly took our breath away by remarking in a placid voice :

"Has Mrs. Protheroe been saying that she committed the crime now ? "

"Upon my soul," said the colonel, "how did you come to guess that, Miss Marple ? "

"Well, I rather thought it might happen," said Miss Marple. "I think dear Lettice thought so, too. She's really a very sharp girl. Not always very scrupulous, I'm afraid. So Anne Protheroe says she killed her husband. Well, well. I don't think it's true. No, I'm almost sure it isn't true. Not with a woman like Anne Protheroe. Although one never can be quite sure about

any one, can one ? At least that's what I've found.
When does she say she shot him ? "

" At twenty minutes past six. Just after speaking to
you."

Miss Marple shook her head slowly and pityingly.
The pity was, I think, for two full-grown men being
so foolish as to believe such a story. At least that is
what we felt like.

" What did she shoot him with ? "

" A pistol."

" Where did she find it ? "

" She brought it with her."

" Well, that she didn't do," said Miss Marple, with
unexpected decision. " I can swear to that. She'd no
such thing with her."

" You mightn't have seen it."

" Of course I should have seen it."

" If it had been in her handbag."

" She wasn't carrying a handbag."

" Well, it might have been concealed—er—upon her
person."

Miss Marple directed a glance of sorrow and scorn
upon him.

" My dear Colonel Melchett, you know what young
women are nowadays. Not ashamed to show exactly
how the creator made them. She hadn't so much as a
handkerchief in the top of her stocking."

Melchett was obstinate.

" You must admit that it all fits in," he said. " The
time, the overturned clock pointing to 6.22——"

Miss Marple turned on me.

" Do you mean you haven't told him about that
clock yet ? "

" What about the clock, Clement ? "

I told him. He showed a good deal of annoyance.

" Why on earth didn't you tell Slack this last night ? "

" Because," I said, " he wouldn't let me."

" Nonsense, you ought to have insisted."

" Probably," I said, " Inspector Slack behaves quite

differently to you than he does to me. I had no earthly chance of insisting."

"It's an extraordinary business altogether," said Melchett. "If a third person comes along and claims to have done this murder, I shall go into a lunatic asylum."

"If I might be allowed to suggest——" murmured Miss Marple.

"Well?"

"If you were to tell Mr. Redding what Mrs. Protheroe has done and then explain that you don't really believe it is her. And then if you were to go to Mrs. Protheroe and tell her that Mr. Redding is all right—why then, they might each of them tell you the truth. And the truth *is* helpful, though I dare say they don't know very much themselves, poor things."

"It's all very well, but they are the only two people who had a motive for making away with Protheroe."

"Oh, I wouldn't say that, Colonel Melchett," said Miss Marple.

"Why, can you think of any one else?"

"Oh! yes, indeed. Why," she counted on her fingers, "one, two, three, four, five, six—yes, and a possible seven. I can think of at least seven people who might be very glad to have Colonel Protheroe out of the way."

The colonel looked at her feebly.

"Seven people? In St. Mary Mead?"

Miss Marple nodded brightly.

"Mind you, I name no names," she said. "That wouldn't be right. But I'm afraid there's a lot of wickedness in the world. A nice honourable upright soldier like you doesn't know about these things, Colonel Melchett."

I thought the Chief Constable was going to have apoplexy.

## CHAPTER X

His remarks on the subject of Miss Marple as we left the house were far from complimentary.

" I really believe that wizened-up old maid thinks she knows everything there is to know. And hardly been out of this village all her life. Preposterous. What can she know of life ? "

I said mildly that though doubtless Miss Marple knew next to nothing of Life with a capital L, she knew practically everything that went on in St. Mary Mead.

Melchett admitted that grudgingly. She was a valuable witness—particularly valuable from Mrs. Protheroe's point of view.

" I suppose there's no doubt about what she says, eh ? "

" If Miss Marple says she had no pistol with her, you can take it for granted that it is so," I said. " If there was the least possibility of such a thing, Miss Marple would have been on to it like a knife."

" That's true enough. We'd better go and have a look at the studio."

The so-called studio was a mere rough shed with a skylight. There were no windows and the door was the only means of entrance or egress. Satisfied on this score, Melchett announced his intention of visiting the Vicarage with the inspector.

" I'm going to the police station now."

As I entered through the front door, a murmur of voices caught my ear. I opened the drawing-room door.

On the sofa beside Griselda, conversing animatedly, sat Miss Gladys Cram. Her legs, which were encased in particularly shiny pink stockings, were crossed, and I had every opportunity of observing that she wore pink striped silk knickers.

"Hullo, Len," said Griselda.

"Good-morning, Mr. Clement," said Miss Cram. "Isn't the news about the colonel reely too awful? Poor old gentleman."

"Miss Cram," said my wife, "very kindly came in to offer to help us with the Guides. We asked for helpers last Sunday, you remember."

I did remember, and I was convinced, and so, I knew from her tone, was Griselda, that the idea of enrolling herself among them would never have occurred to Miss Cram but for the exciting incident which had taken place at the Vicarage.

"I was only just saying to Mrs. Clement," went on Miss Cram, "you could have struck me all of a heap when I heard the news. A murder? I said. In this quiet one-horse village—for quiet it is, you must admit —not so much as a picture house, and as for Talkies! And then when I heard it was Colonel Protheroe—why, I simply couldn't believe it. He didn't seem the kind, somehow, to get murdered."

I don't know what Miss Cram considers are the necessary qualifications for being murdered. It has never struck me that the murdered belong to a special class, but doubtless she had some idea in her golden shingled head.

"And so," said Griselda, "Miss Cram came round to find out all about it."

I feared this plain speaking might offend the lady, but she merely flung her head back and laughed up-roariously, showing every tooth she possessed.

"That's too bad. You're a sharp one, aren't you, Mrs. Clement? But it's only natural, isn't it, to want to hear the ins and outs of a case like this? And I'm sure I'm willing enough to help with the Guides in any way you like. Exciting, that's what it is. I've been stagnating for a bit of fun. I have, really I have. Not that my job isn't a very good one, well paid, and Dr. Stone quite the gentleman in every way. But a girl wants a bit of life out of office hours, and except for

you, Mrs. Clement, who is there in the place to talk
to except a lot of old cats ? "

" There's Lettice Protheroe," I said.

Gladys Cram tossed her head.

" She's too high and mighty for the likes of me.
Fancies herself the county, and wouldn't demean herself
by noticing a girl who had to work for her living. Not
but what I *did* hear her talking of earning her living
herself. And who'd employ her, I should like to know ?
Why, she'd be fired in less than a week. Unless she went
as one of those mannequins, all dressed up and sidling
about. She could do that, I expect."

" She'd make a very good mannequin," said Griselda.
" She's got such a lovely figure." There's nothing of the
cat about Griselda. " When was she talking of earning
her own living ? "

Miss Cram seemed momentarily discomfited, but
recovered herself with her usual archness.

" That would be telling, wouldn't it ? " she said.
" But she did say so. Things not very happy at home,
I fancy. Catch me living at home with a stepmother.
I wouldn't sit down under it for a minute."

" Ah ! but you're so high spirited and independent,"
said Griselda gravely, and I looked at her with suspicion.

Miss Cram was clearly pleased.

" That's right. That's me all over. Can be led, not
driven. A palmist told me that not so very long ago.
No, I'm not one to sit down and be bullied. And I've
made it clear all along to Dr. Stone that I must have
my regular times off. These scientific gentlemen, they
think a girl's a kind of machine—half the time they
just don't notice her or remember she's there."

" Do you find Dr. Stone pleasant to work with ? It
must be an interesting job if you are interested in
archæology."

" Of course, I don't know much about it," confessed
the girl. " It still seems to me that digging up people
that are dead and have been dead for hundreds of years
isn't—well, it seems a bit nosey, doesn't it ? And there's

Dr. Stone so wrapped up in it all that half the time he'd forget his meals if it wasn't for me."

" Is he at the barrow this morning ? " asked Griselda.

Miss Cram shook her head.

" A bit under the weather this morning," she explained. " Not up to doing any work. That means a holiday for little Gladys."

" I'm sorry," I said.

" Oh ! it's nothing much. There's not going to be a second death. But do tell me, Mr. Clement, I hear you've been with the police all the morning. What do they think ? "

" Well," I said slowly, " there is still a little— uncertainty."

" Ah ! " cried Miss Cram. " Then they don't think it is Mr. Lawrence Redding after all. So handsome, isn't he ? Just like a movie star. And such a nice smile when he says good-morning to you. I really couldn't believe my ears when I heard the police had arrested him. Still, one has always heard they're very stupid— the country police."

" You can hardly blame them in this instance," I said. " Mr. Redding came in and gave himself up."

" What ? " the girl was clearly dumbfounded. " Well —of all the poor fish ! If I'd committed a murder, I wouldn't go straight off and give myself up. I should have thought Lawrence Redding would have had more sense. To give in like that ! What did he kill Protheroe for ? Did he say ? Was it just a quarrel ? "

" It's not absolutely certain that he did kill him," I said.

" But surely—if he says he has—why really, Mr. Clement, he ought to know."

" He ought to, certainly," I agreed. " But the police are not satisfied with his story."

" But why should he say he'd done it if he hasn't ? "

That was a point on which I had no intention of enlightening Miss Cram. Instead I said rather vaguely :

" I believe that in all prominent murder cases, the

police receive numerous letters from people accusing themselves of the crime."

Miss Cram's reception of this piece of information was :

" They must be chumps ! " in a tone of wonder and scorn.

She added : " I'd never do a thing like that."

" I'm sure you wouldn't," I said.

" Well," she said with a sigh, " I suppose I must be trotting along." She rose. " Mr. Redding accusing himself of the murder will be a bit of news for Dr. Stone."

" Is he interested ? " asked Griselda.

Miss Cram furrowed her brows perplexedly.

" He's a queer one. You never can tell with him. All wrapped up in the past. He'd a hundred times rather look at a nasty old bronze knife out of one of those humps of ground than he would see the knife Crippen cut up his wife with, supposing he had a chance to."

" Well," I said, " I must confess I agree with him."

Miss Cram's eyes expressed incomprehension and slight contempt. Then, with reiterated good-byes, she took her departure.

" Not such a bad sort, really," said Griselda, as the door closed behind her. " Terribly common, of course, but one of those big, bouncing, good-humoured girls that you can't dislike. I wonder what really brought her here ? "

" Curiosity."

" Yes, I suppose so. Now, Len, tell me all about it. I'm simply dying to hear."

I sat down and recited faithfully all the happenings of the morning, Griselda interpolating the narrative with little exclamations of surprise and interest.

" So it was Anne Lawrence was after all along ! Not Lettice. How blind we've all been ! That must have been what old Miss Marple was hinting at yesterday. Don't you think so ? "

"Yes," I said, averting my eyes.

Mary entered.

"There's a couple of men here—come from a newspaper, so they say. Do you want to see them?"

"No," I said. "certainly not. Refer them to Inspector Slack at the police station."

Mary nodded and turned away.

"And when you've got rid of them," I said, "come back here. There's something I want to ask you."

Mary nodded again.

It was some few minutes before she returned.

"Had a job getting rid of them," she said. "Persistent. You never saw anything like it. Wouldn't take no for an answer."

"I expect we shall be a good deal troubled with them," I said. "Now, Mary, what I want to ask you is this : Are you quite certain you didn't hear the shot yesterday evening?"

"The shot what killed him? No, of course I didn't. if I had of done, I should have gone in to see what had happened."

"Yes, but——" I was remembering Miss Marple's statement that she had heard a shot "in the wood." I changed the form of my question. "Did you hear any other shot—one down in the wood, for instance?"

"Oh! that." The girl paused. "Yes, now I come to think of it, I believe I did. Not a lot of shots, just one. Queer sort of bang it was."

"Exactly," I said. "Now what time was that?"

"Time?"

"Yes, time."

"I couldn't say, I'm sure. Well after tea-time. I do know that."

"Can't you get a little nearer than that?"

"No, I can't. I've got my work to do, haven't I? I can't go on looking at clocks the whole time—and it wouldn't be much good anyway—the alarm loses a good three-quarters every day, and what with putting

F

it on and one thing and another, I'm never exactly sure what time it is."

This perhaps explains why our meals are never punctual. They are sometimes too late and sometimes bewilderingly early.

"Was it long before Mr. Redding came?"

"No, it wasn't long. Ten minutes—a quarter of an hour—not longer than that."

I nodded my head, satisfied.

"Is that all?" said Mary. "Because what I mean to say is, I've got the joint in the oven and the pudding boiling over as likely as not."

"That's all right. You can go."

She left the room, and I turned to Griselda.

"Is it quite out of the question to induce Mary to say sir or m'am?"

"I have told her. She doesn't remember. She's just a raw girl, remember."

"I am perfectly aware of that," I said. "But raw things do not necessarily remain raw for ever. I feel a tinge of cooking might be induced in Mary."

"Well, I don't agree with you," said Griselda. "You know how little we can afford to pay a servant. If once we got her smartened up at all, she'd leave. Naturally. And get higher wages. But as long as Mary can't cook and has those awful manners—well, we're safe, nobody else would have her."

I perceived that my wife's methods of housekeeping were not so entirely haphazard as I had imagined. A certain amount of reasoning underlay them. Whether it was worth while having a maid at the price of her not being able to cook, and having a habit of throwing dishes and remarks at one with the same disconcerting abruptness, was a debatable matter.

"And anyway," continued Griselda, "you must make allowances for her manners being worse than usual just now. You can't expect her to feel exactly sympathetic about Colonel Protheroe's death when he jailed her young man."

" Did he jail her young man ? "

" Yes, for poaching. You know, that man, Archer. Mary has been walking out with him for two years."

" I didn't know that."

" Darling Len, you never know anything."

" It's queer," I said, " that every one says the shot came from the woods."

" I don't think it's queer at all," said Griselda. " You see, one so often does hear shots in the wood. So naturally, when you do hear a shot, you just assume as a matter of course that it *is* in the wood. It probably just sounds a bit louder than usual. Of course, if one were in the next room, you'd realise that it was in the house, but from Mary's kitchen with the window right the other side of the house, I don't believe you'd ever think of such a thing."

The door opened again.

" Colonel Melchett's back," said Mary. " And that police inspector with him, and they say they'd be glad if you'd join them. They're in the study."

# CHAPTER XI

I saw at a glance that Colonel Melchett and Inspector Slack had not been seeing eye to eye about the case. Melchett looked flushed and annoyed and the inspector looked sulky.

" I'm sorry to say," said Melchett, " that Inspector Slack doesn't agree with me in considering young Redding innocent. "

" If he didn't do it, what does he go and say he did it for ? " asked Slack sceptically.

" Mrs. Protheroe acted in an exactly similar fashion, remember, Slack."

" That's different. She's a woman, and women act in that silly way. I'm not saying she did it for a moment. She heard he was accused and she trumped up a story. I'm used to that sort of game. You wouldn't believe the fool things I've known women do. But Redding's different. He's got his head screwed on all right. And if he admits he did it, well, I say he did do it. It's his pistol—you can't get away from that. And thanks to this business of Mrs. Protheroe, we know the motive. That was the weak point before, but now we know it —why, the whole thing's plain sailing."

" You think he can have shot him earlier ?  At six-thirty, say ? "

" He can't have done that."

" You've checked up his movements ? "

The inspector nodded.

" He was in the village near the Blue Boar at ten past six. From there he came along the back lane where you say the old lady next door saw him—she doesn't miss much, I should say—and kept his appointment with Mrs. Protheroe in the studio in the garden. They left there together just after six-thirty, and went along the lane to the village, being joined by Dr. Stone. He corroborates that all right—I've seen him. They all stood talking just by the post office for a few minutes, then Mrs. Protheroe went into Miss Hartnell's to borrow a gardening magazine. That's all right too. I've seen Miss Hartnell. Mrs. Protheroe remained there talking to her till just on seven o'clock, when she exclaimed at the lateness of the hour and said she must get home."

" What was her manner ? "

" Very easy and pleasant, Miss Hartnell said. She seemed in good spirits—Miss Hartnell is quite sure there was nothing on her mind."

" Well, go on."

" Redding, he went with Dr. Stone to the Blue Boar and they had a drink together. He left there at twenty minutes to seven, went rapidly along the village street and down the road to the Vicarage. Lots of people saw him."

" Not down the back lane this time ? " commented the colonel.

" No—he came to the front, asked for the vicar, heard Colonel Protheroe was there, went in—and shot him—just as he said he did ! That's the truth of it, and we needn't look further."

Melchett shook his head.

" There's the doctor's evidence. You can't get away from that. Protheroe was shot not later than six-thirty."

" Oh ! doctors ! " Inspector Slack looked contemptuous. " If you're going to believe doctors. Take out all your teeth—that's what they do nowadays—and then say they're very sorry, but all the time it was appendicitis. Doctors ! "

" This isn't a question of diagnosis. Dr. Haydock was absolutely positive on the point. You can't go against the medical evidence, Slack."

" And there's my evidence for what it is worth," I said, suddenly recalling a forgotten incident. " I touched the body and it was cold. That I can swear to."

" You see, Slack ? " said Melchett.

Inspector Slack gave in with a good grace.

" Well, of course, if that's so. But there it was—a beautiful case. Mr. Redding only too anxious to be hanged, so to speak."

" That, in itself, strikes me as a little unnatural," observed Colonel Melchett.

" Well, there's no accounting for tastes," said the inspector. " There's a lot of gentlemen went a bit balmy after the war. Now, I suppose, it means starting again at the beginning." He turned on me. " Why you went out of your way to mislead me about the clock, sir, I can't think. Obstructing the ends of justice, that's what that was."

I was stung.

" I tried to tell you on three separate occasions," I said. " And each time you shut me up and refused to listen."

" That's just a way of speaking, sir. You could have told me perfectly well if you had had a mind to. The clock and the note seemed to tally perfectly. Now, according to you, the clock was all wrong. I never knew such a case. What's the sense of keeping a clock a quarter of an hour fast anyway ? "

" It is supposed," I said, " to induce punctuality."

The inspector snorted.

" I don't think we need go further into that now, Inspector," said Colonel Melchett tactfully. " What we want now is the true story from both Mrs. Protheroe and young Redding. I telephoned to Haydock and asked him to bring Mrs. Protheroe over here with him. They ought to be here in about a quarter of an hour. I think it would be as well to have Redding here first."

" I'll get on to the station," said Inspector Slack, and took up the telephone.

He spoke down it.

" And now," he said, replacing the receiver, " we'll get to work on this room."

He looked at me in a meaning fashion.

" Perhaps," I said, " you'd like me out of the way."

The inspector immediately opened the door for me. Melchett called out :

" Come back when young Redding arrives, will you, Vicar ? You're a friend of his and you may have sufficient influence to persuade him to speak the truth."

I found my wife and Miss Marple with their heads together.

" We've been discussing all sorts of possibilities," said Griselda. " I wish you'd solve the case, Miss Marple, like you did the way Miss Wetherby's gill of picked shrimps disappeared. And all because it re-minded you of something quite different about a sack of coals."

" You're laughing, my dear," said Miss Marple, " but after all, that is a very sound way of arriving at the truth. It's really what people call intuition and make such a fuss about. Intuition is like reading a word without having to spell it out. A child can't do that because it has had so little experience. But a grown-up person knows the word because they've seen it often before. You catch my meaning, vicar ? "

" Yes," I said slowly, " I think I do. You mean that if a thing reminds you of something else—well, it's probably the same kind of thing."

" Exactly."

" And what precisely does the murder of Colonel Protheroe remind you of ? "

Miss Marple sighed.

" That is just the difficulty. So many parallels come to the mind. For instance, there was Major Hargraves, a churchwarden and a man highly respected in every way. And all the time he was keeping a separate second establishment—a former housemaid, just think of it ! And five children—actually five children—a terrible shock to his wife and daughter."

I tried hard to visualise Colonel Protheroe in the role of secret sinner and failed.

" And then there was that laundry business," went on Miss Marple. " Miss Hartnell's opal pin—left most

imprudently in a frilled blouse and sent to the laundry.
And the woman who took it didn't want it in the least
and wasn't by any means a thief. She simply hid it in
another woman's house and told the police she'd seen
this other woman take it. Spite, you know, sheer spite.
It's an astonishing motive—spite. A man in it, of course.
There always is."

This time I failed to see any parallel, however remote.
Miss Marple went on in a dreamy voice :

" And then there was poor Elwell's daughter—such
a pretty ethereal girl—tried to stifle her little brother.
And there was the money for the Choir Boys' Outing
(before your time, vicar) actually taken by the organist.
His wife was sadly in debt. Yes, this case makes one
think of so many things—too many. It's very hard to
arrive at the truth."

" I wish you would tell me," I said, " who were the
seven suspects ? "

" The seven suspects ? "

" You said you could think of seven people who would
—well, be glad of Colonel Protheroe's death."

" Did I ? Yes, I remember I did."

" Was that true ? "

" Oh ! certainly it was true. But I mustn't mention
names. You can think of them quite easily yourself,
I am sure."

" Indeed I can't. There is Lettice Protheroe, I suppose, since she probably comes into money on her
father's death. But it is absurd to think of her in such
a connection, and outside her I can think of nobody."

" And you, my dear ? " said Miss Marple, turning to
Griselda.

Rather to my surprise Griselda coloured up. Something very like tears started into her eyes. She clenched
both her small hands.

" Oh ! " she cried indignantly. " People are hateful
—hateful. The things they say ! The beastly things
they say. . . ."

I looked at her curiously. It is very unlike Griselda

to be so upset. She noticed my glance and tried to smile.

" Don't look at me as though I were an interesting specimen you didn't understand, Len ? Don't let's get heated and wander from the point. I don't believe that it was Lawrence or Anne, and Lettice is out of the question. There must be some clue or other that would help us."

" There is the note, of course," said Miss Marple. " You will remember my saying this morning that that struck me as exceedingly peculiar."

" It seems to fix the time of his death with remarkable accuracy," I said. " And yet, is that possible ? Mrs. Protheroe would only have just left the study. She would hardly have had time to reach the studio. The only way in which I can account for it is that he consulted his own watch and that his watch was slow. That seems to me a feasible solution."

" I have another idea," said Griselda. " Suppose, Len, that the clock had already been put back—no, that comes to the same thing—how stupid of me ! "

" It hadn't been altered when I left," I said. " I remember comparing it with my watch. Still, as you say, that has no bearing on the present matter."

" What do you think, Miss Marple ? " asked Griselda. The old lady shook her head.

" My dear, I confess I wasn't thinking about it from that point of view at all. What strikes me as so curious, and has done from the first, is the subject matter of that letter."

" I don't see that," I said. " Colonel Protheroe merely wrote that he couldn't wait any longer——"

" At twenty minutes past six ? " said Miss Marple. " Your maid, Mary, had already told him that you wouldn't be in till half-past six at the earliest, and he had appeared to be quite willing to wait until then. And yet at twenty past six he sits down and says he " can't wait any longer."

I stared at the old lady, feeling an increased respect

for her mental powers. Her keen wits had seen what we had failed to perceive. It *was* an odd thing—a very odd thing.

" If only," I said, " the letter hadn't been dated——"

Miss Marple nodded her head.

" Exactly," she said. " If it *hadn't* been dated ! "

I cast my mind back, trying to recall that sheet of notepaper and the blurred scrawl, and at the top that neatly printed 6.20. Surely these figures were on a different scale to the rest of the letter.

I gave a gasp.

" Supposing," I said, " it wasn't dated. Supposing that round about 6.30 Colonel Protheroe got impatient and sat down to say he couldn't wait any longer. And as he was sitting there writing, some one came in through the window——"

" Or through the door," suggested Griselda.

" He'd hear the door and look up."

" Colonel Protheroe was rather deaf, you remember," said Miss Marple.

" Yes, that's true. He wouldn't hear it. Whichever way the murderer came, he stole up behind the colonel and shot him. Then he saw the note and the clock and the idea came to him. He put 6.20 at the top of the letter and he altered the clock to 6.22. It was a clever idea. It gave him, or so he would think, a perfect alibi."

" And what we want to find," said Griselda, " is some one who has a cast-iron alibi for 6.20, but no alibi at all for—well, that isn't so easy. One can't fix the time."

" We can fix it within very narrow limits," I said. " Haydock places 6.30 as the outside limit of time. I suppose one could perhaps shift it to 6.35 from the reasoning we have just been following out, it seems clear that Protheroe would not have got impatient before 6.30. I think we can say we do know pretty well."

" Then that shot I heard—yes, I suppose it is quite possible. And I thought nothing about it—nothing at all. Most vexing. And yet, now I try to recollect, it does seem to me that it was different from the usual sort of shot one hears. Yes, there was a difference."

" Louder ? " I suggested.

No, Miss Marple didn't think it had been louder. In fact, she found it hard to say in what way it had been different, but she still insisted that it was.

I thought she was probably persuading herself of the fact rather than actually remembering it, but she had just contributed such a valuable new outlook to the problem that I felt highly respectful towards her.

She rose, murmuring that she must really get back —it had been so tempting just to run over and discuss the case with dear Griselda. I escorted her to the boundary wall and the back gate and returned to find Griselda wrapped in thought.

" Still puzzling over that note ? " I asked.

" No."

She gave a sudden shiver and shook her shoulders impatiently.

" Len, I've been thinking. How badly some one must have hated Anne Protheroe ! "

" Hated her ? "

" Yes. Don't you see ? There's no real evidence against Lawrence—all the evidence against him is what you might call accidental. He just happens to take it into his head to come here. If he hadn't—well, no one would have thought of connecting him with the crime. But Anne is different. Suppose some one knew that she was here at exactly 6.20—the clock and the time on the letter—everything pointing to her. I don't think it was only because of an alibi it was moved to that exact time—I think there was more in it than that —a direct attempt to fasten the business on her. If it hadn't been for Miss Marple saying she hadn't got the pistol with her and noticing that she was only a moment before going down to the studio—Yes, if it hadn't been for that. . . . " She shivered again. " Len—I feel that some one hated Anne Protheroe very much. I—I don't like it."

# CHAPTER XII

I WAS summoned to the study when Lawrence Redding arrived. He looked haggard, and, I thought, suspicious. Colonel Melchett greeted him with something approaching cordiality.

" We want to ask you a few questions—here, on the spot," he said.

Lawrence sneered slightly.

" Isn't that a French idea ?  Reconstruction of the crime ? "

" My dear boy," said Colonel Melchett, " don't take that tone with us.  Are you aware that some one else has also confessed to committing the crime which you pretend to have committed ? "

The effect of these words on Lawrence was painful and immediate.

" S-s-ome one else ? " he stammered.  " Who—who ? "

" Mrs. Protheroe," said Colonel Melchett, watching him.

" Absurd.  She never did it.  She couldn't have.  It's impossible."

Melchett interrupted him.

" Strangely enough, we did not believe her story. Neither, I may say, do we believe yours.  Dr. Haydock says positively that the murder could not have been committed at the time you say it was."

" Dr. Haydock says that ? "

" Yes, so, you see, you are cleared whether you like it or not.  And now we want you to help us, to tell us exactly what occurred."

Lawrence still hesitated.

" You're not deceiving me about—about Mrs. Protheroe ?  You really don't suspect her ? "

" On my word of honour," said Colonel Melchett.

Lawrence drew a deep breath.

" I've been a fool," he said. " An absolute fool. How could I have thought for one minute that she did it——"

" Suppose you tell us all about it ? " suggested the Chief Constable.

" There's not much to tell. I—I met Mrs. Protheroe that afternoon——"

He paused.

" We know all about that," said Melchett. " You may think that your feeling for Mrs. Protheroe and hers for you was a dead secret, but in reality it was known and commented upon. In any case, everything is bound to come out now."

" Very well, then. I expect you are right. I had promised the vicar here (he glanced at me) to—to go right away. I met Mrs. Protheroe that evening in the studio at a quarter-past six. I told her of what I had decided. She, too, agreed, that it was the only thing to do. We—we said good-bye to each other.

" We left the studio, and almost at once Dr. Stone joined us. Anne managed to seem marvellously natural. I couldn't do it. I went off with Stone to the Blue Boar and had a drink. Then I thought I'd go home, but when I got to the corner of this road, I changed my mind and decided to come along and see the vicar. I felt I wanted some one to talk to about the matter.

" At the door, the maid told me the vicar was out, but would be in shortly, but that Colonel Protheroe was in the study waiting for him. Well, I didn't like to go away again—looked as though I were shirking meeting him. So I said I'd wait too, and I went into the study."

He stopped.

" Well ? " said Colonel Melchett.

" Protheroe was sitting at the writing table—just as you found him. I went up to him—touched him. He was dead. Then I looked down and saw the pistol lying on the floor beside him. I picked it up—*and at once saw that it was my pistol.*

" That gave me a turn. My pistol ! And then,

straightaway I leaped to one conclusion. Anne must have bagged my pistol some time or other—meaning it for herself if she couldn't bear things any longer. Perhaps she had had it with her to-day. After we parted in the village she must have come back here and —and—oh! I suppose I was mad to think of it. But that's what I thought. I slipped the pistol in my pocket and came away. Just outside the Vicarage gate, I met the vicar. He said something nice and normal about seeing Protheroe—suddenly I had a wild desire to laugh. His manner was so ordinary and everyday and there was I all strung up. I remember shouting out something absurd and seeing his face change. I was nearly off my head, I believe. I went walking—walking—at last I couldn't bear it any longer. If Anne had done this ghastly thing, I was, at least, morally responsible. I went and gave myself up."

There was a silence when he had finished. Then the colonel said in a business-like voice:

" I would like to ask just one or two questions. First, did you touch or move the body in any way ? "

" No, I didn't touch it at all. One could see he was dead without touching him."

" Did you notice a note lying on the blotter half concealed by his body ? "

" No."

" Did you interfere in any way with the clock ? "

" I never touched the clock. I seem to remember a clock lying overturned on the table, but I never touched it."

" Now as to this pistol of yours, when did you last see it ? "

Lawrence Redding reflected.

" It's hard to say exactly."

" Where do you keep it ? "

" Oh! in a litter of odds and ends in the sitting-room in my cottage. On one of the shelves of the book-case."

" You left it lying about carelessly ? "

" Yes. I really didn't think about it. It was just there."

" So that any one who came to your cottage could have seen it ? "

" Yes."

" And you don't remember when you last saw it ? "

Lawrence drew his brows together in a frown of recollection.

" I'm almost sure it was there the day before yesterday. I remember pushing it aside to get an old pipe. I think it was the day before yesterday—but it may have been the day before that."

" Who has been to your cottage lately ? "

" Oh ! crowds of people. Some one is always drifting in and out. I had a sort of tea party the day before yesterday. Lettice Protheroe, Dennis, and all their crowd. And then one or other of the old Pussies comes in now and again."

" Do you lock the cottage up when you go out ? "

" No ; why on earth should I ? I've nothing to steal. And no one does lock their houses up round here."

" Who looks after your wants there ? "

" An old Mrs. Archer comes in every morning to ' do for me ' as it's called."

" Do you think she would remember when the pistol was there last ? "

" I don't know. She might. But I don't fancy conscientious dusting is her strong point."

" It comes to this—that almost any one might have taken that pistol ? "

" It seems so—yes."

The door opened and Dr. Haydock came in with Anne Protheroe.

She started at seeing Lawrence. He, on his part, made a tentative step towards her.

" Forgive me, Anne," he said. " It was abominable of me to think what I did."

" I——" She faltered, then looked appealingly at

Colonel Melchett. " It is true, what Dr. Haydock told me ? "

" That Mr. Redding is cleared of suspicion ? Yes. And now what about this story of yours, Mrs. Protheroe ? Eh, what about it ? "

She smiled rather shamefacedly.

" I suppose you think it dreadful of me ? "

" Well, shall we say—very foolish ? But that's all over. What I want now, Mrs. Protheroe, is the truth —the absolute truth."

She nodded gravely.

" I will tell you. I suppose you know about—about everything."

" Yes."

" I was to meet Lawrence—Mr. Redding—that evening at the studio. At a quarter past six. My husband and I drove into the village together. I had some shopping to do. As we parted he mentioned casually that he was going to see the vicar. I couldn't get word to Lawrence, and I was rather uneasy. I—well, it was awkward meeting him in the Vicarage garden whilst my husband was at the Vicarage."

Her cheeks burned as she said this. It was not a pleasant moment for her.

" I reflected that perhaps my husband would not stay very long. To find this out, I came along the back lane and into the garden. I hoped no one would see me, but of course old Miss Marple had to be in her garden ! She stopped me and we said a few words, and I explained I was going to call for my husband. I felt I had to say something. I don't know whether she believed me or not. She looked rather—funny.

" When I left her, I went straight across to the Vicarage and round the corner of the house to the study window. I crept up to it very softly, expecting to hear the sound of voices. But to my surprise there were none. I just glanced in, saw the room was empty, and hurried across the lawn and down to the studio where Lawrence joined me almost at once."

" You say the room was empty, Mrs. Protheroe ? "

" Yes, my husband was not there."

" Extraordinary."

" You mean, m'am, that you didn't see him ? " said the inspector.

" No, I didn't see him."

Inspector Slack whispered to the Chief Constable, who nodded his head.

" Do you mind, Mrs. Protheroe, just showing us exactly what you did ? "

" Not at all."

She rose, Inspector Slack pushed open the window for her, and she stepped out on the terrace and round the house to the left.

Inspector Slack beckoned me imperiously to go and sit at the writing-table.

Somehow I didn't much like doing it. It gave me an uncomfortable feeling. But, of course, I complied.

Presently I heard footsteps outside, they paused for a minute, then retreated. Inspector Slack indicated to me that I could return to the other side of the room. Mrs. Protheroe re-entered through the window.

" Is that exactly how it was ? " asked Colonel Melchett.

" I think exactly."

" Then can you tell us, Mrs. Protheroe, just exactly where the vicar was in the room when you looked in ? " asked Inspector Slack.

" The vicar ? I—no, I'm afraid I can't. I didn't see him."

Inspector Slack nodded.

" That's how you didn't see your husband. He was round the corner at the writing-desk."

" Oh ! " she paused. Suddenly her eyes grew round with horror. " It wasn't there that—that——"

" Yes, Mrs. Protheroe. It was while he was sitting there."

" Oh ! " she shivered.

He went on with his questions.

G

"Did you know, Mrs. Protheroe, that Mr. Redding had a pistol?"

"Yes. He told me so once."

"Did you ever have that pistol in your possession?" She shook her head.

"No."

"Did you know where he kept it?"

"I'm not sure. I think—yes, I think I've seen it on a shelf in his cottage. Didn't you keep it there, Lawrence?"

"When was the last time you were at the cottage, Mrs. Protheroe?"

"Oh! about three weeks ago. My husband and I had tea there with him."

"And you have not been there since?"

"No. I never went there. You see, it would probably cause a lot of talk in the village."

"Doubtless," said Colonel Melchett dryly. "Where were you in the habit of seeing Mr. Redding, if I may ask?"

She blushed.

"He used to come up to the Hall. He was painting Lettice. We—we often met in the woods afterwards."

Colonel Melchett nodded.

"Isn't that enough?" Her voice was suddenly broken. "It's so awful—having to tell you all these things. And—and there wasn't anything wrong about it. There wasn't—indeed, there wasn't. We were just friends. We—we couldn't help caring for each other."

She looked pleadingly at Dr. Haydock, and that soft-hearted man stepped forward.

"I really think, Melchett," he said, "that Mrs. Protheroe has had enough. She's had a great shock—in more ways than one."

The Chief Constable nodded.

"There is really nothing more I want to ask you, Mrs. Protheroe," he said. "Thank you for answering my questions so frankly."

"Then—then I may go?"

"Is your wife in ? " asked Haydock. " I think Mrs. Protheroe would like to see her."

"Yes," I said, " Griselda is in. You'll find her in the drawing-room."

She and Haydock left the room together and Lawrence Redding with them.

Colonel Melchett had pursed up his lips and was playing with a paper knife. Slack was looking at the note. It was then that I mentioned Miss Marple's theory.

Slack looked closely at it.

" My word," he said, " I believe the old lady's right. Look here, sir, don't you see ?—these figures are written in different ink. That date was written with a fountain pen or I'll eat my boots ! "

We were all rather excited.

" You've examined the note for finger-prints, of course," said the Chief Constable.

" What do you think, colonel ? No finger-prints on the note at all. Finger-prints on the pistol those of Mr. Lawrence Redding. May have been some others once before he went fooling round with it and carrying it around in his pocket, but there's nothing clear enough to get hold of now."

" At first the case looked very black against Mrs. Protheroe," said the colonel thoughtfully. " Much blacker than against young Redding. There was that old woman Marple's evidence that she didn't have the pistol with her, but these elderly ladies are often mistaken."

I was silent, but I did not agree with him. I was quite sure that Anne Protheroe had had no pistol with her since Miss Marple had said so. Miss Marple is not the type of elderly lady who makes mistakes. She has got an uncanny knack of being always right.

" What did get me was that nobody heard the shot. If it was fired then—somebody *must* have heard it— wherever they thought it came from. Slack, you'd better have a word with the maid."

Inspector Slack moved with alacrity towards the door.

" I shouldn't ask her if she heard a shot in the house," I said. " Because if you do, she'll deny it. Call it a shot in the wood. That's the only kind of shot she'll admit to hearing."

" I know how to manage them," said Inspector Slack, and disappeared.

" Miss Marple says she heard a shot later," said Colonel Melchett thoughtfully. " We must see if she can fix the time at all precisely. Of course it may be a stray shot that had nothing to do with the case."

" It may be, of course," I agreed.

The colonel took a turn or two up and down the room.

" Do you know, Clement," he said suddenly, " I've a feeling that this is going to turn out a much more intricate and difficult business than any of us think. Dash it all, there's something behind it." He snorted. " Something we don't know about. We're only beginning, Clement. Mark my words, we're only beginning. All these things, the clock, the note, the pistol—they don't make sense as they stand."

I shook my head. They certainly didn't.

" But I'm going to get to the bottom of it. No calling in of Scotland Yard. Slack's a smart man. He's a very smart man. He's a kind of ferret. He'll nose his way through to the truth. He's done several very good things already, and this case will be his *chef d'œuvre*. Some men would call in Scotland Yard. I shan't. We'll get to the bottom of this here in Downshire."

" I hope so, I'm sure," I said.

I tried to make my voice enthusiastic, but I had already taken such a dislike to Inspector Slack that the prospect of his success failed to appeal to me. A successful Slack would, I thought, be even more odious than a baffled one.

" Who has the house next door ? " asked the colonel suddenly.

" You mean at the end of the road ? Mrs. Price Ridley."

" We'll go along to her after Slack has finished with your maid. She might just possibly have heard something. She isn't deaf or anything, is she ? "

" I should say her hearing was remarkably keen. I'm going by the amount of scandal she has started by ' just happening to overhear accidentally.' "

" That's the kind of woman we want. Oh ! here's Slack."

The inspector had the air of one emerging from a severe tussle. He looked hot.

" Phew ! " he said. " That's a tartar you've got, sir."

" Mary is essentially a girl of strong character," I replied.

" Doesn't like the police," he said. " I cautioned her —did what I could to put the fear of the law into her, but no good. She stood right up to me."

" Spirited," I said, feeling more kindly towards Mary.

" But I pinned her down all right. She heard one shot—and one shot only. And it was a good long time after Colonel Protheroe came. I couldn't get her to name a time, but we fixed it at last by means of the fish. The fish was late, and she blew the boy up when he came, and he said it was barely half-past six anyway, and it was just after that she heard the shot. Of course, that's not accurate, so to speak, but it gives us an idea."

" H'm," said Melchett.

" I don't think Mrs. Protheroe's in this after all," said Slack, with a note of regret in his voice. " She wouldn't have had time, to begin with, and then women never like fiddling about with firearms. Arsenic's more in their line. No, I don't think she did it. It's a pity ! "

He sighed.

Melchett explained that he was going round to Mrs. Price Ridley's, and Slack approved.

" May I come with you ? " I asked. " I'm getting interested."

I was given permission, and we set forth. A loud " Hie " greeted us as we emerged from the Vicarage gate, and my nephew, Dennis, came running up the road from the village to join us.

"Look here," he said to the inspector, "what about that footprint I told you about?"

"Gardener's," said Inspector Slack laconically.

"You don't think it might be some one else wearing the gardener's boots?"

"No, I don't!" said Inspector Slack in a discouraging way.

It would take more than that to discourage Dennis, however.

He held out a couple of burnt matches.

"I found these by the Vicarage gate."

"Thank you," said Slack, and put them in his pocket.

Matters appeared now to have reached a deadlock.

"You're not arresting Uncle Len, are you?" inquired Dennis facetiously.

"Why should I?" inquired Slack.

"There's a lot of evidence against him," declared Dennis. "You ask Mary. Only the day before the murder he was wishing Colonel Protheroe out of the world. Weren't you, Uncle Len?"

"Er——" I began.

Inspector Slack turned a slow suspicious stare upon me, and I felt hot all over. Dennis is exceedingly tiresome. He ought to realise that a policeman seldom has a sense of humour.

"Don't be absurd, Dennis," I said irritably.

The innocent child opened his eyes in a stare of surprise.

"I say, it's only a joke," he said. "Uncle Len just said that any one who murdered Colonel Protheroe would be doing the world a service."

"Ah!" said Inspector Slack, "that explains something the maid said.

Servants very seldom have any sense of humour either. I cursed Dennis heartily in my mind for bringing the matter up. That and the clock together will make the inspector suspicious of me for life.

" Come on, Clement," said Colonel Melchett.

" Where are you going ?  Can I come, too ? " asked Dennis.

" No, you can't," I snapped.

We left him looking after us with a hurt expression. We went up to the neat front door of Mrs. Price Ridley's house and the inspector knocked and rang in what I can only describe as an official manner.

A pretty parlourmaid answered the bell.

" Mrs. Price Ridley in ? " inquired Melchett.

" No, sir." The maid paused and added : " She's just gone down to the police station."

This was a totally unexpected development. As we retracted our steps Melchett caught me by the arm and murmured :

" If she's gone to confess to the crime, too, I really shall go off my head."

# CHAPTER XIII

I HARDLY thought it likely that Mrs. Price Ridley had anything so dramatic in view, but I did wonder what had taken her to the police station. Had she really got evidence of importance, or that she thought of importance, to offer? At anyrate, we should soon know.

We found Mrs. Price Ridley talking at a high rate of speed to a somewhat bewildered-looking police constable. That she was extremely indignant I knew from the way the bow in her hat was trembling. Mrs. Price Ridley wears what, I believe, are known as " Hats for Matrons " —they make a speciality of them in our adjacent town of Much Benham. They perch easily on a superstructure of hair and are somewhat overweighted with large bows of ribbon. Griselda is always threatening to get a matron's hat.

Mrs. Price Ridley paused in her flow of words upon our entrance.

" Mrs. Price Ridley ? " inquired Colonel Melchett, lifting his hat.

" Let me introduce Colonel Melchett to you, Mrs. Price Ridley," I said. " Colonel Melchett is our Chief Constable."

Mrs. Price Ridley looked at me coldly, but produced the semblance of a gracious smile for the colonel.

" We've just been round to your house, Mrs. Price Ridley," explained the colonel, " and heard you had come down here."

Mrs. Price Ridley thawed altogether.

" Ah ! " she said, " I'm glad *some* notice is being taken of the occurrence. Disgraceful, I call it. Simply disgraceful."

There is no doubt that murder is disgraceful, but it is not the word I should use to describe it myself. It surprised Melchett too, I could see.

"Have you any light to throw upon the matter?" he asked.

"That's your business. It's the business of the police. What do we pay rates and taxes for, I should like to know?"

One wonders how many times that query is uttered in a year!

"We're doing our best, Mrs. Price Ridley," said the Chief Constable.

"But the man here hadn't even heard of it till I told him about it!" cried the lady.

We all looked at the constable.

"Lady been rung up on the telephone," he said. "Annoyed. Matter of obscene language, I understand."

"Oh! I see." The colonel's brow cleared. "We've been talking at cross purposes. You came down here to make a complaint, did you?"

Melchett is a wise man. He knows that when it is a question of an irate middle-aged lady, there is only one thing to be done—to listen to her. When she has said all that she wants to say, there is a chance that she will listen to you.

Mrs. Price Ridley surged into speech.

"Such disgraceful occurrences ought to be prevented. They ought not to occur. To be rung up in one's own house and insulted—yes, insulted. I'm not accustomed to such things happening. Ever since the war there has been a loosening of moral fibre. Nobody minds what they say, and as to the clothes they wear——"

"Quite," said Colonel Melchett hastily. "What happened exactly?"

Mrs. Price Ridley took breath and started again.

"I was rung up——"

"When?"

"Yesterday afternoon—evening to be exact. About half-past six. I went to the telephone, suspecting nothing. Immediately I was foully attacked, threatened——"

"What actually was said?"

Mrs. Price Ridley got slightly pink.

" That I decline to state."

" Obscene language," murmured the constable in a ruminative bass.

" Was bad language used ? " asked Colonel Melchett.

" It depends on what you call bad language."

" Could you understand it ? " I asked.

" Of course I could understand it."

" Then it couldn't have been bad language," I said.

Mrs. Price Ridley looked at me suspiciously.

" A refined lady," I explained, " is naturally unacquainted with bad language."

" It wasn't that kind of thing," said Mrs. Price Ridley. " At first, I must admit, I was quite taken in. I thought it was a genuine message. Then the—er—person became abusive."

" Abusive ? "

" Most abusive. I was quite alarmed."

" Used threatening language, eh ? "

" Yes. I am not accustomed to being threatened."

" What did they threaten you with ? Bodily damage ? "

" Not exactly."

" I'm afraid, Mrs. Price Ridley, you must be more explicit. In what way were you threatened ? "

This Mrs. Price Ridley seemed singularly reluctant to answer.

" I can't remember exactly. It was all so upsetting. But right at the end—when I was really *very* upset, this—this—*wretch* laughed."

" Was it a man's voice or a woman's ? "

" It was a degenerate voice," said Mrs. Price Ridley, with dignity. " I can only describe it as a kind of perverted voice. Now gruff, now squeaky. Really a very *peculiar* voice."

" Probably a practical joke," said the colonel soothingly.

" A most wicked thing to do, if so. I might have had a heart attack."

"We'll look into it," said the colonel; "eh, inspector? Trace the telephone call. You can't tell me more definitely exactly what was said, Mrs. Price Ridley?"

A struggle began in Mrs. Price Ridley's ample black bosom. The desire for reticence fought against a desire for vengeance. Vengeance triumphed.

"This, of course, will go no further," she began.

"Of course not."

"This creature began by saying—I can hardly bring myself to repeat it——"

"Yes, yes," said Melchett encouragingly.

"'*You are a wicked scandal mongering old woman!*' Me, Colonel Melchett—a scandal-mongering old woman. '*But this time you've gone too far. Scotland Yard are after you for libel.*'"

"Naturally, you were alarmed," said Melchett, biting his moustache to conceal a smile.

"'*Unless you hold your tongue in future, it will be the worse for you—in more ways than one.*' I can't describe to you the menacing way *that* was said. I gasped, 'Who are you?' faintly—like that, and the voice answered, '*The Avenger.*' I gave a little shriek. It sounded so awful, and then—the person laughed. Laughed! Distinctly. And that was all. I heard them hang up the receiver. Of course I asked the exchange what number had been ringing me up, but they said they didn't know. You know what exchanges are. Thoroughly rude and unsympathetic."

"Quite," I said.

"I felt quite faint," continued Mrs. Price Ridley. "All on edge and so nervous that when I heard a shot in the woods, I do declare I jumped almost out of my skin. That will show you."

"A shot in the woods?" said Inspector Slack alertly.

"In my excited state, it simply sounded to me like a cannon going off. 'Oh!' I said, and sank down on the sofa in a state of prostration. Clara had to bring me a glass of Damson Gin."

" Shocking," said Melchett. " Shocking. All very trying for you. And the shot sounded very loud, you say ? As though it were near at hand ? "

" That was simply the state of my nerves."

" Of course. Of course. And what time was all this ? To help us in tracing the telephone call, you know."

" About half-past six."

" You can't give it us more exactly than that ? "

" Well, you see, the little clock on my mantelpiece had just chimed the half-hour, and I said, ' Surely that clock is fast.' (It does gain, that clock.) And I compared it with the watch I was wearing and that only said ten minutes past, but then I put it to my ear and found it had stopped. So I thought : ' Well, if that clock *is* fast, I shall hear the church tower in a moment or two.' And then, of course, the telephone bell rang, and I forgot all about it."

She paused breathless.

" Well, that's near enough," said Colonel Melchett. " We'll have it looked into for you, Mrs. Price Ridley."

" Just think of it as a silly joke, and don't worry, Mrs. Price Ridley," I said.

She looked at me coldly. Evidently the incident of the pound note still rankled.

" Very strange things have been happening in this village lately," she said, addressing herself to Melchett. " Very strange things indeed. Colonel Protheroe was going to look into them, and what happened to him, poor man ? Perhaps I shall be the next ? "

And on that she took her departure, shaking her head with a kind of ominous melancholy. Melchett muttered under his breath : " No such luck." Then his face grew grave, and he looked inquiringly at Inspector Slack.

That worthy nodded his head slowly.

" This about settles it, sir. That's three people who heard the shot. We've got to find out now who fired it. This business of Mr. Redding's has delayed us. But we've got several starting points. Thinking Mr. Redding was guilty, I didn't bother to look into them. But that's all changed now. And now one of the first things to do is to look up that telephone call."

" Mrs. Price Ridley's ? "

The inspector grinned.

" No—though I suppose we'd better make a note of that or else we shall have the old girl bothering in here again. No, I meant that fake call that got the vicar out of the way."

" Yes," said Melchett, " that's important."

" And the next thing is to find out what every one was doing that evening between six and seven. Every one at Old Hall, I mean, and pretty well every one in the village as well."

I gave a sigh.

" What wonderful energy you have, Inspector Slack."

" I believe in hard work. We'll begin by just noting down your own movements, Mr. Clement."

" Willingly. The telephone call came through about half-past five."

" A man's voice, or a woman's ? "

" A woman's. At least it sounded like a woman's. But of course I took it for granted it was Mrs. Abbott speaking."

" You didn't recognise it as being Mrs. Abbott's ? "

" No, I can't say I did. I didn't notice the voice particularly or think about it."

" And you started right away ? Walked ? Haven't you got a bicycle ? "

" No."

" I see. So it took you—how long ? "

" It's very nearly two miles, whichever way you go."

" Through Old Hall woods is the shortest way, isn't it ? "

" Actually, yes. But it's not particularly good going. I went and came back by the footpath across the fields."

" The one that comes out opposite the Vicarage gate ? "

" Yes."

" And Mrs. Clement ? "

" My wife was in London. She arrived back by the 6.50 train."

" Right. The maid I've seen. That finishes with the Vicarage. I'll be off to Old Hall next. And then I want an interview with Mrs. Lestrange. Queer, her going to see Protheroe the night before he was killed. A lot of queer things about this case."

I agreed.

Glancing at the clock, I realised that it was nearly lunch time. I invited Melchett to partake of pot luck with us, but he excused himself on the plea of having to go to tne Blue Boar. The Blue Boar gives you a first-rate meal of the joint and two-vegetable type. I thought his choice was a wise one. After her interview with the police, Mary would probably be feeling more temperamental than usual.

# CHAPTER XIV

On my way home, I ran into Miss Hartnell and she detained me at least ten minutes, declaiming in her deep bass voice against the improvidence and ungratefulness of the lower classes. The crux of the matter seemed to be that The Poor did not want Miss Hartnell in their houses. My sympathies were entirely on their side. I am debarred by my social standing from expressing my prejudices in the forceful manner they do.

I soothed her as best I could and made my escape.

Haydock overtook me in his car at the corner of the Vicarage road.

"I've just taken Mrs. Protheroe home," he called.

He waited for me at the gate of his house.

"Come in a minute," he said.

I complied.

"This is an extraordinary business," he said, as he threw his hat on a chair and opened the door into his surgery.

He sank down on a shabby leather chair and stared across the room. He looked harried and perplexed.

I told him that we had succeeded in fixing the time of the shot. He listened with an almost abstracted air.

"That lets Anne Protheroe out," he said. "Well, well, I'm glad it's neither of those two. I like 'em both."

I believed him, and yet it occurred to me to wonder why, since, as he said, he liked them both, their freedom from complicity seemed to have had the result of plunging him in gloom. This morning he had looked like a man with a weight lifted from his mind, now he looked thoroughly rattled and upset.

And yet I was convinced that he meant what he said. He was fond of both Anne Protheroe and Lawrence Redding. Why, then, this gloomy absorption?

He roused himself with an effort.

" I meant to tell you about Hawes. All this business has driven him out of my mind."

" Is he really ill ? "

" There's nothing radically wrong with him. You know, of course, that he's had Encephalitis Lethargica, sleepy sickness, as it's commonly called ? "

" No," I said, very much surprised, " I didn't know anything of the kind. He never told me anything about it. When did he have it ? "

" About a year ago. He recovered all right—as far as one ever recovers. It's a strange disease—has a queer moral effect. The whole character may change after it."

He was silent for a moment or two, and then said :

" We think with horror now of the days when we burnt witches. I believe the day will come when we will shudder to think that we ever hanged criminals."

" You don't believe in capital punishment ? "

" It's not so much that." He paused. " You know," he said slowly, " I'd rather have my job than yours.

" Why ?

" Because your job deals very largely with what we call right and wrong—and I'm not at all sure that there's any such thing. Suppose it's all a question of glandular secretion. Too much of one gland, too little of another —and you get your murderer, your thief, your habitual criminal. Clement, I believe the time will come when we'll be horrified to think of the long centuries in which we've indulged in what you may call moral reprobation, to think how we've punished people for disease—which they can't help, poor devils. You don't hang a man for having tuberculosis."

" He isn't dangerous to the community."

" In a sense he is. He infects other people. Or take a man who fancies he's the Emperor of China. You don't say how wicked of him. I take your point about the community. The community must be protected. Shut up these people where they can't do any harm —even put them peacefully out of the way—yes, I'd go as far as that.  But don't call it punishment.  Don't bring shame on them and their innocent families."

I looked at him curiously.

" I've never heard you speak like this before."

" I don't usually air my theories abroad.  To-day I'm riding my hobby.  You're an intelligent man, Clement, which is more than some parsons are.  You won't admit, I dare say, that there's no such thing as what is technically termed ' Sin,' but you're broadminded enough to consider the possibility of such a thing."

" It strikes at the root of all our accepted ideas," I said.

" Yes, we're a narrow-minded, self-righteous lot, only too keen to judge matters we know nothing about.  I honestly believe crime is a case for the doctor, not the policeman and not the parson.  In the future, perhaps, there won't be any such thing."

" You'll have cured it ? "

" We'll have cured it.  Rather a wonderful thought. Have you ever studied the statistics of crime ?  No— very few people have.  I have, though.  You'd be amazed at the amount there is of adolescent crime, glands again, you see.  Young Neil, the Oxfordshire murderer—killed five little girls before he was suspected. Nice lad—never given any trouble of any kind.  Lily Rose, the little Cornish girl—killed her uncle because he docked her of sweets.  Hit him when he was asleep with a coal hammer.  Went home and a fortnight later killed her elder sister who had annoyed her about some trifling matter.  Neither of them hanged, of course. Sent to a home.  May be all right later—may not.  Doubt if the girl will.  The only thing she cares about is seeing the pigs killed.  Do you know when suicide is commonest ?  Fifteen to sixteen years of age.  From self-murder to murder of some one else isn't a very long step.  But it's not a moral lack—it's a physical one."

" What you say is terrible ! "

" No—it's only new to you.  New truths have to be

H

faced. One's ideas adjusted. But sometimes—it makes life difficult."

He sat there frowning, yet with a strange look of weariness.

"Haydock," I said, "if you suspected—if you knew —that a certain person was a murderer, would you give that person up to the law, or would you be tempted to shield them?"

I was quite unprepared for the effect of my question. He turned on me angrily and suspiciously.

"What makes you say that, Clement? What's in your mind? Out with it, man."

"Why, nothing particular," I said, rather taken aback. "Only—well, murder is in our minds, just now. If by any chance you happened to discover the truth —I wondered how you would feel about it, that was all."

His anger died down. He stared once more straight ahead of him like a man trying to read the answer to a riddle that perplexes him, yet which exists only in his own brain.

"If I suspected—if I knew—I should do my duty, Clement. At least, I hope so."

"The question is—which way would you consider your duty lay?"

He looked at me with inscrutable eyes.

"That question comes to every man some time in his life, I suppose, Clement. And every man has to decide it in his own way."

"You don't know?"

"No, I don't know. . . ."

I felt the best thing was to change the subject.

"That nephew of mine is enjoying this case thoroughly," I said. "Spends his entire time looking for footprints and cigarette ash."

Haydock smiled.

"What age is he?"

"Just sixteen. You don't take tragedies seriously at that age. It's all Sherlock Holmes and Arsene Lupin to you."

Haydock said thoughtfully ·

" He's a fine-looking boy. What are you going to do with him ? "

" I can't afford a University education, I'm afraid. The boy himself wants to go into the Merchant Service. He failed for the Navy."

" Well—it's a hard life—but he might do worse. Yes, he might do worse."

" I must be going," I exclaimed, catching sight of the clock. " I'm nearly half an hour late for lunch."

My family were just sitting down when I arrived. They demanded a full account of the morning's activities, which I gave them, feeling, as I did so, that most of it was in the nature of an anticlimax.

Dennis, however, was highly entertained by the history of Mrs. Price Ridley's telephone call, and went into fits of laughter as I enlarged upon the nervous shock her system had sustained and the necessity for reviving her with damson gin.

" Serve the old cat right," he exclaimed. " She's got the worst tongue in the place. I wish I'd thought of ringing her up and giving her a fright. I say, Uncle Len, what about giving her a second dose ? "

I hastily begged him to do nothing of the sort. Nothing is more dangerous than the well-meant efforts of the younger generation to assist you and show their sympathy.

Dennis's mood changed suddenly. He frowned and put on his man of the world air.

" I've been with Lettice most of the morning," he said. " You know, Griselda, she's really *very* worried. She doesn't want to show it, but she is. Very worried indeed."

" I should hope so," said Griselda, with a toss of her head.

Griselda is not too fond of Lettice Protheroe.

" I don't think you're ever quite fair to Lettice."

" Don't you ? " said Griselda.

" Lots of people don't wear mourning."

Griselda was silent and so was I. Dennis continued:

"She doesn't talk to most people, but she *does* talk to me. She's awfully worried about the whole thing, and she thinks something ought to be done about it."

"She will find," I said, "that Inspector Slack shares her opinion. He is going up to Old Hall this afternoon, and will probably make the life of everybody there quite unbearable to them in his efforts to get at the truth."

"What do you think *is* the truth, Len?" asked my wife suddenly.

"It's hard to say, my dear. I can't say that at the moment I've any idea at all."

"Did you say that Inspector Slack was going to trace that telephone call—the one that took you to the Abbotts?"

"Yes."

"But can he do it? Isn't it a very difficult thing to do?"

"I should not imagine so. The Exchange will have a record of the calls."

"Oh!" My wife relapsed into thought.

"Uncle Len," said my nephew, "why were you so ratty with me this morning for joking about your wishing Colonel Protheroe to be murdered?"

"Because," I said, "there is a time for everything. Inspector Slack has no sense of humour. He took your words quite seriously, will probably cross-examine Mary, and will get out a warrant for my arrest."

"Doesn't he know when a fellow's ragging?"

"No," I said, "he does not. He has attained to his present position through hard work and zealous attention to duty. That has left him no time for the minor recreations of life."

"Do you like him, Uncle Len?"

"No," I said, "I do not. From the first moment I saw him I disliked him intensely. But I have no doubt that he is a highly successful man in his profession."

"You think he'll find out who shot old Protheroe?"

" If he doesn't," I said, " it will not be for the want of trying."

Mary appeared and said :

" Mr. Hawes wants to see you. I've put him in the drawing-room, and here's a note. Waiting for an answer. Verbal will do."

I tore open the note and read it.

" DEAR MR. CLEMENT,—I should be so very grateful if you could come and see me this afternoon as early as possible. I am in great trouble and would like your advice.

" Sincerely yours,<br>" ESTELLE LESTRANGE."

" Say I will come round in about half an hour," I said to Mary.

Then I went into the drawing-room to see Hawes.

CHAPTER XV

HAWES's appearance distressed me very much. His
hands were shaking and his face kept twitching nervously. In my opinion he should have been in bed, and
I told him so. He insisted that he was perfectly well.

" I assure you, sir, I never felt better. Never in my
life."

This was so obviously wide of the truth that I hardly
knew how to answer. I have a certain admiration for a
man who will not give in to illness, but Hawes was
carrying the thing rather too far.

" I called to tell you how sorry I was—that such a
thing should happen in the Vicarage."

" Yes," I said, " it's not very pleasant."

" It's terrible—quite terrible. It seems they haven't
arrested Mr. Redding after all ? "

" No. That was a mistake. He made—er—rather a
foolish statement."

" And the police are now quite convinced that he is
innocent ? "

" Perfectly."

" Why is that, may I ask ? Is it—I mean, do they
suspect any one else ? "

I should never have suspected that Hawes would take
such a keen interest in the details of a murder case.
Perhaps it is because it happened in the Vicarage. He
appeared as eager as a reporter.

" I don't know that I am completely in Inspector
Slack's confidence. So far as I know, he does not suspect
any one in particular. He is at present engaged in making
inquiries."

" Yes. Yes—of course. But who can one imagine
doing such a dreadful thing ? "

I shook my head.

" Colonel Protheroe was not a popular man, I know

that. But murder! For murder—one would need a very strong motive."

" So I should imagine," I said.

" Who could have such a motive ? Have the police any idea ? "

" I couldn't say."

" He might have made enemies, you know. The more I think about it, the more I am convinced that he was the kind of man to have enemies. He had a reputation on the Bench for being very severe."

" I suppose he had."

" Why, don't you remember, sir ? He was telling you yesterday morning about having been threatened by that man Archer."

" Now I come to think of it, so he did," I said. " Of course, I remember. You were quite near us at the time."

" Yes, I overheard what he was saying. Almost impossible to help it with Colonel Protheroe. He had such a very loud voice, hadn't he ? I remember being impressed by your own words. That when his time came, he might have justice meted out to him instead of mercy."

" Did I say that ? " I asked, frowning. My remembrance of my own words was slightly different.

" You said it very impressively, sir. I was struck by your words. Justice is a terrible thing. And to think the poor man was struck down shortly afterwards. It's almost as though you had a premonition."

" I had nothing of the sort," I said shortly. I rather dislike Hawes's tendency to mysticism. There is a touch of the visionary about him.

" Have you told the police about this man Archer, sir ? "

" I know nothing about him."

" I mean, have you repeated to them what Colonel Protheroe said—about Archer having threatened him."

" No," I said slowly, " I have not."

" But you are going to do so ? "

I was silent. I dislike hounding a man down who has already got the forces of law and order against him. I held no brief for Archer. He is an inveterate poacher —one of those cheerful ne'er-do-weels that are to be found in any parish. Whatever he may have said in the heat of anger when he was sentenced I had no definite knowledge that he felt the same when he came out of prison.

" You heard the conversation," I said at last. " If you feel it your duty to go to the police with it, you must do so."

" It would come better from you, sir."

" Perhaps—but to tell the truth—well, I've no fancy for doing it. I might be helping to put the rope round the neck of an innocent man."

" But if he shot Colonel Protheroe——"

" Oh, if I    There's no evidence of any kind that he did."

" His threats."

" Strictly speaking, the threats were not his, but Colonel Protheroe's. Colonel Protheroe was threatening to show Archer what vengeance was worth next time he caught him."

" I don't understand your attitude, sir."

" Don't you ? " I said wearily. " You're a young man. You're zealous in the cause of right. When you get to my age, you'll find that you like to give people the benefit of the doubt."

" It's not—I mean——"

He paused, and I looked at him in surprise.

" You haven't any—any ideas of your own—as to the identity of the murderer, I mean ? "

" Good heavens, no."

Hawes persisted.

" Or as to the—the motive ? "

" No. Have you ? "

" I ? No, indeed. I just wondered. If Colonel Protheroe had—had confided in you in any way— mentioned anything. . . ."

" His confidences, such as they were, were heard by the whole village street yesterday morning," I said dryly.

" Yes. Yes—of course. And you don't think—about Archer ? "

" The police will know all about Archer soon enough," I said. " If I'd heard him threaten Colonel Protheroe myself, that would be a different matter. But you may be sure that if he actually has threatened him, half the people in the village will have heard him, and the news will get to the police all right. You, of course, must do as you like about the matter."

But Hawes seemed curiously unwilling to do anything himself.

The man's whole attitude was nervous and queer. I recalled what Haydock had said about his illness. There, I supposed, lay the explanation.

He took his leave unwillingly, as though he had more to say, and didn't know how to say it.

Before he left, I arranged with him to take the service for the Mothers' Union, followed by the meeting of District Visitors. I had several projects of my own for the afternoon.

Dismissing Hawes and his troubles from my mind I started off for Mrs. Lestrange.

On the table in the hall lay the *Guardian* and the *Church Times* unopened.

As I walked, I remembered that Mrs. Lestrange had had an interview with Colonel Protheroe the night before his death. It was possible that something had transpired in that interview which would throw light upon the problem of his murder.

I was shown straight into the little drawing-room, and Mrs. Lestrange rose to meet me. I was struck anew by the marvellous atmosphere that this woman could create. She wore a dress of some dead black material that showed off the extraordinary fairness of her skin. There was something curiously dead about her face. Only the eyes were burningly alive. There was a watchful look in them to-day. Otherwise she showed no signs of animation.

"It was very good of you to come, Mr. Clement," she said, as she shook hands. "I wanted to speak to you the other day. Then I decided not to do so. I was wrong."

"As I told you then, I shall be glad to do anything that can help you."

"Yes, you said that. And you said it as though you meant it. Very few people, Mr. Clement, in this world have ever sincerely wished to help me."

"I can hardly believe that, Mrs. Lestrange."

"It is true. Most people—most men, at anyrate, are out for their own hand."

There was a bitterness in her voice.

I did not answer, and she went on:

"Sit down, won't you?"

I obeyed, and she took a chair facing me. She hesitated a moment and then began to speak very slowly and thoughtfully, seeming to weigh each word as she uttered it.

"I am in a very peculiar position, Mr. Clement, and I want to ask your advice. That is, I want to ask your advice as to what I should do next. What is past is past and cannot be undone. You understand?"

Before I could reply, the maid who had admitted me opened the door and said with a scared face:

"Oh! please, m'am, there a police inspector here, and he says he must speak to you, please."

There was a pause. Mrs. Lestrange's face did not change. Only her eyes very slowly closed and opened again. She seemed to swallow once or twice, then she said in exactly the same clear, calm voice:

"Show him in, Hilda."

I was about to rise, but she motioned me back again with an imperious hand.

"If you do not mind—I should be much obliged if you would stay."

I resumed my seat.

"Certainly, if you wish it," I murmured, as Slack entered with a brisk regulation tread.

"Good-afternoon, madam," he began.

"Good-afternoon, Inspector."

At this moment, he caught sight of me and scowled. There is no doubt about it, Slack does not like me.

"You have no objection to the vicar's presence, I hope?"

I suppose that Slack could not very well say he had.

"No-o," he said grudgingly. "Though, perhaps, it might be better——"

Mrs. Lestrange paid no attention to the hint.

"What can I do for you, inspector?" she asked.

"It's this way, madam. Murder of Colonel Protheroe. I'm in charge of the case and making inquiries."

Mrs. Lestrange nodded.

"Just as a matter of form, I'm asking every one just where they were yesterday evening between the hours of 6 and 7 p.m. Just as a matter of form, you understand."

Mrs. Lestrange did not seem in the least discomposed.

"You want to know where I was yesterday evening between six and seven?"

"If you please, madam."

"Let me see." She reflected a moment. "I was here. In this house."

"Oh!" I saw the inspector's eyes flash. "And your maid—you have only one maid, I think—can confirm that statement?"

"No, it was Hilda's afternoon out."

"I see."

"So, unfortunately, you will have to take my word for it," said Mrs. Lestrange pleasantly.

"You seriously declare that you were at home all the afternoon?"

"You said between six and seven, inspector. I was out for a walk early in the afternoon. I returned some time before five o'clock."

"Then if a lady—Miss Hartnell, for instance—were

to declare that she came here about six o'clock, rang the bell, but could make no one hear and was compelled to go away again—you'd say she was mistaken, eh ? "

" Oh ! no," Mrs. Lestrange shook her head.

" But——"

" If your maid is in, she can say not at home. If one is alone and does not happen to want to see callers —well, the only thing to do is to let them ring."

Inspector Slack looked slightly baffled.

" Elderly women bore me dreadfully," said Mrs. Lestrange. " And Miss Hartnell is particularly boring. She must have rung at least half a dozen times before she went away."

She smiled sweetly at Inspector Slack.

The inspector shifted his ground.

" Then if any one were to say they'd seen you out and about then——"

" Oh ! but they didn't, did they ? " She was quick to sense his weak point. " No one saw me out, because I was in, you see."

" Quite so, madam."

The inspector hitched his chair a little nearer.

" Now I understand, Mrs. Lestrange, that you paid a visit to Colonel Protheroe at Old Hall the night before his death."

Mrs. Lestrange said calmly :

" That is so."

" Can you indicate to me the nature of that interview ? "

" It concerned a private matter, inspector."

" I'm afraid I must ask you to tell me the nature of that private matter."

" I shall not tell you anything of the kind. I will only assure you that nothing which was said at that interview could possibly have any bearing upon the crime."

" I don't think you are the best judge of that."

" At anyrate, you will have to take my word for it, inspector."

"In fact, I have to take your word about everything."

"It does seem rather like it," she agreed, still with the same smiling calm.

Inspector Slack grew very red.

"This is a serious matter, Mrs. Lestrange. I want the truth——" He banged his fist down on a table. "And I mean to get it."

Mrs. Lestrange said nothing at all.

"Don't you see, madam, that you're putting yourself in a very fishy position?"

Still Mrs. Lestrange said nothing.

"You'll be required to give evidence at the inquest."

"Yes."

Just the monosyllable. Unemphatic, uninterested. The inspector altered his tactics.

"You were acquainted with Colonel Protheroe?"

"Yes, I was acquainted with him."

"Well acquainted?"

There was a pause before she said:

"I had not seen him for several years."

"You were acquainted with Mrs. Protheroe?"

"No."

"You'll excuse me, but it was a very unusual time to make a call."

"Not from my point of view."

"What do you mean by that?"

She said clearly and distinctly:

"I wanted to see Colonel Protheroe alone. I did not want to see Mrs. Protheroe or Miss Protheroe. I considered this the best way of accomplishing my object."

"Why didn't you want to see Mrs. or Miss Protheroe?"

"That, inspector, is my business."

"Then you refuse to say more?"

"Absolutely."

Inspector Slack rose.

"You'll be putting yourself in a nasty position, madam, if you're not careful. All this looks bad—it looks very bad."

She laughed. I could have told Inspector Slack that this was not the kind of woman who is easily frightened.

"Well," he said, extricating himself with dignity, "don't say I haven't warned you, that's all. Good-afternoon, madam, and mind you, we're going to get at the truth."

He departed. Mrs. Lestrange rose and held out her hand.

"I am going to send you away—yes, it is better so. You see, it is too late for advice now. I have chosen my part."

She repeated in a rather forlorn voice :

"I have chosen my part."

## CHAPTER XVI

As I went out I ran into Haydock on the doorstep. He glanced sharply after Slack, who was just passing through the gate, and demanded :

" Has he been questioning her ? "

" Yes."

" He's been civil, I hope ? "

Civility, to my mind, is an art which Inspector Slack has never learnt, but I presumed that according to his own lights, civil he had been, and anyway, I didn't want to upset Haydock any further. He was looking worried and upset as it was. So I said he had been quite civil.

Haydock nodded and passed on into the house, and I went on down the village street, where I soon caught up the inspector. I fancy that he was walking slowly on purpose. Much as he dislikes me, he is not the man to let dislike stand in the way of acquiring any useful information.

" Do you know anything about the lady ? " he asked me point blank.

I said I knew nothing whatever.

" She's never said anything about why she came here to live ? "

" No."

" Yet you go and see her ? "

" It is one of my duties to call on my parishioners," I replied, evading to remark that I had been sent for.

" H'm, I suppose it is." He was silent for a minute or two and then, unable to resist discussing his recent failure, he went on : " Fishy business, it looks to me."

" You think so ? "

" If you ask me, I say ' blackmail.'; Seems funny, when you think of what Colonel Protheroe was always supposed to be. But there, you never can tell. He wouldn't be the first churchwarden who'd led a double life."

Faint remembrances of Miss Marple's remarks on the same subject floated through my mind.

" You really think that's likely ? "

" Well, it fits the facts, sir. Why did a smart, well-dressed lady come down to this quiet little hole ? Why did she go and see him at that funny time of day ? Why did she avoid seeing Mrs. and Miss Protheroe ? Yes, it all hangs together. Awkward for her to admit —blackmail's a punishable offence. But we'll get the truth out of her. For all we know it may have a very important bearing on the case. If Colonel Protheroe had some guilty secret in his life—something disgraceful —well, you can see for yourself what a field it opens up."

I suppose it did.

" I've been trying to get the butler to talk. He might have overheard some of the conversation between Colonel Protheroe and Lestrange. Butlers do some-times. But he swears he hasn't the least idea of what the conversation was about. By the way, he got the sack through it. The colonel went for him, being angry at his having let her in. The butler retorted by giving notice. Says he didn't like the place anyway and had been thinking of leaving for some time."

" Really."

" So that gives us another person who had a grudge against the colonel."

" You don't seriously suspect the man—what's his name, by the way ? "

" His name's Reeves, and I don't say I do suspect him. What I say is, you never know. I don't like that soapy, oily manner of his."

I wonder what Reeves would say of Inspector Slack's manner.

" I'm going to question the chauffeur now."

" Perhaps, then," I said, " you'll give me a lift in your car. I want a short interview with Mrs. Protheroe."

" What about ? "

" The funeral arrangements."

" Oh ! " Inspector Slack was slightly taken aback. " The inquest's to-morrow, Saturday."

" Just so. The funeral will probably be arranged for Tuesday."

Inspector Slack seemed to be a little ashamed of himself for his brusqueness. He held out an olive branch in the shape of an invitation to be present at the interview with the chauffeur, Manning.

Manning was a nice lad, not more than twenty-five or six years of age. He was inclined to be awed by the inspector.

" Now, then, my lad," said Slack, " I want a little information from you."

" Yes, sir," stammered the chauffeur. " Certainly, sir."

If he had committed the murder himself he could not have been more alarmed.

" You took your master to the village yesterday ? "

" Yes, sir."

" What time was that ? "

" Five-thirty."

" Mrs. Protheroe went too ? "

" Yes, sir."

" You went straight to the village ? "

" Yes, sir."

" You didn't stop anywhere on the way ? "

" No, sir."

" What did you do when you got there ? "

" The colonel got out and told me he wouldn't want the car again. He'd walk home. Mrs. Protheroe had some shopping to do. The parcels were put in the car. Then she said that was all, and I drove home."

" Leaving her in the village ? "

" Yes, sir."

" What time was that ? "

" A quarter past six, sir. A quarter past exactly."

" Where did you leave her ? "

" By the church, sir."

I

" Had the colonel mentioned at all where he was going ? "

" He said something about having to see the vet— something to do with one of the horses."

" I see. And you drove straight back here ? "

" Yes, sir."

" There are two entrances to Old Hall, by the South Lodge and by the North Lodge. I take it that going to the village you would go by the South Lodge ? "

" Yes, sir, always."

" And you came back the same way ? "

" Yes, sir."

"H'm. I think that's all. Ah ! here's Miss Protheroe." Lettice drifted towards us.

" I want the Fiat, Manning," she said. " Start her for me, will you ? "

" Very good, miss."

He went towards a two-seater and lifted the bonnet.

" Just a minute, Miss Protheroe," said Slack. " It's necessary that I should have a record of everybody's movements yesterday afternoon. No offence meant."

Lettice stared at him.

" I never know the time of anything," she said.

" I understand you went out soon after lunch yesterday ? "

She nodded.

" Where to, please ? "

" To play tennis."

" Who with ? "

" The Hartley Napiers."

" At Much Benham ? "

" Yes."

" And you returned ? "

" I don't know. I tell you I never know these things."

" You returned," I said, " about seven-thirty."

" That's right," said Lettice. " In the middle of the shemozzle. Anne having fits and Griselda supporting her.

" Thank you, miss," said the inspector. " That's all I want to know."

" How queer," said Lettice. " It seems so uninteresting."

She moved towards the Fiat.

The inspector touched his forehead in a surreptitious manner.

" A bit wanting ? " he suggested.

" Not in the least," I said. " But she likes to be thought so."

" Well, I'm off to question the maids now."

One cannot really like Slack, but one can admire his energy.

We parted company, and I inquired of Reeves if I could see Mrs. Protheroe.

" She is lying down, sir, at the moment."

" Then I'd better not disturb her."

" Perhaps if you would wait, sir, I know that Mrs. Protheroe is anxious to see you. She was saying as much at luncheon."

He showed me into the drawing-room, switching on the electric lights since the blinds were down.

" A very sad business all this," I said.

" Yes, sir."

His voice was cold and respectful.

I looked at him. What feelings were at work under that impassive demeanour. Were there things that he knew and could have told us ? There is nothing so inhuman as the mask of the good servant.

" Is there anything more, sir ? "

Was there just a hint of anxiety to be gone behind that correct expression.

" There's nothing more," I said.

I had a very short time to wait before Anne Protheroe came to me. We discussed and settled a few arrangements and then :

" What a wonderfully kind man Dr. Haydock is ! " she exclaimed.

" Haydock is the best fellow I know."

" He has been amazingly kind to me.  But he looks very sad, doesn't he ? "

It had never occurred to me to think of Haydock as sad.  I turned the idea over in my mind.

" I don't think I've ever noticed it," I said at last.

" I never have, until to-day."

" One's own troubles sharpen one's eyes sometimes," I said.

" That's very true."

She paused and then said :

" Mr. Clement, there's one thing I absolutely *cannot* make out.  If my husband were shot immediately after I left him, how was it that I didn't hear the shot ? "

" They have reason to believe that the shot was fired later."

" But the 6.20 on the note ? "

" Was possibly added by a different hand—the murderer's."

Her cheek paled.

" How horrible ! "

" It didn't strike you that the date was not in his handwriting ? "

" None of it looked like his handwriting."

There was some truth in this observation.  It was a somewhat illegible scrawl, not so precise as Protheroe's writing usually was.

" You are sure they don't still suspect Lawrence ? "

" I think he is definitely cleared."

" But, Mr. Clement, who can it be ?  Lucius was not popular, I know, but I don't think he had any real enemies.  Not—not that kind of enemy."

I shook my head.

" It's a mystery."

I thought wonderingly of Miss Marple's seven suspects.  Who could they be ?

After I took leave of Anne, I proceeded to put a certain plan of mine into action.

I returned from Old Hall by way of the private path.  When I reached the stile, I retraced my steps, and choosing a place where I fancied the undergrowth showed signs of being disturbed, I turned aside from the path and forced my way through the bushes. The wood was a thick one, with a good deal of tangled undergrowth. My progress was not very fast, and I suddenly became aware that some one else was moving amongst the bushes not very far from me. As I paused irresolutely, Lawrence Redding came into sight. He was carrying a large stone.

I suppose I must have looked surprised, for he suddenly burst out laughing.

" No," he said, " it's not a clue, it's a peace offering."

" A peace offering ? "

" Well, a basis for negotiations, shall we say ? I want an excuse for calling on your neighbour, Miss Marple, and I have been told that there is nothing she likes so much as a nice bit of rock or stone for the Japanese gardens she makes."

" Quite true," I said. " But what do you want with the old lady ? "

" Just this. If there was anything to be seen yesterday evening Miss Marple saw it. I don't mean anything necessarily connected with the crime—that she would think connected with the crime. I mean some outré or bizarre incident, some simple little happening that might give us a clue to the truth. Something that she wouldn't think worth while mentioning to the police."

" It's possible, I suppose."

" It's worth trying anyhow. Clement, I'm going to get to the bottom of this business. For Anne's sake, if nobody's else. And I haven't any too much confidence in Slack—he's a zealous fellow, but zeal can't really take the place of brains."

" I see," I said, " that you are that favourite character of fiction, the amateur detective. I don't know that they really hold their own with the professional in real life."

He looked at me shrewdly and suddenly laughed.

" What are you doing in the wood, padre ? "

I had the grace to blush.

" Just the same as I am doing, I dare swear. We've got the same idea, haven't we ? *How did the murderer come to the study ?* First way, along the lane and through the gate, second way, by the front door, third way—is there a third way ? My idea was to see if there was any signs of the bushes being disturbed or broken anywhere near the wall of the Vicarage garden."

" That was just my idea," I admitted.

" I hadn't really got down to the job, though," continued Lawrence. " Because it occurred to me that I'd like to see Miss Marple first, to make quite sure that no one did pass along the lane yesterday evening whilst we were in the studio."

I shook my head.

" She was quite positive that nobody did."

" Yes, nobody whom she would call anybody—sounds mad, but you see what I mean. But there might have been some one like a postman or a milkman or a butcher's boy—some one whose presence would be so natural that you wouldn't think of mentioning it."

" You've been reading G. K. Chesterton," I said, and Lawrence did not deny it.

" But don't you think there's just possibly something in the idea ? "

" Well, I suppose there might be," I admitted.

Without further ado, we made our way to Miss Marple's. She was working in the garden, and called out to us as we climbed over the stile.

" You see," murmured Lawrence, " she sees everybody."

She received us very graciously and was much pleased with Lawrence's immense rock, which he presented with all due solemnity.

" It's very thoughtful of you, Mr. Redding. Very thoughtful indeed."

Emboldened by this, Lawrence embarked on his questions. Miss Marple listened attentively.

" Yes, I see what you mean, and I quite agree, it is

the sort of thing no one mentions or bothers to mention. But I can assure you that there was nothing of the kind. Nothing whatever."

" You are sure, Miss Marple ? "

" Quite sure."

" Did you see any one go by the path into the wood that afternoon ? " I asked. " Or come from it ? "

" Oh ! yes, quite a number of people. Dr. Stone and Miss Cram went that way—it's the nearest way to the Barrow for them. That was a little after two o'clock. And Dr. Stone returned that way—as you know, Mr. Redding, since he joined you and Mrs. Protheroe."

" By the way," I said. " That shot—the one you heard, Miss Marple. Mr. Redding and Mrs. Protheroe must have heard it too."

I looked inquiringly at Lawrence.

" Yes," he said, frowning. " I believe I did hear some shots. Weren't there one or two shots ? "

" I only heard one," said Miss Marple.

" It's only the vaguest impression in my mind," said Lawrence. " Curse it all, I wish I could remember. If only I'd known. You see, I was so completely taken up with—with——"

He paused, embarrassed.

I gave a tactful cough. Miss Marple with a touch of prudishness, changed the subject.

" Inspector Slack has been trying to get me to say whether I heard the shot after Mr. Redding and Mrs. Protheroe had left the studio or before. I've had to confess that I really could not say definitely, but I have the impression—which is growing stronger the more I think about it—that it was after."

" Then that lets the celebrated Dr. Stone out anyway," said Lawrence, with a sigh. " Not that there has ever been the slightest reason why he should be suspected of shooting poor old Protheroe."

" Ah ! " said Miss Marple. " But I always find it prudent to suspect everybody just a little. What I say is, you really never *know*, do you ? "

This was typical of Miss Marple. I asked Lawrence if he agreed with her about the shot.

" I really can't say. You see, it was such an ordinary sound. I should be inclined to think it had been fired when we were in the studio. The sound would have been deadened and—and one would have noticed it less there."

For other reasons than the sound being deadened, I thought to myself !

" I must ask Anne," said Lawrence. " She may remember. By the way, there seems to me to be one curious fact that needs explanation. Mrs. Lestrange, the Mystery Lady of St. Mary Mead, paid a visit to old Protheroe after dinner on Wednesday night. And nobody seems to have any idea what it was all about. Old Protheroe said nothing to either his wife or Lettice."

" Perhaps the vicar knows," said Miss Marple.

Now how did the woman know that I had been to visit Mrs. Lestrange that afternoon ? The way she always knows things is uncanny.

I shook my head and said I could throw no light upon the matter.

" What does Inspector Slack think ? " asked Miss Marple.

" He's done his best to bully the butler—but apparently the butler wasn't curious enough to listen at the door. So there it is—no one knows."

" I expect some one overheard something, though, don't you ? " said Miss Marple. " I mean, somebody always *does*. I think that is where Mr. Redding might find out something."

" But Mrs. Protheroe knows nothing."

" I didn't mean Anne Protheroe," said Miss Marple. " I meant the women servants. They do so hate telling anything to the police. But a nice-looking young man —you'll excuse me, Mr. Redding—and one who has been unjustly subjected—oh ! I'm sure they'd tell him at once."

" I'll go and have a try this evening," said Lawrence

with vigour. " Thanks for the hint, Miss Marple. I'll go after—well, after a little job the vicar and I are going to do."

It occurred to me that we had better be getting on with it. I said good-bye to Miss Marple and we entered the woods once more.

First we went up the path till we came to a new spot where it certainly looked as though some one had left the path on the right-hand side. Lawrence explained that he had already followed this particular trail and found it led nowhere, but he added that we might as well try again. He might have been wrong.

It was, however, as he had said. After about ten or twelve yards any sign of broken and trampled leaves petered out. It was from this spot that Lawrence had broken back towards the path to meet me earlier in the afternoon.

We emerged on the path again and walked a little farther along it. Again we came to a place where the bushes seemed disturbed. The signs were very slight but, I thought, unmistakable. This time the trail was more promising. By a devious course, it wound steadily nearer to the Vicarage. Presently we arrived at where the bushes grew thickly up to the wall. The wall is a high one and ornamented with fragments of broken bottles on the top. If any one had placed a ladder against it, we ought to find traces of their passage.

We were working our way slowly along the wall when a sound came to our ears of a breaking twig. I pressed forward, forcing my way through a thick tangle of shrubs—and came face to face with Inspector Slack.

" So it's you," he said. " And Mr. Redding. Now what do you think you two gentlemen are doing ? "

Slightly crestfallen, we explained.

" Quite so," said the inspector. " Not being the fools we're usually thought to be, I had the same idea myself. I've been here over an hour. Would you like to know something ? "

" Yes," I said meekly.

" Whoever murdered Colonel Protheroe didn't come this way to do it ! There's not a sign either on this side of the wall, nor the other. Whoever murdered Colonel Protheroe came through the front door. There's no other way he could have come "

" Impossible," I cried.

" Why impossible ? Your door stands open. Any one's only got to walk in. They can't be seen from the kitchen. They know you're safely out of the way, they know Mrs. Clement is in London, they know Mr. Dennis is at a tennis party. Simple as A.B.C. And they don't need to go or come through the village. Just opposite the Vicarage gate is a public footpath, and from it you can turn into these same woods and come out whichever way you choose. Unless Mrs. Price Ridley were to come out of her front gate at that particular minute, it's all clear sailing. A great deal more so than climbing over walls. The side windows of the upper story or Mrs. Price Ridley's house do overlook most of that wall. No, depend upon it, that's the way he came."

It really seemed as though he must be right.

# CHAPTER XVII

Inspector Slack came round to see me the following morning. He is, I think, thawing towards me. In time, he may forget the incident of the clock.

" Well, sir," he greeted me. " I've traced that telephone call that you received."

" Indeed ? " I said eagerly.

" It's rather odd. It was put through from the North Lodge of Old Hall. Now that lodge is empty, the lodge-keepers have been pensioned off and the new lodge-keepers aren't in yet. The place was empty and convenient—a window at the back was open. No finger-prints on the instrument itself—it had been wiped clear. That's suggestive."

" How do you mean ? "

" I mean that it shows that call was put through deliberately to get you out of the way. Therefore the murder was carefully planned in advance. If it had been just a harmless practical joke, the fingerprints wouldn't have been wiped off so carefully."

" No, I see that."

" It also shows that the murderer was well acquainted with Old Hall and its surroundings. It wasn't Mrs. Protheroe who put that call through. I've accounted for every moment of her time that afternoon. There are half a dozen servants who can swear that she was at home up till five-thirty. Then the car came round and drove Colonel Protheroe and her to the village. The colonel went to see Quinton, the vet, about one of the horses. Mrs. Protheroe did some ordering at the grocers and at the fish shop, and from there came straight down the back lane where Miss Marple saw her. All the shops agree she carried no handbag with her. The old lady was right."

" She usually is," I said mildly.

"And Miss Protheroe was over at Much Benham at 5.30."

"Quite so," I said. "My nephew was there too."

"That disposes of her. The maids seem all right—a bit hysterical and upset, but what can you expect? Of course, I've got my eye on the butler—what with giving notice and all. But I don't think he knows anything about it."

"Your inquiries seem to have had rather a negative result, inspector."

"They do and they do not, sir. There's one very queer thing has turned up—quite unexpectedly, I may say."

"Yes?"

"You remember the fuss that Mrs. Price Ridley, who lives next door to you, was kicking up yesterday morning? About being rung up on the telephone?"

"Yes?" I said.

"Well, we traced the call just to calm her—and where on this earth do you think it was put through from?"

"A call office?" I hazarded.

"No, Mr. Clement. That call was put through from Mr. Lawrence Redding's cottage."

"What?" I exclaimed, surprised.

"Yes. A bit odd, isn't it? Mr. Redding had nothing to do with it. At that time, 6.30, he was on his way to the Blue Boar with Dr. Stone in full view of the village. But there it is. Suggestive, eh? Some one walked into that empty cottage and used the telephone, who was it? That's two queer telephone calls in one day. Makes you think there's some connection between them. I'll eat my hat if they weren't both put through by the same person."

"But with what object?"

"Well, that's what we've got to find out. There seems no particular point in the second one, but there must be a point somewhere. And you see the significance? Mr. Redding's house used to telephone from.

Mr. Redding's pistol. All throwing suspicion on Mr. Redding."

"It would be more to the point to have put through the *first* call from his house," I objected.

"Ah! but I've been thinking that out. What did Mr. Redding do most afternoons? He went up to Old Hall and painted Miss Protheroe. And from his cottage he'd go on his motor bicycle, passing through the North Gate. Now you see the point of the call being put through from there. *The murderer is some one who didn't know about the quarrel and that Mr. Redding wasn't going up to Old Hall any more.*"

I reflected a moment to let the inspector's points sink into my brain. They seemed to me logical and unavoidable.

"Were there any fingerprints on the receiver in Mr. Redding's cottage?" I asked.

"There were not," said the inspector bitterly. "That dratted old woman who goes and does for him had been and dusted them off yesterday morning." He reflected wrathfully for a few minutes. "She's a stupid old fool, anyway. Can't remember when she saw the pistol last. It might have been there on the morning of the crime, or it might not. 'She couldn't say, she's sure.' They're all alike!

"Just as a matter of form, I went round and saw Dr. Stone," he went on. "I must say he was pleasant as could be about it. He and Miss Cram went up to that mound—or barrow—or whatever you call it, about half-past two yesterday, and stayed there all the afternoon. Dr. Stone came back alone, and she came later. He says he didn't hear any shot, but admits he's absent-minded. But it all bears out what we think."

"Only," I said, "you haven't caught the murderer."

"H'm," said the inspector. "It was a woman's voice you heard through the telephone. It was in all probability a woman's voice Mrs. Price Ridley heard. If only that shot hadn't come hard on the close of the telephone call—well, I'd know where to look."

" Where ? "

" Ah ! that's just what it's best not to say, sir."

Unblushingly, I suggested a glass of old port. I have some very fine old vintage port. Eleven o'clock in the morning is not the usual time for drinking port, but I did not think that mattered with Inspector Slack. It was, of course, cruel abuse of the vintage port, but one must not be squeamish about such things.

When Inspector Slack had polished off the second glass, he began to unbend and become genial. Such is the effect of that particular port.

" I don't suppose it matters with you, sir," he said. " You'll keep it to yourself ? No letting it get round the parish."

I reassured him.

" Seeing as the whole thing happened in your house, it almost seems as though you had a right to know."

" Just what I feel myself," I said.

" Well, then, sir, what about the lady who called on Colonel Protheroe the night before the murder ? "

" Mrs. Lestrange," I cried, speaking rather loud in my astonishment.

The inspector threw me a reproachful glance.

" Not so loud, sir. Mrs. Lestrange is the lady I've got my eye on. You remember what I told you—blackmail."

" Hardly a reason for murder. Wouldn't it be a case of killing the goose that laid the golden eggs ? That is, assuming that your hypothesis is true, which I don't for a minute admit."

The inspector winked at me in a common manner.

" Ah ! she's the kind the gentlemen will always stand up for. Now look here, sir. Suppose she's successfully blackmailed the old gentleman in the past. After a lapse of years, she gets wind of him, comes down here and tries it on again. *But*, in the meantime, things have changed. The law has taken up a very different stand. Every facility is given nowadays to people prosecuting for blackmail—names are not allowed to be reported in the press. Suppose Colonel Protheroe turns round and says he'll have the law on her. She's in a nasty position. They give a very severe sentence for blackmail. The boot's on the other leg. The only thing to do to save herself is to put him out good and quick."

I was silent. I had to admit that the case the inspector had built up was plausible. Only one thing to my mind made it inadmissible—the personality of Mrs. Lestrange.

"I don't agree with you, inspector," I said. "Mrs. Lestrange doesn't seem to me to be a potential blackmailer. She's—well, it's an old-fashioned word, but she's a—lady."

He threw me a pitying glance.

"Ah! well, sir," he said tolerantly, "you're a clergyman. You don't know half of what goes on. Lady indeed! You'd be surprised if you knew some of the things I know."

"I'm not referring to mere social position. Anyway, I should imagine Mrs. Lestrange to be a *declassée*. What I mean is a question of—personal refinement."

"You don't see her with the same eyes as I do, sir. I may be a man—but I'm a police officer, too. They can't get over me with their personal refinement. Why, that woman is the kind who could stick a knife into you without turning a hair."

Curiously enough, I could believe Mrs. Lestrange guilty of murder much more easily than I could believe her capable of blackmail.

"But, of course, she can't have been telephoning to the old lady next door and shooting Colonel Protheroe at one and the same time," continued the inspector.

The words were hardly out of his mouth when he slapped his leg ferociously.

"Got it," he exclaimed. "That's the point of the telephone call. Kind of *alibi*. Knew we'd connect it with the first one. I'm going to look into this. She may have bribed some village lad to do the phoning for her. *He'd* never think of connecting it with the murder."

The inspector hurried off.

"Miss Marple wants to see you," said Griselda, putting her head in. "She sent over a very incoherent note—all spidery and underlined. I couldn't read most of it. Apparently she can't leave home herself. Hurry up and go across and see her and find out what it is. I've got my old women coming in two minutes or I'd come myself. I do hate old women—they tell you about their bad legs and sometimes insist on showing them to you. What luck that the inquest is this afternoon! You won't have to go and watch the Boys' Club Cricket Match."

I hurried off, considerably exercised in my mind as to the reason for this summons.

I found Miss Marple in what, I believe, is described as a fluster. She was very pink and slightly incoherent.

"My nephew," she explained. "My nephew, Raymond West, the author. He is coming down to-day. Such a to-do. I have to see to everything myself. You cannot trust a maid to air a bed properly and we must, of course, have a meat meal to-night. Gentlemen require such a lot of meat, do they not? And drink. There certainly should be some drink in the house—and a siphon."

"If I can do anything——" I began.

"Oh! how very kind. But I did not mean that. There is plenty of time really. He brings his own pipe and tobacco, I am glad to say. Glad because it saves me from knowing which kind of cigarettes are right to buy. But rather sorry, too, because it takes so long for the smell to get out of the curtains. Of course, I open the window and shake them well very early every morning. Raymond gets up very late—I think writers often do. He writes very clever books, I believe, though people are not really nearly so unpleasant as he makes out. Clever young men know so little of life, don't you think?"

"Would you like to bring him to dinner at the

Vicarage ? " I asked, still unable to gather why I had been summoned.

" Oh ! no, thank you," said Miss Marple. " It's very kind of you," she added.

" There was—er—something you wanted to see me about, I think," I suggested desperately.

" Oh ! of course. In all the excitement it had gone right out of my head." She broke off and called to her maid. " Emily—Emily. Not those sheets. The frilled ones with the monogram, and don't put them too near the fire."

She closed the door and returned to me on tiptoe.

" It's just rather a curious thing that happened last night," she explained. " I thought you would like to hear about it, though at the moment it doesn't seem to make sense. I felt very wakeful last night—wondering about all this sad business. And I got up and looked out of my window. And what do you think I saw ? "

I looked, inquiring.

" Gladys Cram," said Miss Marple, with great emphasis. " As I live, going into the wood with a suit-case."

" A suit-case ? "

" Isn't it extraordinary ? What should she want with a suit-case in the wood at twelve o'clock at night ? "

We both stared at each other.

" You see," said Miss Marple. " I daresay it has nothing to do with the murder. But it is a Peculiar Thing. And just at present we all feel we must take notice of Peculiar Things."

" Perfectly amazing," I said. " Was she going to—er—sleep in the barrow by any chance ? "

" She didn't, at anyrate," said Miss Marple. " Because quite a short time afterwards she came back, and she hadn't got the suit-case with her."

We stared at each other again.

K

# CHAPTER XVIII

THE inquest was held that afternoon (Saturday) at two o'clock at the Blue Boar. The local excitement was, I need hardly say, tremendous. There had been no murder in St. Mary Mead for at least fifteen years. And to have some one like Colonel Protheroe murdered actually in the Vicarage study is such a feast of sensation as rarely falls to the lot of a village population.

Various comments floated to my ears which I was probably not meant to hear.

"There's vicar. Looks pale, don't he? I wonder if he had a hand in it. 'Twas done at Vicarage, after all." "How can you, Mary Adams? And him visiting Henry Abbott at the time." "Ah! but they do say him and the colonel had words. There's Mary Hill. Giving herself airs, she is, on account of being in service there. Hush, here's coroner."

The coroner was Dr. Roberts of our adjoining town of Much Benham. He cleared his throat, adjusted his eyeglasses, and looked important.

To recapitulate all the evidence would be merely tiresome. Lawrence Redding gave evidence of finding the body, and identified the pistol as belonging to him. To the best of his belief he had seen it on the Tuesday, two days previously. It was kept on a shelf in his cottage, and the door of the cottage was habitually unlocked.

Mrs. Protheroe gave evidence that she had last seen her husband at about a quarter to six when they separated in the village street. She agreed to call for him at the Vicarage later. She had gone to the Vicarage about a quarter past six, by way of the back lane and the garden gate. She had heard no voices in the study and had imagined that the room was empty, but her husband might have been sitting at the writing-table, in which case she would not have seen him. As far as she knew, he had been in his usual health and spirits. She knew of no enemy who might have had a grudge against him.

I gave evidence next, told of my appointment with Protheroe and my summons to the Abbotts. I described how I had found the body and my summoning of Dr. Haydock.

"How many people, Mr. Clement, were aware that Colonel Protheroe was coming to see you that evening?"

"A good many, I should imagine. My wife knew, and my nephew, and Colonel Protheroe himself alluded to the fact that morning when I met him in the village. I should think several people might have overheard him, as being slightly deaf, he spoke in a loud voice."

"It was then, a matter of common knowledge? Any one might know?"

I agreed.

Haydock followed. He was an important witness. He described carefully and technically the appearance of the body and the exact injuries. It was his opinion that deceased had been shot whilst actually in the act of writing. He placed the time of death at approximately 6.20 to 6.30—certainly not later than 6.35. That was the outside limit. He was positive and emphatic on that point. There was no question of suicide, the wound could not have been self-inflicted.

Inspector Slack's evidence was discreet and abridged. He described his summons and the circumstances under which he had found the body. The unfinished letter was produced and the time on it—6.20—noted. Also the clock. It was tacitly assumed that the time of death was 6.22. The police were giving nothing away. Anne Protheroe told me afterwards that she had been told to suggest a slightly earlier period of time than 6.20 for her visit.

Our maid, Mary, was the next witness, and proved a somewhat truculent one. She hadn't heard anything, and didn't want to hear anything. It wasn't as though gentlemen who came to see the vicar usually got shot. They didn't. She'd got her own jobs to look after. Colonel Protheroe had arrived at a quarter past six exactly. No, she didn't look at the clock. She heard the church chime after she had shown him into the study. She didn't hear any shot. If there had been a shot she'd have heard it. Well, of course, she knew there must have been a shot, since the gentleman was found shot—but there it was. She hadn't heard it.

The coroner did not press the point. I realised that he and Colonel Melchett were working in agreement.

Mrs. Lestrange had been subpœned to give evidence, but a medical certificate, signed by Dr. Haydock, was produced saying she was too ill to attend.

There was only one other witness, a somewhat doddering old woman. The one who, in Slack's phrase, " did for " Lawrence Redding.

Mrs Archer was shown the pistol and recognised it as the one she had seen in Mr. Redding's sitting-room " over against the bookcase, he kept it, lying about." She had last seen it on the day of the murder. Yes—in answer to a further question—she was quite sure it was there at lunch time on Thursday—quarter to one when she left.

I remembered what the inspector had told me, and I was mildly surprised. However vague she might have been when he questioned her, she was quite positive about it now.

The coroner summed up in a negative manner, but with a good deal of firmness. The verdict was given almost immediately :

Murder by Person or Persons unknown.

As I left the room I was aware of a small army of young men with bright, alert faces and a kind of superficial resemblance to each other. Several of them were already known to me by sight as having haunted the Vicarage the last few days. Seeking to escape, I plunged back into the Blue Boar and was lucky enough to run straight

into the archæologist, Dr. Stone. I clutched at him
without ceremony.

" Journalists," I said briefly and expressively. " If
you could deliver me from their clutches ? "

" Why, certainly, Mr. Clement. Come upstairs with
me."

He led the way up the narrow staircase and into his
sitting-room, where Miss Cram was sitting rattling the
keys of a typewriter with a practised touch. She greeted
me with a broad smile of welcome and seized the opportunity to stop work.

" Awful, isn't it ? " she said. " Not knowing who did
it, I mean. Not but that I'm disappointed in an inquest.
Tame, that's what I call it. Nothing what you might
call spicy from beginning to end."

" You were there, then, Miss Cram ? "

" I was there all right. Fancy your not seeing me.
Didn't you see me ? I feel a bit hurt about that. Yes,
I do. A gentleman, even if he is a clergyman, ought
to have eyes in his head."

" Were you present also ? " I asked Dr. Stone, in an
effort to escape from this playful badinage. Young
women like Miss Cram always make me feel awkward.

" No, I'm afraid I feel very little interest in such
things. I am a man very wrapped up in his own
hobby."

" It must be a very interesting hobby," I said.

" You know something of it, perhaps ? "

I was obliged to confess that I knew next to nothing.

Dr. Stone was not the kind of man whom a confession
of ignorance daunts. The result was exactly the same
as though I had said that the excavation of barrows was
my only relaxation. He surged and eddied into speech.
Long barrows, round barrows, stone age, bronze age,
paleolithic, neolithic, kistvæns and cromlechs, it burst
forth in a torrent. I had little to do save nod my head
and look intelligent—and that last is perhaps over
optimistic. Dr. Stone boomed on. He was a little man.
His head was round and bald, his face was round and rosy,

and he beamed at you through very strong glasses. I have never known a man so enthusiastic on so little encouragement. He went into every argument for and against his own pet theory—which, by the way, I quite failed to grasp !

He detailed at great length his difference of opinion with Colonel Protheroe.

" An opinionated boor," he said with heat. " Yes, yes, I know he is dead, and one should speak no ill of the dead. But death does not alter facts. An opinionated boor describes him exactly. Because he had read a few books, he set himself up as an authority—against a man who has made a lifelong study of the subject. My whole life, Mr. Clement, has been given up to this work. My whole life——"

He was spluttering with excitement. Gladys Cram brought him back to earth with a terse sentence.

" You'll miss your train if you don't look out," she observed.

" Oh ! " The little man stopped in mid speech and dragged a watch from his pocket. " Bless my soul. Quarter to ? Impossible."

" Once you start talking you never remember the time. What you'd do without me to look after you, I reely don't know."

" Quite right, my dear, quite right." He patted her affectionately on the shoulder. " This is a wonderful girl, Mr. Clement. Never forgets anything. I consider myself extremely lucky to have found her. "

" Oh ! go on, Dr. Stone," said the lady. " You spoil me, you do."

I could not help feeling that I should be in a material position to add my support to the second school of thought—that which foresees lawful matrimony as the future of Dr. Stone and Miss Cram. I imagined that in her own way Miss Cram was rather a clever young woman.

" You'd better be getting along," said Miss Cram.

" Yes, yes, so I must."

He vanished into the room next door and returned carrying a suit-case.

" You are leaving ? " I asked in some surprise.

" Just running up to town for a couple of days," he explained. " My old mother to see to-morrow, some business with my lawyers on Monday. On Tuesday I shall return. By the way, I suppose that Colonel Protheroe's death will make no difference to our arrangements. As regards the barrow, I mean. Mrs. Protheroe will have no objection to our continuing the work ? "

" I should not think so."

As he spoke, I wondered who actually would be in authority at Old Hall. It was just possible that Protheroe might have left it to Lettice. I felt that it would be interesting to know the contents of Protheroe's will.

" Causes a lot of trouble in a family, a death does," remarked Miss Cram, with a kind of gloomy relish. " You wouldn't believe what a nasty spirit there sometimes is."

" Well I must really be going." Dr. Stone made ineffectual attempts to control the suit-case, a large rug and an unwieldy umbrella. I came to his rescue. He protested.

" Don't trouble—don't trouble. I can manage perfectly. Doubtless there will be somebody downstairs."

But down below there was no trace of a boots or any one else. I suspect that they were being regaled at the expense of the Press. Time was getting on, so we set out together to the station, Dr. Stone carrying the suit-case, and I holding the rug and umbrella.

Dr. Stone ejaculated remarks in between panting breaths as we hurried along.

" Really too good of you—didn't mean—to trouble you. . . . Hope we shan't miss—the train—Gladys is a good girl—really a wonderful girl—a very sweet nature —not too happy at home, I'm afraid—absolutely—the heart of a child—heart of a child, I do assure you,

in spite of—difference in our ages—find a lot in
common. . . ."

I felt that several well-known parallels would have
occurred to Miss Marple, had she been there.

We saw Lawrence Redding's cottage just as we turned
off to the station. It stands in an isolated position with
no other house near it. I observed two young men of
smart appearance standing on the doorstep and a
couple more peering in at the windows. It was a busy
day for the Press.

" Nice fellow, young Redding," I remarked, to see
what my companion would say.

He was so out of breath by this time that he found it
difficult to say anything, but he puffed out a word which
I did not at first quite catch.

" Dangerous," he gasped, when I asked him to repeat
his remark.

" Dangerous ? "

" Most dangerous. Innocent girls—know no better—
taken in by a fellow like that—always hanging round
women. . . . No good."

From which I deduced that the only young man in
the village had not passed unnoticed by the fair Gladys.

" Goodness," ejaculated Dr. Stone. " The train ! "

We were close to the station by this time and we
broke into a fast sprint. A down train was standing in
the station and the up London train was just coming in.

At the door of the booking office we collided with a
rather exquisite young man, and I recognised Miss
Marple's nephew just arriving. He is, I think, a young
man who does not like to be collided with. He prides
himself on his poise and general air of detachment, and
there is no doubt that vulgar contact is detrimental
to poise of any kind. He staggered back. I apologised
hastily and we passed in. Dr. Stone climbed on the train
and I handed up his baggage just as the train gave an
unwilling jerk and started.

I waved to him and then turned away. Raymond
West had departed, but our local chemist, who rejoices

in the name of Cherubim, was just setting out for the village. I walked beside him.

" Close shave that," he observed. " Well, how did the inquest go, Mr. Clement ? "

I gave him the verdict.

" Oh ! so that's what happened. I rather thought that would be the verdict.   Where's Dr. Stone off to ? "

I repeated what he had told me.

" Lucky not to miss the train. Not that you ever know on this line. I tell you, Mr. Clement, it's a crying shame. Disgraceful, that's what I call it. Train I came down by was ten minutes late. And that on a Saturday with no traffic to speak of. And on Wednesday —no, Thursday—yes, Thursday it was—I remember it was the day of the murder because I meant to write a strongly-worded complaint to the company—and the murder put it out of my head—yes, last Thursday. I had been to a meeting of the Pharmaceutical Society. How late do you think the 6.50 was ? *Half an hour.* Half an hour exactly ! What do you think of that ? Ten minutes I don't mind. But if the train doesn't get in till twenty past seven, well, you can't get home before half-past. What I say is, why call it the 6.50 ? "

" Quite so," I said, and wishing to escape from the monologue I broke away with the excuse that I had something to say to Lawrence Redding whom I saw approaching us on the other side of the road.

# CHAPTER XIX

" Very glad to have met you," said Lawrence. " Come to my place."

We turned in at the little rustic gate, went up the path, and he drew a key from his pocket and inserted it in the lock.

" You keep the door locked now," I observed.

" Yes." He laughed rather bitterly. " Case of stable door when the steed is gone, eh ? It is rather like that. You know, padre," he held the door open and I passed inside, " there's something about all this business that I don't like. It's too much of—how shall I put it—an inside job. Some one knew about that pistol of mine. That means that the murderer, whoever he was, must have actually been in this house—perhaps even had a drink with me."

" Not necessarily," I objected. " The whole village of St. Mary Mead probably knows exactly where you keep your toothbrush and what kind of tooth powder you use."

" But why should it interest them ? "

" I don't know," I said, " but it does. If you change your shaving cream it will be a topic of conversation."

" They must be very hard up for news."

" They are. Nothing exciting ever happens here."

" Well, it has now—with a vengeance."

I agreed.

" And who tells them all these things anyway ? Shaving cream and things like that ? "

" Probably old Mrs. Archer."

" That old crone ? She's practically a half wit, as far as I can make out."

" That's merely the camouflage of the poor," I explained. " They take refuge behind a mask of stupidity. You'll probably find that the old lady has all her wits about her. By the way, she seems very certain now that the pistol was in its proper place midday Thursday. What's made her so positive all of a sudden ? "

" I haven't the least idea. '

" Do you think she's right ? "

" There again I haven't the least idea. I don't go round taking an inventory of my possessions every day."

I looked round the small living room. Every shelf and table was littered with miscellaneous articles. Lawrence lived in the midst of an artistic disarray that would have driven me quite mad.

" It's a bit of a job finding things sometimes," he said, observing my glance. " On the other hand, everything is handy—not tucked away."

" Nothing is tucked away, certainly," I agreed. " It might perhaps have been better if the pistol had been."

" Do you know I rather expected the coroner to say something of the sort. Coroners are such asses. I expected to be censured or whatever they call it."

" By the way," I asked, " was it loaded ? "

Lawrence shook his head.

" I'm not quite so careless as that. It was unloaded, but there was a box of cartridges beside it."

" It was apparently loaded in all six chambers and one shot had been fired."

Lawrence nodded.

" And whose hand fired it ? It's all very well, sir, but unless the real murderer is discovered I shall be suspected of the crime to the day of my death."

" Don't say that, my boy."

" But I do say it."

He became silent, frowning to himself. He roused himself at last and said :

" But let me tell you how I got on last night. You know, old Miss Marple knows a thing or two."

" She is, I believe, rather unpopular on that account."

Lawrence proceeded to recount his story.

He had, following Miss Marple's advice, gone up to

Old Hall. There, with Anne's assistance, he had had an interview with the parlourmaid.

Anne had said simply :

"Mr. Redding wants to ask you a few questions, Rose."

Then she had left the room.

Lawrence had felt somewhat nervous. Rose, a pretty girl of twenty-five, gazed at him with a limpid gaze which he found rather disconcerting.

"It's—it's about Colonel Protheroe's death."

"Yes, sir ? "

"I'm very anxious, you see, to get at the truth."

"Yes, sir."

"I feel that there may be—that some one might—that—that there might be some incident——"

At this point Lawrence felt that he was not covering himself with glory, and heartily cursed Miss Marple and her suggestions.

"I wondered if you could help me ? "

"Yes, sir ? "

Rose's demeanour was still that of the perfect servant, polite, anxious to assist, and completely uninterested.

"Dash it all," said Lawrence, "haven't you talked the thing over in the servants' hall ? "

This method of attack flustered Rose slightly. Her perfect poise was shaken.

"In the servants' hall, sir ? "

"Or the housekeeper's room, or the bootboy's dug-out, or wherever you do talk ? There must be *some* place."

Rose displayed a very faint disposition to giggle, and Lawrence felt encouraged.

"Look here, Rose, you're an awfully nice girl. I'm sure you must understand what I'm feeling like. I don't want to be hanged. I didn't murder your master, but a lot of people think I did. Can't you help me in any way ? "

I can imagine at this point that Lawrence must have looked extremely appealing. His handsome head thrown back, his Irish blue eyes appealing. Rose softened and capitulated.

"Oh! sir, I'm sure—if any of us could help in any way. None of us think you did it, sir. Indeed we don't."

"I know, my dear girl, but that's not going to help me with the police."

"The police!" Rose tossed her head. "I can tell you, sir, we don't think much of that inspector. Slack, he calls himself. The police indeed."

"All the same, the police are very powerful. Now, Rose, you say you'll do your best to help me. I can't help feeling that there's a lot we haven't got at yet. The lady, for instance, who called to see Colonel Protheroe the night before he died."

"Mrs. Lestrange?"

"Yes, Mrs. Lestrange. I can't help feeling there's something rather odd about that visit of hers."

"Yes, indeed, sir, that's what we all said."

"You did?"

"Coming the way she did. And asking for the colonel. And of course there's been a lot of talk—nobody knowing anything about her down here. And Mrs. Simmons, she's the housekeeper, sir, she gave it as her opinion that she was a regular bad lot. But after hearing what Gladdie said, well, I didn't know what to think."

"What did Gladdie say?"

"Oh! nothing, sir. It was just—we were talking, you know."

Lawrence looked at her. He had the feeling of something kept back.

"I wonder very much what her interview with Colonel Protheroe was about."

"Yes, sir."

"I believe you know, Rose?"

"Me? Oh! no, sir. Indeed I don't. How could I?"

"Look here, Rose. You said you'd help me. If you overheard anything, anything at all—it mightn't seem

important, but anything . . . I'd be so awfully grateful
to you. After all, any one might—might chance—just
*chance* to overhear something."

" But I didn't, sir, really I didn't."

" Then somebody else did," said Lawrence acutely.

" Well, sir——"

" Do tell me, Rose."

" I don't know what Gladdie would say, I'm sure."

" She'd want you to tell me. Who *is* Gladdie, by the
way ? "

" She's the kitchenmaid, sir. And you see, she'd just
stepped out to speak to a friend, and she was passing
the window—the study window—and the master was
there with the lady. And of course he did speak very
loud, the master did, always. And naturally, feeling a
little curious—I mean——"

" Awfully natural," said Lawrence, " I mean one
would simply have to listen."

" But of course she didn't tell any one—except me.
And we both thought it very odd. But Gladdie couldn't
say anything, you see, because if it was known she'd
gone out to meet a—a friend—well, it would have
meant a lot of unpleasantness with Mrs. Pratt, that's
the cook, sir. But I'm sure she'd tell you anything,
sir, willing."

" Well, can I go to the kitchen and speak to her ? "

Rose was horrified by the suggestion.

" Oh ! no, sir, that would never do. And Gladdie's
a very nervous girl anyway."

At last the matter was settled, after a lot of discussion
over difficult points. A clandestine meeting was
arranged in the shrubbery.

Here, in due course, Lawrence was confronted by the
nervous Gladdie whom he described as more like a
shivering rabbit than anything human. Ten minutes
were spent in trying to put the girl at her ease, the
shivering Gladys explaining that she couldn't ever—
that she didn't ought, that she didn't think Rose would
have given her away, that anyway she hadn't meant

no harm, indeed she hadn't, and that she'd catch it badly if Mrs. Pratt ever came to hear of it.

Lawrence reassured, cajoled, persuaded—at last Gladys consented to speak.

"If you'll be sure it'll go no further, sir."

"Of course it won't."

"And it won't be brought up against me in a court of law."

"Never."

"And you won't tell the mistress ? "

"Not on any account."

"If it were to get to Mrs. Pratt's ears——"

"It won't. Now tell me, Gladys."

"If you're sure it's all right ? "

"Of course it is. You'll be glad some day you've saved me from being hanged."

Gladys gave a little shriek.

"Oh ! indeed, I wouldn't like that, sir. Well, it's very little I heard—and that entirely by accident as you might say——"

"I quite understand."

"But the master, he was evidently very angry. ' After all these years '—that's what he was saying— ' you dare to come here——'   ' It's an outrage——' I couldn't hear what the lady said—but after a bit he said, ' I utterly refuse—utterly——'' I can't remember everything—seemed as though they were at it hammer and tongs, she wanting him to do something and he refusing. ' It's a disgrace that you should have come down here,' that's one thing he said. And ' You shall not see her—I forbid it—— ' and that made me prick up my ears. Looked as though the lady wanted to tell Mrs. Protheroe a thing or two, and he was afraid about it. And I thought to myself, ' Well, now, fancy the master. Him so particular. And maybe no beauty himself when all's said and done. Fancy ! ' I said. And ' Men are all alike,' I said to my friend later. Not that he'd agree. Argued, he did. But he did admit he was surprised at Colonel Protheroe—him being a churchwarden and handing round the plate and reading the lessons on Sundays. ' But there,' I said, ' that's very often the worst.' For that's what I've heard my mother say, many a time."

Gladdie paused out of breath, and Lawrence tried tactfully to get back to where the conversation had started.

" Did you hear anything else ? "

" Well, it's difficult to remember exactly, sir. It was all much the same. He said once or twice, ' I don't believe it.' Just like that. ' Whatever Haydock says, I don't believe it.' "

" He said that, did he ? ' Whatever Haydock says ? ' "

" Yes. And he said it was all a plot."

" You didn't hear the lady speak at all ? "

" Only just at the end. She must have got up to go and come nearer the window. And I heard what she said. Made my blood run cold, it did. I'll never forget it. ' *By this time to-morrow night, you may be dead,*' she said. Wicked the way she said it. As soon as I heard the news, ' There,' I said to Rose. ' There ! ' "

Lawrence wondered. Principally he wondered how much of Gladys's story was to be depended upon. True in the main, he suspected that it had been embellished and polished since the murder. In especial he doubted the accuracy of the last remark. He thought it highly possible that it owed its being to the fact of the murder.

He thanked Gladys, rewarded her suitably, reassured her as to her misdoings being made known to Mrs. Pratt, and left Old Hall with a good deal to think over.

One thing was clear, Mrs. Lestrange's interview with Colonel Protheroe had certainly not been a peaceful one, and it was one which he was anxious to keep from the knowledge of his wife.

I thought of Miss Marple's churchwarden with his separate establishment. Was this a case resembling that ?

I wondered more than ever where Haydock came in ? He had saved Mrs. Lestrange from having to give evidence at the inquest.  He had done his best to protect her from the police.

How far would he carry that protection ?

Supposing he suspected her of crime—would he still try and shield her ?

She was a curious woman—a woman of very strong magnetic charm.  I myself hated the thought of connecting her with the crime in any way.

Something in me said, " It can't be her ! "

Why ?

And an imp in my brain replied : " Because she's a very beautiful and attractive woman.  That's why ? "

There is, as Miss Marple would say, a lot of human nature in all of us.

# CHAPTER XX

WHEN I got back to the Vicarage I found that we were in the middle of a domestic crisis.

Griselda met me in the hall and with tears in her eyes dragged me into the drawing-room.

" She's going."

" Who's going ? "

" Mary. She's given notice."

I really could not take the announcement in a tragic spirit.

" Well," I said, " we'll have to get another servant."

It seemed to me a perfectly reasonable thing to say. When one servant goes, you get another. I was at a loss to understand Griselda's look of reproach.

" Len—you are absolutely heartless. You don't *care*."

I didn't. In fact, I felt almost light-hearted at the prospect of no more burnt puddings and undercooked vegetables.

" I'll have to look about for a girl, and find one, and train her," continued Griselda in a voice of acute self-pity.

" Is Mary trained ? " I said.

" Of course she is."

" I suppose," I said, " that somebody has heard her address us as sir or m'am and has immediately wrested her from us as a paragon. All I can say is, they'll be disappointed.

" It isn t that," said Griselda. " Nobody else wants her. I don't see how they could. It's her feelings. They're upset because Lettice Protheroe said she didn't dust properly."

Griselda often comes out with surprising statements, but this seemed to me so surprising that I questioned it. It seemed to me the most unlikely thing in the world that Lettice Protheroe should go out of her way to interfere in our domestic affairs and reprove our maid for slovenly housework. It was completely un-Lettice-like, and I said so.

"I don't see," I said, "what our dust has to do with Lettice Protheroe."

"Nothing at all," said my wife. "That's why it's so unreasonable. I wish you'd go and talk to Mary yourself. She's in the kitchen."

I had no wish to talk to Mary on the subject, but Griselda, who is very energetic and quick, fairly pushed me through the baize door into the kitchen before I had time to rebel.

Mary was peeling potatoes at the sink.

"Er—good-afternoon," I said nervously.

Mary looked up and snorted, but made no other response.

"Mrs. Clement tells me that you wish to leave us," I said.

Mary condescended to reply to this.

"There's some things," she said darkly, "as no girl can be asked to put up with."

"Will you be more explicit, please?"

"Eh?"

"Will you tell me exactly what it is that has upset you?"

"Tell you that in two words, I can." (Here, I may say, she vastly underestimated.) "People coming snooping round here when my back's turned. Poking round. And what business of hers is it, how often the study is dusted or turned out? If you and the missus don't complain, it's nobody else's business. If I give satisfaction to you that's all that matters, I say."

Mary has never given satisfaction to me. I confess that I have a hankering after a room thoroughly dusted and tidied every morning. Mary's practice of flicking off the more obvious deposit on the surface of low tables is to my thinking grossly inadequate. However, I realised that at the moment it was no good to go into side issues.

" Had to go to that inquest, didn't I ? Standing up before twelve men, a respectable girl like me ! And who knows what questions you may be asked. I'll tell you this. I've never before been in a place where they had a murder in the house, and I never want to be again.''

" I hope you won't," I said. " On the law of averages, I should say it was very unlikely."

" I don't hold with the law. *He* was a magistrate. Many a poor fellow sent to jail for potting at a rabbit —and him with his pheasants and what not. And then, before he's so much as decently buried, that daughter of his comes round and says I don't do my work properly."

" Do you mean that Miss Protheroe has been here ? "

" Found her here when I come back from the Blue Boar. In the study she was. And ' Oh ! ' she says. ' I'm looking for my little yellow berry—a little yellow hat. I left it here the other day.' ' Well,' I says, ' I haven't seen no hat. It wasn't here when I done the room on Thursday morning,' I says. And ' Oh ! ' she says, ' but I dare say you wouldn't see it. You don't spend much time doing a room, do you ? ' And with that she draws her finger along the mantelshelf and looks at it. As though I had time on a morning like this to take off all them ornaments and put them back, with the police only unlocking the room the night before. ' If the vicar and his lady are satisfied that's all that matters, I think, miss,' I said. And she laughs and goes out of the window and says, ' Oh ! but are you sure they are ? ' "

" I see," I said.

" And there it is ! A girl has her feelings ! I'm sure I'd work my fingers to the bone for you and the missus. And if she wants a new-fangled dish tried, I'm always ready to try it."

" I'm sure you are," I said soothingly.

" But she must have heard something or she wouldn't have said what she did. And if I don't give satisfaction I'd rather go. Not that I take any notice of what Miss

Protheroe says. She's not loved up at the Hall, I can tell you. Never a please or a thank you, and everything scattered right and left. I wouldn't set any store by Miss Lettice Protheroe myself for all that Mr. Dennis is so set upon her. But she's the kind that can always twist a young gentleman round her little finger."

During all this, Mary had been extracting eyes from potatoes with such energy that they had been flying round the kitchen like hailstones. At this moment one hit me in the eye and caused a momentary pause in the conversation.

" Don't you think," I said, as I dabbed my eye with my handkerchief, " that you have been rather too inclined to take offence where none is meant ? You know, Mary, your mistress will be very sorry to lose you."

" I've nothing against the mistress—or against you, sir, for that matter."

" Well, then, don't you think you're being rather silly ? "

Mary sniffed.

" I was a bit upset like—after the inquest and all. And a girl has her feelings. But I wouldn't like to cause the mistress inconvenience."

" Then that's all right," I said.

I left the kitchen to find Griselda and Dennis waiting for me in the hall.

" Well ? " exclaimed Griselda.

" She's staying," I said, and sighed.

" Len," said my wife, " you *have* been clever."

I felt rather inclined to disagree with her. I did not think I had been clever. It is my firm opinion that no servant could be a worse one than Mary. Any change, I consider, would have been a change for the better.

But I like to please Griselda. I detailed the heads of Mary's grievance.

" How like Lettice," said Dennis. " She couldn't have left that yellow beret of hers here on Wednesday. She was wearing it for tennis on Thursday."

" That seems to me highly probable," I said.

" She never knows where she's left anything," said Dennis, with a kind of affectionate pride and admiration that I felt was entirely uncalled for. " She loses about a dozen things every day."

" A remarkably attractive trait," I observed.

Any sarcasm missed Dennis.

" She *is* attractive," he said, with a deep sigh. " People are always proposing to her—she told me so."

" They must be illicit proposals if they're made to her down here," I remarked. " We haven't got a bachelor in the place."

" There's Dr. Stone," said Griselda, her eyes dancing.

" He asked her to come and see the barrow the other day," I admitted.

" Of course he did," said Griselda. " She *is* attractive, Len. Even bald-headed archæologists feel it."

" Lots of S.A.," said Dennis sapiently.

And yet Lawrence Redding is completely untouched by Lettice's charm. Griselda, however, explained that with the air of one who knew she was right.

" Lawrence has got lots of S.A. himself. That kind always likes the—how shall I put it—the Quaker type. Very unrestrained and diffident. The kind of women whom everybody calls cold. I think Anne is the only woman who could ever hold Lawrence. I don't think they'll ever tire of each other. All the same, I think he's been rather stupid in one way. He's rather made use of Lettice, you know. I don't think he ever dreamed she cared—he's awfully modest in some ways—but I have a feeling she does."

" She can't bear him," said Dennis positively. " She told me so."

I have never seen anything like the pitying silence with which Griselda received this remark.

I went into my study. There was, to my fancy, still a rather eerie feeling in the room. I knew that I must get over this. Once give in to that feeling, and I should probably never use the study again. I walked thoughtfully over to the writing table. Here Protheroe had sat, red faced, hearty, self-righteous, and here, in a moment of time, he had been struck down. Here, where I was standing, an enemy had stood. . . .

And so—no more Protheroe. . . .

Here was the pen his fingers had held.

On the floor was a faint dark stain—the rug had been sent to the cleaners, but the blood had soaked through.

I shivered.

" I can't use this room," I said aloud. " I can't use it."

Then my eye was caught by something—a mere speck of bright blue. I bent down. Between the floor and the desk I saw a small object. I picked it up.

I was standing staring at it in the palm of my hand when Griselda came in.

" I forgot to tell you, Len. Miss Marple wants us to go over to-night after dinner. To amuse the nephew. She's afraid of his being dull. I said we'd go."

" Very well, my dear."

" What are you looking at ? "

" Nothing."

I closed my hand, and looking at my wife, observed :

" If you don't amuse Master Raymond West, my dear, he must be very hard to please."

My wife said : " Don't be ridiculous, Len," and turned pink.

She went out again, and I unclosed my hand.

In the palm of my hand was a blue lapis lazuli ear-ring set in seed pearls.

It was rather an unusual jewel, and I knew very well where I had seen it last.

# CHAPTER XXI

I CANNOT say that I have at any time a great admiration for Mr. Raymond West. He is, I know, supposed to be a brilliant novelist and has made quite a name as a poet. His poems have no capital letters in them, which is, I believe, the essence of modernity. His books are about unpleasant people leading lives of surpassing dullness.

He has a tolerant affection for " Aunt Jane," whom he alludes to in her presence as a " survival."

She listens to his talk with a flattering interest, and if there is sometimes an amused twinkle in her eye I am sure he never notices it.

He fastened on Griselda at once with flattering abruptness. They discussed modern plays and from there went on to modern schemes of decoration. Griselda affects to laugh at Raymond West, but she is, I think, susceptible to his conversation.

During my (dull) conversation with Miss Marple, I heard at intervals the reiteration " buried as you are down here."

It began at last to irritate me. I said suddenly :

" I suppose you consider us very much out of things down here ? "

Raymond West waved his cigarette.

" I regard St. Mary Mead," he said authoritatively, " as a stagnant pool."

He looked at us, prepared for resentment at his statement, but somewhat, I think, to his chagrin, no one displayed annoyance.

" That is really not a very good simile, dear Raymond," said Miss Marple briskly. " Nothing, I believe, is so full of life under the microscope as a drop of water from a stagnant pool."

" Life—of a kind," admitted the novelist.

"It's all much the same kind, really, isn't it?" said Miss Marple.

"You compare yourself to a denizen of a stagnant pond, Aunt Jane?"

"My dear, you said something of the sort in your last book, I remember."

No clever young man likes having his works quoted against himself. Raymond West was no exception.

"That was entirely different," he snapped.

"Life is, after all, very much the same everywhere," said Miss Marple in her placid voice. "Getting born, you know, and growing up—and coming into contact with other people—getting jostled—and then marriage and more babies——"

"And finally death," said Raymond West. "And not death with a death certificate always. Death in life."

"Talking of death," said Griselda. "You know we've had a murder here?"

Raymond West waved murder away with his cigarette.

"Murder is so crude," he said. "I take no interest in it."

That statement did not take me in for a moment. They say all the world loves a lover—apply that saying to murder and you have an even more infallible truth. No one can fail to be interested in a murder. Simple people like Griselda and myself can admit the fact, but any one like Raymond West has to pretend to be bored—at anyrate for the first five minutes.

Miss Marple, however, gave her nephew away by remarking:

"Raymond and I have been discussing nothing else all through dinner."

"I take a great interest in all the local news," said Raymond hastily. He smiled benignly and tolerantly at Miss Marple.

"Have you a theory, Mr. West?" asked Griselda.

"Logically," said Raymond West, again flourishing

his cigarette, "only one person could have killed Protheroe."

"Yes?" said Griselda.

We hung upon his words with flattering attention.

"The vicar," said Raymond, and pointed an accusing finger at me.

I gasped.

"Of course," he reassured me, "I know you didn't do it. Life is never what it should be. But think of the drama—the fitness—churchwarden murdered in the vicar's study by the vicar. Delicious!"

"And the motive?" I inquired.

"Oh! that's interesting." He sat up—allowed his cigarette to go out. "Inferiority complex, I think. Possibly too many inhibitions. I should like to write the story of the affair. Amazingly complex. Week after week, year after year, he's seen the man—at vestry meetings—at choir-boys' outings—handing round the bag in church—bringing it to the altar. Always he dislikes the man—always he chokes down his dislike. It's un-Christian, he won't encourage it. And so it festers underneath, and one day——"

He made a graphic gesture.

Griselda turned to me.

"Have you ever felt like that, Len?"

"Never," I said truthfully.

"Yet I hear you were wishing him out of the world not so long ago," remarked Miss Marple.

(That miserable Dennis! But my fault, of course, for ever making the remark.)

"I'm afraid I was," I said. "It was a stupid remark to make, but really I'd had a very trying morning with him."

"That's disappointing," said Raymond West. "Because, of course, if your subconscious were really planning to do him in, it would never have allowed you to make that remark."

He sighed.

"My theory falls to the ground. This is probably a

very ordinary murder—a revengeful poacher or something of that sort."

"Miss Cram came to see me this afternoon," said Miss Marple. "I met her in the village and I asked her if she would like to see my garden."

"Is she fond of gardens?" asked Griselda.

"I don't think so," said Miss Marple, with a faint twinkle. "But it makes a very useful excuse for talk, don't you think?"

"What did you make of her?" asked Griselda. "I don't believe she's really so bad."

"She volunteered a lot of information—really a lot of information," said Miss Marple. "About herself, you know, and her people. They all seem to be dead or in India. Very sad. By the way, she has gone to Old Hall for the week-end."

"What?"

"Yes, it seems Mrs. Protheroe asked her—or she suggested it to Mrs. Protheroe—I don't quite know which way about it was. To do some secretarial work for her—there are so many letters to cope with. It turned out rather fortunately. Dr. Stone being away, she has nothing to do. What an excitement this barrow has been."

"Stone?" said Raymond. "Is that the archæologist fellow?"

"Yes, he is excavating a barrow. On the Protheroe property."

"He's a good man," said Raymond. "Wonderfully keen on his job. I met him at a dinner not long ago and we had a most interesting talk. I must look him up."

"Unfortunately," I said, "he's just gone to London for the week-end. Why, you actually ran into him at the station this afternoon."

"I ran into you. You had a little fat man with you —with glasses on."

"Yes—Dr. Stone."

"But, my dear fellow—that wasn't Stone."

" Not Stone ? "

" Not the archæologist. I know him quite well. The man wasn't Stone—not the faintest resemblance."

We stared at each other. In particular I stared at Miss Marple.

" Extraordinary," I said.

" The suit-case," said Miss Marple.

" But why ? " said Griselda.

" It reminds me of the time the man went round pretending to be the gas inspector," murmured Miss Marple. " Quite a little haul, he got."

" An impostor," said Raymond West. " Now this is really interesting."

" The question is, has it anything to do with the murder ? " said Griselda.

" Not necessarily," I said. " But——" I looked at Miss Marple.

" It is," she said, " a Peculiar Thing. Another Peculiar Thing."

" Yes," I said, rising. " I rather feel the inspector ought to be told about this at once."

# CHAPTER XXII

INSPECTOR SLACK'S orders, once I had got him on the telephone, were brief and emphatic. Nothing was to "get about." In particular, Miss Cram was not to be alarmed. In the meantime, a search was to be instituted for the suit-case in the neighbourhood of the barrow.

Griselda and I returned home very excited over this new development. We could not say much with Dennis present, as we had faithfully promised Inspector Slack to breathe no word to anybody.

In any case, Dennis was full of his own troubles. He came into my study and began fingering things and shuffling his feet and looking thoroughly embarrassed.

"What is it, Dennis?" I said at last.

"Uncle Len, I don't want to go to sea."

I was astonished. The boy had been so very decided about his career up to now.

"But you were so keen on it."

"Yes, but I've changed my mind."

"What do you want to do?"

"I want to go into finance."

I was even more surprised.

"What do you mean—finance?"

"Just that. I want to go into the city."

"But, my dear boy, I am sure you would not like the life. Even if I obtained a post for you in a bank——"

Dennis said that wasn't what he meant. He didn't want to go into a bank. I asked him what exactly he did mean, and of course, as I suspected, the boy didn't really know.

By "going into finance" he simply meant getting rich quickly, which with the optimism of youth he imagined was a certainty if one "went into the city." I disabused him of this notion as gently as I could.

" What's put it into your head ? " I asked. " You were so satisfied with the idea of going to sea."

" I know, Uncle Len, but I've been thinking. I shall want to marry some day—and, I mean, you've got to be rich to marry a girl."

" Facts disprove your theory," I said.

" I know—but a real girl. I mean, a girl who's used to things."

It was very vague, but I thought I knew what he meant.

" You know," I said gently, " all girls aren't like Lettice Protheroe."

He fired up at once.

" You're awfully unfair to her. You don't like her. Griselda doesn't either. She says she's tiresome."

From the feminine point of view Griselda is quite right. Lettice *is* tiresome. I could quite realise, however, that a boy would resent the adjective.

" If only people made a few allowances. Why even the Hartley Napiers are going about grousing about her at a time like this ! Just because she left their old tennis party a bit early. Why should she stay if she was bored ? Jolly decent of her to go at all, I think."

" Quite a favour," I said, but Dennis suspected no malice. He was full of his own grievance on Lettice's behalf.

" She's awfully unselfish really. Just to show you, she made me stay. Naturally I wanted to go too. But she wouldn't hear of it. Said it was too bad on the Napiers. So, just to please her, I stopped on a quarter of an hour."

The young have very curious views on unselfishness.

" And now I hear Susan Hartley Napier is going about everywhere saying Lettice has rotten manners."

" If I were you," I said, " I shouldn't worry."

" It's all very well, but——"

He broke off.

" I'd—I'd do anything for Lettice."

" Very few of us can do anything for any one else," I said. "However much we wish it, we are powerless."

" I wish I were dead," said Dennis.

Poor lad. Calf love is a virulent disease. I forebore to say any of the obvious and probably irritating things which come so easily to one's lips. Instead, I said good-night, and went up to bed.

I took the eight o'clock service the following morning and when I returned found Griselda sitting at the breakfast table with an open note in her hand. It was from Anne Protheroe.

" DEAR GRISELDA,—If you and the vicar could come up and lunch here quietly to-day, I should be so very grateful. Something very strange has occurred, and I should like Mr. Clement's advice.

" Please don't mention this when you come, as I have said nothing to any one.

" With love,

" Yours affectionately,

" ANNE PROTHEROE."

" We must go, of course," said Griselda.

I agreed.

" I wonder what can have happened ? "

I wondered too.

" You know," I said to Griselda, " I don't feel we are really at the end of this case yet."

" You mean not till some one has really been arrested ? "

" No," I said, " I didn't mean that. I mean that there are ramifications, under-currents, that we know nothing about. There are a whole lot of things to clear up before we get at the truth."

" You mean things that don't really matter, but that get in the way ? "

" Yes, I think that expresses my meaning very well."

" I think we're all making a great fuss," said Dennis, helping himself to marmalade. " It's a jolly good thing old Protheroe is dead. Nobody liked him. Oh! I know the police have got to worry—it's their job. But I rather hope myself they'll never find out. I should hate to see Slack promoted going about swelling with importance over his cleverness."

I am human enough to feel that I agreed over the matter of Slack's promotion. A man who goes about systematically rubbing people up the wrong way cannot hope to be popular.

" Dr. Haydock thinks rather like I do," went on Dennis. " He'd never give a murderer up to justice. He said so."

I think that that is the danger of Haydock's views. They may be sound in themselves—it is not for me to say—but they produce an impression on the young, careless mind which I am sure Haydock himself never meant to convey.

Griselda looked out of the window and remarked that there were reporters in the garden.

" I suppose they're photographing the study windows again," she said, with a sigh.

We had suffered a good deal in this way. There was first the idle curiosity of the village—every one had come to gape and stare. There were next the reporters armed with cameras, and the village again to watch the reporters. In the end we had to have a constable from Much Benham on duty outside the window.

" Well," I said, " the funeral is to-morrow morning. After that, surely, the excitement will die down."

I noticed a few reporters hanging about Old Hall when we arrived there. They accosted me with various queries to which I gave the invariable answer (we had found it the best), that, " I had nothing to say."

We were shown by the butler into the drawing-room, the sole occupant of which turned out to be Miss Cram —apparently in a state of high enjoyment.

" This is a surprise, isn't it ? " she said, as she shook hands. " I never should have thought of such a thing, but Mrs. Protheroe is kind, isn't she ? And, of course, it isn't what you might call nice for a young girl to be staying alone at a place like the Blue Boar, reporters about and all. And, of course, it's not as though I haven't been able to make myself useful—you really need a secretary at a time like this, and Miss Protheroe doesn't do anything to help, does she ? "

I was amused to notice that the old animosity against Lettice persisted, but that the girl had apparently become a warm partisan of Anne's. At the same time I wondered if the story of her coming here was strictly accurate. In her account the initiative had come from Anne, but I wondered if that were really so. The first mention of disliking to be at the Blue Boar alone might have easily come from the girl herself. Whilst keeping an open mind on the subject, I did not fancy that Miss Cram was strictly truthful.

At that moment Anne Protheroe entered the room.

She was dressed very quietly in black. She carried in her hand a Sunday paper which she held out to me with a rueful glance.

" I've never had any experience of this sort of thing. It's pretty ghastly, isn't it ? I saw a reporter at the inquest. I just said that I was terribly upset and had nothing to say, and then he asked me if I wasn't very anxious to find my husband's murderer, and I said " Yes." And then whether I had any suspicions, and I said " No." And whether I didn't think the crime showed local knowledge, and I said it seemed to certainly. And that was all. And now look at this ! "

In the middle of the page was a photograph, evidently taken at least ten years ago—Heaven knows where they had dug it out. There were large headlines :

" WIDOW DECLARES SHE WILL NEVER REST TILL SHE HAS HUNTED DOWN HUSBAND'S MURDERER.

" *Mrs. Protheroe, the widow of the murdered man, is certain that the murderer must be looked for locally. She has suspicions, but no certainty. She declared herself*

M

*prostrated with grief, but reiterated her determination to
hunt down the murderer."*

" It doesn't sound like me, does it ? " said Anne.

" I dare say it might have been worse," I said, handing
back the paper.

" Impudent, aren't they ? " said Miss Cram.   " I'd
like to see one of those fellows trying to get something
out of me."

By the twinkle in Griselda's eye, I was convinced
that she regarded this statement as being more literally
true than Miss Cram intended it to appear.

Luncheon was announced, and we went in.   Lettice
did not come in till half-way through the meal, when she
drifted into the empty place with a smile for Griselda
and a nod for me.   I watched her with some attention,
for reasons of my own, but she seemed much the same
vague creature as usual.   Extremely pretty—that in
fairness I had to admit.   She was still not wearing
mourning, but was dressed in a shade of pale green
that brought out all the delicacy of her fair colour-
ing.

After we had had coffee, Anne said quietly :

" I want to have a little talk with the vicar.   I will
take him up to my sitting-room."

At last I was to learn the reason of our summons.
I rose and followed her up the stairs.   She paused at the
door of the room.   As I was about to speak, she stretched
out a hand to stop me.   She remained listening, looking
down towards the hall.

" Good.   They are going out into the garden.   No—
don't go in there.   We can go straight up."

Much to my surprise she led the way along the corridor
to the extremity of the wing.   Here a narrow ladder-like
staircase rose to the floor above, and she mounted it,
I following.   We found ourselves in a dusty boarded
passage.   Anne opened a door and led me into a large
dim attic which was evidently used as a lumber room.
There were trunks there, old broken furniture, a few

stacked pictures, and the many countless odds and ends which a lumber room collects.

My surprise was so evident that she smiled faintly.

" First of all, I must explain. I am sleeping very lightly just now. Last night—or rather this morning about three o'clock, I was convinced that I heard some one moving about the house. I listened for some time, and at last got up and came out to see. Out on the landing I realised that the sounds came, not from down below, but from up above. I came along to the foot of these stairs. Again I thought I heard a sound. I called up, " Is anybody there ? " But there was no answer, and I heard nothing more, so I assumed that my nerves had been playing tricks on me, and went back to bed.

" However, early this morning, I came up here—simply out of curiosity. And I found *this !* "

She stooped down and turned round a picture that was leaning against the wall with the back of the canvas towards us.

I gave a gasp of surprise. The picture was evidently a portrait in oils, but the face had been hacked and cut in such a savage way as to render it unrecognisable. Moreover, the cuts were clearly quite fresh.

" What an extraordinary thing," I said.

" Isn't it ? Tell me, can you think of any explanation ? "

I shook my head.

" There's a kind of savagery about it," I said, " that I don't like. It looks as though it had been done in a fit of maniacal rage."

" Yes, that's what I thought."

" What is the portrait ? "

" I haven't the least idea. I have never seen it before. All these things were in the attic when I married Lucius and came here to live. I have never been through them or bothered about them."

" Extraordinary," I commented.

I stooped down and examined the other pictures. They were very much what you would expect to find

—some very mediocre landscapes, some oleographs and a few cheaply-framed reproductions.

There was nothing else helpful. A large old-fashioned trunk, of the kind that used to be called an " ark " had the initials E.P. upon it. I raised the lid. It was empty. Nothing else in the attic was the least suggestive.

" It really is a most amazing occurrence," I said. " It's so—senseless."

" Yes," said Anne. " That frightens me a little."

There was nothing more to see. I accompanied her down to her sitting-room where she closed the door.

" Do you think I ought to do anything about it ? Tell the police ? "

I hesitated.

" It's hard to say on the face of it whether——"

" It has anything to do with the murder or not," finished Anne. " I know. That's what is so difficult. On the face of it, there seems no connection whatever."

" No," I said, " but it is another Peculiar Thing."

We both sat silent with puzzled brows.

" What are your plans, if I may ask ? " I said presently.

She lifted her head.

" I'm going to live here for at least another six months ! " She said it defiantly. " I don't want to. I hate the idea of living here. But I think it's the only thing to be done. Otherwise people will say that I ran away—that I had a guilty conscience."

" Surely not."

" Oh ! yes, they will. Especially when——" She paused and then said : " When the six months are up —I am going to marry Lawrence." Her eyes met mine. " We're neither of us going to wait any longer."

" I supposed," I said, " that that would happen."

Suddenly she broke down, burying her head in her hands.

" You don't know how grateful I am to you—you don't know. We'd said good-bye to each other—he was going away. I feel—I feel not so awful about Lucius's death. If we'd been planning to go away together, and he'd died then—it would be so awful now. But you made us both see how wrong it would be. That's why I'm grateful.

" I, too, am thankful," I said gravely.

" All the same, you know," she sat up. " Unless the real murderer is found, they'll always think it was Lawrence—oh ! yes, they will. And especially when he marries me."

" My dear, Dr. Haydock's evidence made it perfectly clear——"

" What do people care about evidence ? They don't even know about it. And medical evidence never means anything to outsiders anyway. That's another reason why I'm staying on here. Mr. Clement, *I'm going to find out the truth.*"

Her eyes flashed as she spoke. She added :

" That's why I asked that girl here."

" Miss Cram ? "

" Yes."

" You did ask her, then. I mean, it was your idea ? "

" Entirely. Oh ! as a matter of fact, she whined a bit. At the inquest—she was there when I arrived. No, I asked her here deliberately."

" But surely," I cried, " you don't think that that silly young woman could have anything to do with the crime ? "

" It's awfully easy to appear silly, Mr. Clement. It's one of the easiest things in the world."

" Then you really think—— ? "

" No, I don't. Honestly, I don't. What I do think is that that girl knows something—or might know something. I wanted to study her at close quarters."

" And the very night she arrives, that picture is slashed," I said thoughtfully.

" You think she did it ? But why ? It seems so utterly absurd and impossible."

" It seems to me utterly impossible and absurd that

your husband should have been murdered in my study,"
I said bitterly. "But he was."

"I know." She laid her hand on my arm. "It's
dreadful for you. I do realise that, though I haven't
said very much about it."

I took the blue lapis lazuli ear-ring from my pocket
and held it out to her.

"This is yours, I think?"

"Oh! yes." She held out her hand for it with a
pleased smile. "Where did you find it?"

But I did not put the jewel into her outstretched
hand.

"Would you mind," I said, "if I kept it a little
longer?"

"Why, certainly." She looked puzzled and a little
inquiring. I did not satisfy her curiosity.

Instead I asked her how she was situated financially.

"It is an impertinent question," I said, "but I
really do not mean it as such."

"I don't think it's impertinent at all. You and
Griselda are the best friends I have here. And I like
that funny old Miss Marple. Lucius was very well off,
you know. He left things pretty equally divided between
me and Lettice. Old Hall goes to me, but Lettice is to
be allowed to choose enough furniture to furnish a small
house, and she is left a separate sum for the purpose of
buying one, so as to even things up."

"What are her plans, do you know?"

Anne made a comical grimace.

"She doesn't tell them to me. I imagine she will
leave here as soon as possible. She doesn't like me—
she never has. I dare say it's my fault, though I've
really always tried to be decent. But I suppose any
girl resents a young stepmother."

"Are you fond of her?" I asked bluntly.

She did not reply at once, which convinced me that
Anne Protheroe is a very honest woman.

"I was at first," she said. "She was such a pretty
little girl. I don't think I am now. I don't know why

Perhaps it's because she doesn't like me. I like being liked, you know."

" We all do," I said, and Anne Protheroe smiled.

I had one more task to perform. That was to get a word alone with Lettice Protheroe. I managed that easily enough, catching sight of her in the deserted drawing-room. Griselda and Gladys Cram were out in the garden.

I went in and shut the door.

" Lettice," I said, " I want to speak to you about something."

She looked up indifferently.

" Yes ? "

I had thought beforehand what to say. I held out the lapis ear-ring and said quietly :

" Why did you drop that in my study ? "

I saw her stiffen for a moment—it was almost instantaneous. Her recovery was so quick that I myself could hardly have sworn to the movement. Then she said carelessly :

" I never dropped anything in your study. That's not mine. That's Anne's."

" I know that," I said.

" Well, why ask me, then ? Anne must have dropped it."

" Mrs. Protheroe has only been in my study once since the murder, and then she was wearing black and so would not have been likely to have had on a blue ear-ring."

" In that case," said Lettice, " I suppose she must have dropped it before." She added : " That's only logical."

" It's very logical," I said. " I suppose you don't happen to remember when your stepmother was wearing these ear-rings last ? "

" Oh ! " She looked at me with a puzzled, trustful gaze. " Is it very important ? "

" It might be," I said.

" I'll try and think." She sat there knitting her

brows. I have never seen Lettice Protheroe look more charming than she did at that moment. " Oh ! yes," she said suddenly. " She had them on—on Thursday. I remember now."

" Thursday," I said slowly, "was the day of the murder. Mrs. Protheroe came to the study in the garden that day, but if you remember, in her evidence, she only came as far as the study window, not inside the room."

" Where did you find this ? "

" Rolled underneath the desk."

" Then it looks, doesn't it," said Lettice coolly, " as though she hadn't spoken the truth ? "

" You mean that she came right in and stood by the desk ? "

" Well, it looks like it, doesn't it ? "

Her eyes met mine serenely.

" If you want to know," she said calmly, " I never have thought she was speaking the truth."

" And I *know you* are not, Lettice."

" What do you mean ? "

She was startled.

" I mean," I said, " that the last time I saw this earring was on Friday morning when I came up here with Colonel Melchett. It was lying with its fellow on your stepmother's dressing-table. I actually handled them both."

" Oh—— ! " She wavered, then suddenly flung herself sideways over the arm of her chair and burst into tears. Her short fair hair hung down almost touching the floor. It was a strange attitude—beautiful and unrestrained.

I let her sob for some moments in silence and then I said very gently :

" Lettice, why did you do it ? "

" What ? "

She sprang up, flinging her hair wildly back. She looked wild—almost terrified.

" What do you mean ? "

"What made you do it? Was it jealousy? Dislike of Anne?"

"Oh!—oh! yes." She pushed the hair back from her face and seemed suddenly to regain complete self-possession. "Yes, you can call it jealousy. I've always disliked Anne—ever since she came queening it here. I put the damned thing under the desk. I hoped it would get her into trouble. It would have done if you hadn't been such a Nosey Parker, fingering things on dressing-tables. Anyway, it isn't a clergyman's business to go about helping the police."

It was a spiteful, childish outburst. I took no notice of it. Indeed, at that moment, she seemed a very pathetic child indeed.

Her childish attempt at vengeance against Anne seemed hardly to be taken seriously. I told her so, and added that I should return the earring to her and say nothing of the circumstances in which I had found it. She seemed rather touched by that.

"That's nice of you," she said.

She paused a minute and then said, keeping her face averted and evidently choosing her words with care.

"You know, Mr. Clement, I should—I should get Dennis away from here soon, if I were you. I—I think it would be better."

"Dennis?" I raised my eyebrows in slight surprise but with a trace of amusement too.

"I think it would be better." She added, still in the same awkward manner: "I'm sorry about Dennis. I didn't think he—anyway, I'm sorry."

We left it at that.

## CHAPTER XXIII

On the way back, I proposed to Griselda that we should make a detour and go round by the barrow. I was anxious to see if the police were at work and if so, what they had found. Griselda, however, had things to do at home, so I was left to make the expedition on my own.

I found Constable Hurst in charge of operations.

" No sign so far, sir," he reported. " And yet it stands to reason that this is the only place for a *cache.*"

His use of the word cache puzzled me for a moment, as he pronounced it catch, but his real meaning occurred to me almost at once.

" Whatimeantersay is, sir, where else could the young woman be going starting into the wood by that path ? It leads to Old Hall, and it leads here, and that's about all."

" I suppose," I said, " that Inspector Slack would disdain such a simple course as asking the young lady straight out.

" Anxious not to put the wind up her," said Hurst. " Anything she writes to Stone or he writes to her may throw light on things—once she knows we're on to her, she'd shut up like *that.*"

Like *what* exactly was left in doubt, but I personally doubted Miss Gladys Cram ever being shut up in the way described. It was impossible to imagine her as other than overflowing with conversation.

" When a man's an h'impostor, you want to know *why* he's an h'impostor," said Constable Hurst didactically.

" Naturally," I said.

" And the answer is to be found in this here barrow —or else why was he for ever messing about with it ? "

" A *raison d'etre* for prowling about," I suggested, but

this bit of French was too much for the constable. He revenged himself for not understanding it by saying coldly :

" That's the h'amateur's point of view."

" Anyway, you haven't found the suit-case," I said.

" We shall do, sir. Not a doubt of it."

" I'm not so sure," I said. " I've been thinking. Miss Marple said it was quite a short time before the girl reappeared empty-handed. In that case, she wouldn't have had time to get up here and back."

" You can't take any notice of what old ladies say. When they've seen something curious, and are waiting all eager like, why, time simply flies for them. And anyway, no lady knows anything about time."

I often wonder why the whole world is so prone to generalise. Generalisations are seldom or ever true and are usually utterly inaccurate. I have a poor sense of time myself (hence the keeping of my clock fast) and Miss Marple, I should say, has a very acute one. Her clocks keep time to the minute and she herself is rigidly punctual on every occasion.

However, I had no intention of arguing with Constable Hurst on the point. I wished him good-afternoon and good luck and went on my way.

It was just as I was nearing home that the idea came to me. There was nothing to lead up to it. It just flashed into my brain as a possible solution.

You will remember that on my first search of the path, the day after the murder, I had found the bushes disturbed in a certain place. They proved, or so I thought at the time, to have been disturbed by Lawrence, bent on the same errand as myself.

But I remembered that afterwards he and I together had come upon another faintly marked trail which proved to be that of the inspector. On thinking it over, I distinctly remembered that the first trail (Lawrence's) had been much more noticeable than the second, as though more than one person had been passing that way. And I reflected that that was probably what had drawn Lawrence's attention to it in the first instance. Supposing that it had originally been made by either Dr. Stone or else Miss Cram ?

I remembered, or else I imagined remembering, that there had been several withered leaves on broken twigs. If so, the trail could not have been made the afternoon of our search.

I was just approaching the spot in question. I recognised it easily enough and once more forced my way through the bushes. This time I noticed fresh twigs broken. Some one *had* passed this way since Lawrence and myself.

I soon came to the place where I had encountered Lawrence. The faint trail, however, persisted farther, and I continued to follow it. Suddenly it widened out into a little clearing which showed signs of recent upheaval. I say a clearing, because the denseness of the undergrowth was thinned out there, but the branches of the trees met overhead and the whole place was not more than a few feet across.

On the other side, the undergrowth grew densely again, and it seemed quite clear that no one had forced a way through it recently. Nevertheless, it seemed to have been disturbed in one place.

I went across and kneeled down, thrusting the bushes aside with both hands. A glint of a shiny brown surface rewarded me. Full of excitement, I thrust my arm in and with a good deal of difficulty I extracted a small brown suitcase.

I uttered an ejaculation of triumph. I had been successful. Coldly snubbed by Constable Hurst, I had yet proved right in my reasoning. Here without doubt was the suitcase carried by Miss Cram. I tried the hasp, but it was locked.

As I rose to my feet I noticed a small brownish crystal lying on the ground. Almost automatically, I picked it up and slipped it into my pocket.

Then grasping my find by the handle, I retraced my steps to the path.

As I climbed over the stile into the lane, an agitated voice near at hand called out :

" Oh ! Mr. Clement. You've found it ! How clever of you ! "

Mentally registering the fact that in the art of seeing without being seen, Miss Marple had no rival, I balanced my find on the palings between us.

" That's the one,' said Miss Marple. " I'd know it anywhere."

This, I thought, was a slight exaggeration. There are thousands of cheap shiny suit-cases all exactly alike. No one could recognise one particular one seen from such a distance away by moonlight, but I realised that the whole business of the suit-case was Miss Marple's particular triumph and, as such, she was entitled to a little pardonable exaggeration.

" It's locked, I suppose, Mr. Clement ? "

" Yes. I'm just going to take it down to the police station."

" You don't think it would be better to telephone ? "

Of course unquestionably it would be better to telephone. To stride through the village, suit-case in hand, would be to court a probably undesirable publicity.

So I unlatched Miss Marple's garden gate and entered the house by the French window, and from the sanctity of the drawing-room with the door shut, I telephoned my news.

The result was that Inspector Slack announced he would be up himself in a couple of jiffies.

When he arrived it was in his most cantankerous mood.

" So we've got it, have we ? " he said. " You know, sir, you shouldn't keep things to yourself. If you've any reason to believe you know where the article in question was hidden, you ought to have reported it to the proper authorities."

" It was a pure accident," I said. " The idea just happened to occur to me."

" And that's a likely tale. Nearly three-quarters of

a mile of woodland, and you go right to the proper spot and lay your hand upon it."

I would have given Inspector Slack the steps in reasoning which led me to this particular spot, but he had achieved his usual result of putting my back up. I said nothing.

"Well?" said Inspector Slack, eyeing the suit-case with dislike and wouldbe indifference, "I suppose we might as well have a look at what's inside."

He had brought an assortment of keys and wire with him. The lock was a cheap affair. In a couple of seconds the case was open.

I don't know what we had expected to find—something sternly sensational, I imagine. But the first thing that met our eyes was a greasy plaid scarf. The inspector lifted it out. Next came a faded dark blue overcoat, very much the worse for wear. A checked cap followed.

"A shoddy lot," said the inspector.

A pair of boots very down at heel and battered came next. At the bottom of the suit-case was a parcel done up in newspaper.

"Fancy shirt, I suppose," said the inspector bitterly, as he tore it open.

A moment later he had caught his breath in surprise.

For inside the parcel were some demure little silver objects and a round platter of the same metal.

Miss Marple gave a shrill exclamation of recognition.

"The trencher salts," she exclaimed. "Colonel Protheroe's trencher salts, and the Charles II. tazza. Did you ever hear of such a thing!"

The inspector had got very red.

"So that was the game," he muttered. "Robbery. But I can't make it out. There's been no mention of these things being missing."

"Perhaps they haven't discovered the loss," I suggested. "I presume these valuable things would not have been kept out in common use. Colonel Protheroe probably kept them locked away in a safe."

"I must investigate this," said the inspector. "I'll

go right up to Old Hall now. So that's why our Dr.
Stone made himself scarce. What with the murder and
one thing and another, he was afraid we'd get wind of
his activities. As likely as not his belongings might
have been searched. He got the girl to hide them in
the wood with a suitable change of clothing. He meant
to come back by a roundabout route and go off with
them one night whilst she stayed here to disarm
suspicion. Well, there's one thing to the good. This
lets him out over the murder. He'd nothing to do with
that. Quite a different game."

He repacked the suit-case and took his departure,
refusing Miss Marple's offer of a glass of sherry.

" Well, that's one mystery cleared up," I said with
a sigh. " What Slack says is quite true ; there are no
grounds for suspecting him of the murder. Everything's
accounted for quite satisfactorily."

" It really would seem so," said Miss Marple.
" Although one never can be quite certain, can one ? "

" There's a complete lack of motive," I pointed out.
" He'd got what he came for and was clearing out."

" Y—es."

She was clearly not quite satisfied, and I looked at
her in some curiosity. She hastened to answer my
inquiring gaze with a kind of apologetic eagerness.

" I've no doubt I am *quite* wrong. I'm so stupid
about these things. But I just wondered—I mean this
silver is very valuable, is it not ? "

" A tazza sold the other day for over a thousand
pounds, I believe."

" I mean—it's not the value of the metal."

" No, it's what one might call a connoisseur's value."

" That's what I mean. The sale of such things would
take a little time to arrange, or even if it was arranged,
it couldn't be carried through without secrecy. I mean
—if the robbery were reported and a hue and cry were
raised, well, the things couldn't be marketed at all."

" I don't quite see what you mean ? " I said.

" I know I'm putting it badly." She became more

flustered and apologetic. " But it seems to me that—
that the things couldn't just have been abstracted, so
to speak. The only satisfactory thing to do would be
to replace these things with copies. Then, perhaps,
the robbery wouldn't be discovered for some time."

" That's a very ingenious idea," I said.

" It would be the only way to do it, wouldn't it ?
And if so, of course, as you say, once the substitution
had been accomplished there wouldn't have been any
reason for murdering Colonel Protheroe —quite the
reverse."

" Exactly," I said. " That's what I said."

" Yes, but I just wondered—I don't know, of course
—and Colonel Protheroe always talked a lot about
doing things before he actually did do them, and, of
course, sometimes never did them at all, but he did
say——"

" Yes ? "

" That he was going to have all his things valued—a
man down from London. For probate—no, that's when
you're dead—for insurance. Some one told him that
was the thing to do. He talked about it a great deal,
and the importance of having it done. Of course, I
don't know if he had made any actual arrangements,
but if he had . . ."

" I see," I said slowly.

" Of course, the moment the expert saw the silver,
he'd know, and then Colonel Protheroe would remember
having shown the things to Dr. Stone—I wonder if it
was done then—legerdemain, don't they call it ? So
clever—and then, well, the fat would be in the fire, to
use an old-fashioned expression."

" I see your idea," I said. " I think we ought to find
out for certain."

I went once more to the telephone. In a few minutes
I was through to Old Hall and speaking to Anne
Protheroe.

" No, it's nothing very important. Has the inspector
arrived yet ? Oh ! well, he's on his way. Mrs. Protheroe,

can you tell me if the contents of Old Hall were ever valued ? What's that you say ? "

Her answer came clear and prompt. I thanked her, replaced the receiver, and turned to Miss Marple.

" That's very definite. Colonel Protheroe had made arrangements for a man to come down from London on Monday—to-morrow—to make a full valuation. Owing to the colonel's death, the matter has been put off."

" Then there *was* a motive," said Miss Marple softly.

" A motive, yes. But that's all. You forget. When the shot was fired, Dr. Stone had just joined the others, or was climbing over the stile in order to do so.

" Yes," said Miss Marple thoughtfully. " So that rules him out."

# CHAPTER XXIV

I RETURNED to the Vicarage to find Hawes waiting for me in my study. He was pacing up and down nervously, and when I entered the room he started as though he had been shot.

"You must excuse me," he said, wiping his forehead. "My nerves are all to pieces lately."

"My dear fellow," I said, "you positively must get away for a change. We shall have you breaking down altogether and that will never do."

"I can't desert my post. No, that is a thing I will never do."

"It's not a case of desertion. You are ill. I'm sure Haydock would agree with me."

"Haydock—Haydock. What kind of a doctor is he? An ignorant country practitioner."

"I think you're unfair to him. He has always been considered a very able man in his profession."

"Oh! perhaps. Yes, I daresay. But I don't like him. However, that's not what I came to say. I came to ask you if you would be kind enough to preach to-night instead of me. I—I really do not feel equal to it."

"Why, certainly. I will take the service for you."

"No, no. I wish to take the service. I am perfectly fit. It is only the idea of getting up in the pulpit, of all those eyes staring at me. . . ."

He shut his eyes and swallowed convulsively.

It is clear to me that there is something very wrong indeed the matter with Hawes. He seemed aware of my thoughts, for he opened his eyes and said quickly :

"There is nothing really wrong with me. It is just these headaches—these awful racking headaches. I wonder if you could let me have a glass of water."

"Certainly," I said.

I went and fetched it myself from the tap. Ringing
bells is a profitless form of exercise in our house.

I brought the water to him and he thanked me. He
took from his pocket a small cardboard box, and
opening it, extracted a rice paper capsule, which he
swallowed with the aid of the water.

"A headache powder," he explained.

I suddenly wondered whether Hawes might have
become addicted to drugs. It would explain a great
many of his peculiarities.

"You don't take too many, I hope," I said.

"No—oh, no. Dr. Haydock warned me against that.
But it is really wonderful. They bring instant relief."

Indeed he already seemed calmer and more composed.

He stood up.

"Then you will preach to-night? It's very good of
you, sir."

"Not at all. And I insist on taking the service too.
Get along home and rest. No, I won't have any
argument. Not another word."

He thanked me again. Then he said, his eyes sliding
past me to the window:

"You—you have been up at Old Hall to-day, haven't
you, sir?"

"Yes."

"Excuse me—but were you sent for?"

I looked at him in surprise, and he flushed.

"I'm sorry, sir. I—I just thought some new development might have arisen and that that was why Mrs.
Protheroe had sent for you."

I had not the faintest intention of satisfying Hawes's
curiosity.

"She wanted to discuss the funeral arrangements
and one or two other small matters with me," I said.

"Oh! that was all. I see."

I did not speak. He fidgeted from foot to foot, and
finally said:

" Mr. Redding came to see me last night. I—I can't imagine why."

" Didn't he tell you ? "

" He—he just said he thought he'd look me up. Said it was a bit lonely in the evenings. He's never done such a thing before."

" Well, he's supposed to be pleasant company," I said, smiling.

" What does he want to come and see me for ? I don't like it." His voice rose shrilly. " He spoke of dropping in again. What does it all mean ? What idea do you think he has got into his head ? "

" Why should you suppose he has any ulterior motive ? " I asked.

" I don't like it," repeated Hawes obstinately. " I've never gone against *him* in any way. I never suggested that *he* was guilty—even when he accused himself I said it seemed most incomprehensible. If I've had suspicions of anybody it's been of Archer—never of him. Archer is a totally different proposition—a godless irreligious ruffian. A drunken blackguard."

" Don't you think you're being a little harsh ? " I said. " After all, we really know very little about the man."

" A poacher, in and out of prison, capable of anything."

" Do you really think he shot Colonel Protheroe ? " I asked curiously.

Hawes has an inveterate dislike of answering yes or no. I have noticed it several times lately.

" Don't you think yourself, sir, that it's the only possible solution ? "

" As far as we know," I said, " there's no evidence of any kind against him."

" His threats," said Hawes eagerly. " You forget about his threats."

I am sick and tired of hearing about Archer's threats. As far as I can make out, there is no direct evidence that he ever made any.

" He was determined to be revenged on Colonel Protheroe. He primed himself with drink and then shot him."

" That's pure supposition."

" But you will admit that it's perfectly probable ? "

" No, I don't."

" Possible, then ? "

" Possible, yes."

Hawes glanced at me sideways.

" Why don't you think it's probable ? "

" Because," I said, " a man like Archer wouldn't think of shooting a man with a pistol. It's the wrong weapon."

Hawes seemed taken aback by my argument. Evidently it wasn't the objection he had expected.

" Do you really think the objection is feasible ? " he asked doubtingly.

" To my mind it is a complete stumbling block to Archer's having committed the crime," I said.

In face of my positive assertion, Hawes said no more. He thanked me again and left.

I had gone as far as the front door with him, and on the hall table I saw four notes. They had certain characteristics in common. The handwriting was almost unmistakably feminine, they all bore the words, " By hand, Urgent," and the only difference I could see was that one was noticeably dirtier than the rest.

Their similarity gave me a curious feeling of seeing —not double, but quadruple.

Mary came out of the kitchen and caught me staring at them.

" Come by hand since lunch time," she volunteered. " All but one. I found that in the box."

I nodded, gathered them up, and took them into the study.

The first one ran thus :

" DEAR MR. CLEMENT,—Something has come to my knowledge which I feel you ought to know. It concerns the death of poor Colonel Protheroe. I should much appreciate your advice on the matter—whether to go to the police or not. Since my dear husband's death, I have such a shrinking from every kind of publicity. Perhaps you could run in and see me for a few minutes this afternoon.

> " Yours sincerely,
> " MARTHA PRICE RIDLEY."

I opened the second :

> " DEAR MR. CLEMENT,—I am so troubled—so *exercised* in my mind—to know what I ought to do. Something has come to my ears that I feel may be important. I have such a *horror* of being mixed up with the police in any way. I am so disturbed and distressed. Would it be asking too much of you, dear vicar, to drop in for a few minutes and solve my doubts and perplexities for me in the wonderful way you always do ?
> " Forgive my troubling you,
> " Yours very sincerely,
> " CAROLINE WETHERBY."

The third, I felt, I could almost have recited beforehand.

> " DEAR MR. CLEMENT,—Something most important has come to my ears. I feel you should be the first to know about it. Will you call in and see me this afternoon sometime. I will wait in for you."

This militant epistle was signed " AMANDA HARTNELL."
I opened the fourth missive. It has been my good fortune to be troubled with very few anonymous letters. An anonymous letter is, I think, the meanest and cruellest weapon there is. This one was no exception. It purported to be written by an illiterate person, but several things inclined me to disbelieve that assumption.

> " DEAR VICAR,—I think you ought to know what is

Going On. Your lady has been seen coming out of
Mr. Redding's cottage in a surreptitious manner. You
know wot i mean. The two are Carrying On together.
i think you ought to know.

" A FRIEND."

I made a faint exclamation of disgust and crumpling
up the paper tossed it into the open grate just as
Griselda entered the room.

"What's that you're throwing down so contemp-
tuously ? " she asked.

"Filth," I said.

Taking a match from my pocket, I struck one and
bent down. Griselda, however, was too quick for me.
She had stooped down and caught up the crumpled
ball of paper and smoothed it out before I could stop
her.

She read it, gave a little exclamation of disgust, and
tossed it back to me, turning away as she did so. I
lighted it and watched it burn.

Griselda had moved away. She was standing by the
window looking out into the garden.

"Len," she said, without turning round.

"Yes, my dear."

"I'd like to tell you something. Yes, don't stop me.
I want to, please. When—when Lawrence Redding
came here, I let you think that I had only known him
slightly before. That wasn't true. I—had known him
rather well. In fact, before I met you, I had been rather
in love with him. I think most people are with Lawrence.
I was—well absolutely silly about him at one time.
I don't mean I wrote him compromising letters or anything idiotic like they do in books. But I was rather
keen on him once."

"Why didn't you tell me ? " I asked.

"Oh ! because ! I don't know exactly except that
—well, you're foolish in some ways. Just because you're
so much older than I am, you think that I—well, that
I'm likely to like other people. I thought you'd be

tiresome, perhaps, about me and Lawrence being friends."

"You're very clever at concealing things," I said, remembering what she had told me in that room less than a week ago, and the ingenuous natural way she had talked.

"Yes, I've always been able to hide things. In a way, I like doing it."

Her voice held a childlike ring of pleasure in it.

"But it's quite true what I said. I didn't know about Anne, and I wondered why Lawrence was so different, not—well, really not noticing me. I'm not used to it."

There was a pause.

"You do understand, Len?" said Griselda anxiously.

"Yes," I said, "I understand."

But did I?

# CHAPTER XXV

I FOUND it hard to shake off the impression left by the anonymous letter. Pitch soils.

However, I gathered up the other three letters, glanced at my watch, and started out.

I wondered very much what this might be that had " come to the knowledge " of three ladies simultaneously. I took it to be the same piece of news. In this, I was to realise that my psychology was at fault.

I cannot pretend that my calls took me past the police station. My feet gravitated there of their own accord. I was anxious to know whether Inspector Slack had returned from Old Hall.

I found that he had, and further, that Miss Cram had returned with him. The fair Gladys was seated in the police station carrying off matters with a high hand. She denied absolutely having taken the suitcase to the woods.

" Just because one of these gossiping old cats has nothing better to do than look out of her window all night you go and pitch upon me. She's been mistaken once, remember, when she said she saw me at the end of the lane on the afternoon of the murder, and if she was mistaken then, in daylight, how can she possibly have recognised me by moonlight.

" Wicked it is, the way these old ladies go on down here. Say anything, they will. And me asleep in my bed as innocent as can be. You ought to be ashamed of yourselves, the lot of you."

" And supposing the landlady of the Blue Boar identifies the suitcase as yours, Miss Cram ? "

" If she says anything of the kind, she's wrong. There's no name on it. Nearly everybody's got a suit-case like that. As for poor Dr. Stone, accusing him of being a common burglar ! And he with a lot of letters after his name."

" You refuse to give us any explanation, then, Miss Cram ? "

" No refusing about it. You've made a mistake, that's all. You and your meddlesome Marples. I won't say a word more—not without my solicitor present. I'm going this minute—unless you're going to arrest me."

For answer, the inspector rose and opened the door for her, and with a toss of the head, Miss Cram walked out.

" That's the line she takes," said Slack, coming back to his chair. " Absolute denial. And, of course, the old lady *may* have been mistaken. No jury would believe you could recognise any one from that distance on a moonlit night. And, of course, as I say, the old lady may have made a mistake."

" She may," I said, " but I don't think she did. Miss Marple is usually right. That's what makes her unpopular."

The inspector grinned.

" That's what Hurst says. Lord, these villages ! "

" What about the silver, inspector ? "

" Seemed to be perfectly in order. Of course, that meant one lot or the other must be a fake. There's a very good man in Much Benham, an authority on old silver. I've phoned over to him and sent a car to fetch him. We'll soon know which is which. Either the burglary was an accomplished fact, or else it was only planned. Doesn't make a frightful lot of difference either way—I mean as far as we're concerned. Robbery's a small business compared with murder. These two aren't concerned with the murder. We'll maybe get a line on him through the girl—that's why I let her go without any more fuss."

" I wondered," I said.

" A pity about Mr. Redding. It's not often you find a man who goes out of his way to oblige you."

" I suppose not," I said, smiling slightly.

" Women cause a lot of trouble," moralised the inspector.

He sighed and then went on, somewhat to my surprise : " Of course, there's Archer."

" Oh ! " I said. " You've thought of him ? "

" Why, naturally, sir, first thing. It didn't need any anonymous letters to put me on his track."

" Anonymous letters," I said sharply. " Did you get one, then ? "

" That's nothing new, sir. We get a dozen a day, at least. Oh ! yes, we were put wise to Archer. As though the police couldn't look out for themselves ! Archer's been under suspicion from the first. The trouble of it is, he's got an alibi. Not that it amounts to anything, but it's awkward to get over."

" What do you mean by its not amounting to anything ? " I asked.

" Well, it appears he was with a couple of pals all the afternoon. Not, as I say, that that counts much. Men like Archer and his pals would swear to anything. There's no believing a word they say. *We* know that. But the public doesn't, and the jury's taken from the public, more's the pity. They know nothing, and ten to one believe everything that's said in the witness box, no matter who it is that says it. And of course Archer himself will swear till he's black in the face that he didn't do it."

" Not so obliging as Mr. Redding," I said with a smile.

" Not he," said the inspector, making the remark as a plain statement of fact.

" It is natural, I suppose, to cling to life," I mused.

" You'd be surprised if you knew the murderers that have got off through the soft-heartedness of the jury," said the inspector gloomily.

" But do you really think that Archer did it ? " I asked.

It has struck me as curious all along that Inspector

Slack never seems to have any personal views of his own on the murder. The easiness or difficulty of getting a conviction are the only points that seem to appeal to him.

" I'd like to be a bit surer," he admitted. " A finger-print now, or a footprint, or seen in the vicinity about the time of the crime. Can't risk arresting him without something of that kind. He's been seen round Mr. Redding's house once or twice, but he'd say that was to speak to his mother. A decent body, she is. No, on the whole, I'm for the lady. If I could only get definite proof of blackmail—but you can't get definite proof of anything in this crime ! It's theory, theory, theory. It's a sad pity that there's not a single spinster lady living along your road, Mr. Clement. I bet she'd have seen something if there had been."

His words reminded me of my calls, and I took leave of him. It was about the solitary instance when I had seen him in a genial mood.

My first call was on Miss Hartnell. She must have been watching for me from the window, for before I had time to ring, she had opened the front door, and clasping my hand firmly in hers, had led me over the threshold.

" So good of you to come. In here. More private."

We entered a microscopic room, about the size of a hencoop. Miss Hartnell shut the door and with an air of deep secrecy waved me to a seat (there were only three). I perceived that she was enjoying herself.

" I'm never one to beat about the bush," she said in her jolly voice, the latter slightly toned down to meet the requirements of the situation. " You know how things go the round in a village like this."

" Unfortunately," I said, " I do."

" I agree with you. Nobody dislikes gossip more than I do. But there it is. I thought it my duty to tell the police inspector that I'd called on Mrs. Lestrange the afternoon of the murder and that she was out. I don't expect to be thanked for doing my duty, I just do it. Ingratitude is what you meet with first and last in this life. Why only yesterday that impudent Mrs. Baker——"

" Yes, yes," I said, hoping to avert the usual tirade. " Very sad, very sad. But you were saying."

" The lower classes don't know who are their best friends," said Miss Hartnell. " I always say a word in season when I'm visiting. Not that I'm ever thanked for it."

" You were telling the inspector about your call upon Mrs. Lestrange," I prompted.

" Exactly—and by the way, he didn't thank me. Said he'd ask for information when he wanted it—not those words exactly, but that was the spirit. There's a different class of men in the police force nowadays."

" Very probably," I said. " But you were going on to say something ? "

" I decided that this time I wouldn't go near any wretched inspector. After all, a clergyman is a gentleman —at least some are," she added.

I gathered that the qualification was intended to include me.

" If I can help you in any way," I began.

" It's a matter of duty," said Miss Hartnell, and closed her mouth with a snap. " I don't want to have to say these things. No one likes it less. But duty is duty."

I waited.

" I've been given to understand," went on Miss Hartnell, turning rather red, " that Mrs. Lestrange gives out that she was at home all the time—that she didn't answer the door because—well, because she didn't choose. Such airs and graces. I only called as a matter of duty, and to be treated like that ! "

" She has been ill," I said mildly.

" Ill ? Fiddlesticks. You're too unworldly, Mr. Clement. There's nothing the matter with that woman. Too ill to attend the inquest indeed ! Medical certificate from Dr. Haydock ! She can wind him round her little finger, every one knows that. Well, where was I ? "

I didn't quite know. It is difficult with Miss Hartnell to know where narrative ends and vituperation begins.

"Oh! about calling on her that afternoon. Well, it's fiddlesticks to say she was in the house. She wasn't. I know."

"How can you possibly know?"

Miss Hartnell's face turned a little redder. In some one less truculent, her demeanour might have been called embarrassed.

"I'd knocked and rung," she explained. "Twice. If not three times. And it occurred to me suddenly that the bell might be out of order."

She was, I was glad to note, unable to look me in the face when saying this. The same builder builds all our houses and the bells he installs are always clearly audible when standing on the mat outside the front door. Both Miss Hartnell and I knew this perfectly well, but I suppose decencies have to be preserved.

"Yes"? I murmured.

"I didn't want to push my card through the letter box. That would seem so rude, and whatever I am, I am never rude."

She made this amazing statement without a tremor.

"So I thought I would just go round the house and —and tap on the window pane," she continued unblushingly. "I went all round the house and looked in at all the windows, but there was no one in the house at all."

I understood her perfectly. Taking advantage of the fact that the house was empty, Miss Hartnell had given unbridled rein to her curiosity and had gone round the house, examining the garden and peering in at all the windows to see as much as she could of the interior. She had chosen to tell her story to me, believing that I should be a more sympathetic and lenient audience than the police. The clergy are supposed to give the benefit of the doubt to their parishioners.

I made no comment on the situation. I merely asked a question.

" What time was this, Miss Hartnell ? "

" As far as I can remember," said Miss Hartnell, " it must have been close on six o'clock. I went straight home afterwards, and I got in about ten past six, and Mrs. Protheroe came in somewhere round about the half-hour, leaving Dr. Stone and Mr. Redding outside, and we talked about bulbs. And all the time the poor colonel lying murdered. It's a sad world."

" It is sometimes a rather unpleasant one," I said.

I rose.

" And that is all you have to tell me ?"

" I just thought it might be important."

" It might," I agreed.

And refusing to be drawn further, much to Miss Hartnell's disappointment, I took my leave.

Miss Wetherby, whom I visited next, received me in a kind of flutter.

" Dear vicar, how truly kind. You've had tea ? Really, you won't ? A cushion for your back ? It is so kind of you to come round so promptly. Always willing to put yourself out for others."

There was a good deal of this before we came to the point, and even then it was approached with a good deal of circumlocution.

" You must understand that I heard this on the best authority."

In St. Mary Mead the best authority is always somebody else's servant.

" You can't tell me who told you ? "

" I promised, dear Mr. Clement. And I always think a promise should be a sacred thing."

She looked very solemn.

" Shall we say a little bird told me ? That is safe, isn't it ? "

I longed to say, " It's damned silly." I rather wish I had. I should have liked to observe the effect on Miss Wetherby.

" Well, this little bird told that she saw a certain lady, who shall be nameless."

" Another kind of bird ? " I inquired.

To my great surprise Miss Wetherby went off into paroxysms of laughter and tapped me playfully on the arm saying :

" Oh ! vicar, you must not be so naughty."

When she had recovered, she went on.

" A certain lady, and where do you think this certain lady was going ? She turned into the Vicarage road, but before she did so, she looked up and down the road in a most peculiar way—to see if any one she knew were noticing her, I imagine."

" And the little bird ? " I inquired.

" Paying a visit to the fishmonger's—in the room over the shop."

I now know where maids go on their days out. I know there is one place they never go if they can help —anywhere in the open air.

" And the time," continued Miss Wetherby, leaning forward mysteriously, " was just before six o'clock."

" On which day ? "

Miss Wetherby gave a little scream.

" The day of the murder, of course, didn't I say so ? "

" I inferred it," I replied.   " And the name of the lady ? "

" Begins with an L," said Miss Wetherby, nodding her head several times.

Feeling that I had got to the end of the information Miss Wetherby had to impart, I rose to my feet.

" You won't let the police cross-question me, will you ? " said Miss Wetherby, pathetically, as she clasped my hand in both of hers.  " I do shrink from publicity. And to stand up in court ! "

" In special cases," I said, " they let witnesses sit down."

And I escaped.

There was still Mrs. Price Ridley to see. That lady put me in my place at once.

" I will not be mixed up in any police court business," she said firmly, after shaking my hand coldly.  " You understand that. On the other hand, having come across a circumstance which needs explaining, I think it should be brought to the notice of the authorities."

"Does it concern Mrs. Lestrange?" I asked.

"Why should it?" demanded Mrs. Price Ridley coldly. She had me at a disadvantage there.

"It's a very simple matter," she continued. "My maid, Clara, was standing at the front gate, she went down there for a minute or two—*she* says to get a breath of fresh air. Most unlikely, I should say. Much more probable that she was looking out for the fishmonger's boy—if he calls himself a boy—impudent young jacka-napes, thinks because he's seventeen he can joke with all the girls. Anyway, as I say, she was standing at the gate and she heard a sneeze."

"Yes," I said, waiting for more.

"That's all. I tell you she heard a sneeze. And don't, start telling me I'm not so young as I once was and may have made a mistake, because it was Clara who heard it and she's only nineteen."

"But," I said, "why shouldn't she have heard a sneeze?"

Mrs. Price Ridley looked at me in obvious pity for my poorness of intellect.

"She heard a sneeze on the day of the murder at a time when there was no one in your house. Doubtless the murderer was concealed in the bushes waiting his opportunity. What you have to look for is a man with a cold in his head."

"Or a sufferer from hay fever," I suggested. "But as a matter of fact, Mrs. Price Ridley, I think that mystery has a very easy solution. Our maid, Mary, has been suffering from a severe cold in the head. In fact, her sniffing has tried us very much lately. It must have been her sneeze your maid heard."

"It was a man's sneeze," said Mrs. Price Ridley firmly. "And you couldn't hear your maid sneeze in your kitchen from our gate."

"You couldn't hear any one sneezing in the study from your gate," I said. "Or at least, I very much doubt it."

" I said the man might have been concealed in the shrubbery," said Mrs. Price Ridley. "Doubtless when Clara had gone in, he effected an entrance by the front door."

" Well, of course, that's possible," I said.

I tried not to make my voice consciously soothing, but I must have failed, for Mrs. Price Ridley glared at me suddenly.

" I am accustomed not to be listened to, but I might mention also that to leave a tennis racquet carelessly flung down on the grass without a press completely ruins it. And tennis racquets are very expensive nowadays."

There did not seem to be rhyme or reason in this flank attack. It bewildered me utterly.

" But perhaps you don't agree," said Mrs. Price Ridley.

" Oh ! I do—certainly."

" I am glad. Well, that is all I have to say. I wash my hands of the whole affair."

She leaned back and closed her eyes like one weary of this world. I thanked her and said good-bye.

On the doorstep, I ventured to ask Clara about her mistress's statement.

" It's quite true, sir, I heard a sneeze. And it wasn't an ordinary sneeze—not by any means."

Nothing about a crime is ever ordinary. The shot was not an ordinary kind of shot. The sneeze was not a usual kind of sneeze. It was, I presume, a special murderer's sneeze. I asked the girl what time this had been, but she was very vague—sometime between a quarter and half-past six, she thought. Anyway, " it was before the mistress had the telephone call and was took bad."

I asked her if she had heard a shot of any kind. And she said the shots had been something awful. After that, I placed very little credence in her statements.

I was just turning in at my own gate when I decided to pay a friend a visit.

Glancing at my watch, I saw that I had just time for it before taking Evensong. I went down the road to Haydock's house. He came out on the doorstep to meet me.

I noticed afresh how worried and haggard he looked. This business seemed to have aged him out of all knowledge.

" I'm glad to see you," he said. " What's the news ? "

I told him the latest Stone development.

" A high-class thief," he commented. " Well, that explains a lot of things. He'd read up his subject, but he made slips from time to time to me. Protheroe must have caught him out once. You remember the row they had. What do you think about the girl ? Is she in it too ? "

" Opinion as to that is undecided," I said. " For my own part, I think the girl is all right.

" She's such a prize idiot," I added.

" Oh ! I wouldn't say that. She's rather shrewd, is Miss Gladys Cram. A remarkably healthy specimen. Not likely to trouble members of my profession."

I told him that I was worried about Hawes, and that I was anxious that he should get away for a real rest and change.

Something evasive came into his manner when I said this. His answer did not ring quite true.

" Yes," he said slowly. " I suppose that would be the best thing. Poor chap. Poor chap."

" I thought you didn't like him."

" I don't—not much. But I'm sorry for a lot of people I don't like." He added after a minute or two : " I'm even sorry for Protheroe. Poor fellow—nobody ever liked him much. Too full of his own rectitude and too self-assertive. It's an unlovable mixture. He was always the same—even as a young man."

" I didn't know you knew him then ? "

" Oh, yes ! When he lived in Westmorland, I had a practice not far away. That's a long time ago now. Nearly twenty years."

I sighed. Twenty years ago Griselda was five years old.
Time is an odd thing. . . .

" Is that all you came to say to me, Clement ? "

I looked up with a start. Haydock was watching me
with keen eyes.

" There's something else, isn't there ? " he said.

I nodded.

I had been uncertain whether to speak or not when
I came in, but now I decided to do so. I like Haydock
as well as any man I know. He is a splendid fellow in
every way. I felt that what I had to tell might be useful
to him.

I recited my interviews with Miss Hartnell and Miss
Wetherby.

He was silent for a long time after I'd spoken.

" It's quite true, Clement," he said at last. " I've
been trying to shield Mrs. Lestrange from any inconvenience that I could. As a matter of fact, she's an old
friend. But that's not my only reason. That medical
certificate of mine isn't the put-up job you all think
it was."

He paused, and then said gravely :

" This is between you and me, Clement. Mrs.
Lestrange is doomed."

" What ? "

" She's a dying woman. I give her a month at
longest. Do you wonder that I want to keep her from
being badgered and questioned ? "

He went on :

" When she turned into this road that evening it was
here she came—to this house."

" You haven't said so before."

" I didn't want to create talk. Six to seven isn't my
time for seeing patients, and every one knows that.
But you can take my word for it that she was here."

" She wasn't here when I came for you, though. I
mean, when we discovered the body."

" No," he seemed perturbed. " She'd left—to keep
an appointment."

" In what direction was the appointment ?  In her own house ? "

"I don't know, Clement.  On my honour, I don't know."

I believed him, but——

" And supposing an innocent man is hanged ? " I said. He shook his head.

" No," he said.  " No one will be hanged for the murder of Colonel Protheroe.  You can take my word for that."

But that is just what I could not do.  And yet the certainty in his voice was very great.

" No one will be hanged," he repeated.

" This man, Archer——"

He made an impatient movement.

" Hasn't got brains enough to wipe his finger-prints off the pistol."

" Perhaps not," I said dubiously.

Then I remembered something, and taking the little brownish crystal I had found in the wood from my pocket, I held it out to him and asked him what it was.

" H'm," he hesitated.  " Looks like picric acid.  Where did you find it ? "

" That," I replied, " is Sherlock Holmes's secret."

He smiled.

" What is picric acid ? "

" Well, it's an explosive."

" Yes, I know that, but it's got another use, hasn't it ? "

He nodded.

" It's used medically—in solution for burns.  Wonderful stuff."

I held out my hand, and rather reluctantly he handed it back to me.

" It's of no consequence probably," I said.  " But I found it in rather an unusual place."

" You won't tell me where ? "

Rather childishly, I wouldn't.

He had his secrets.  Well, I would have mine.

I was a little hurt that he had not confided in me more fully.

## CHAPTER XXVI

I WAS in a strange mood when I mounted the pulpit that night.

The church was unusually full. I cannot believe that it was the prospect of Hawes preaching which had attracted so many. Hawes's sermons are dull and dogmatic. And if the news had got round that I was preaching instead, that would not have attracted them either. For my sermons are dull and scholarly. Neither, I am afraid, can I attribute it to devotion.

Everybody had come, I concluded, to see who else was there, and possibly to exchange a little gossip in the church porch afterwards.

Haydock was in church, which is unusual, and also Lawrence Redding. And to my surprise, beside Lawrence I saw the white, strained face of Hawes. Anne Protheroe was there, but she usually attends Evensong on Sundays, though I had hardly thought she would to-day. I was far more surprised to see Lettice. Church-going was compulsory on Sunday morning—Colonel Protheroe was adamant on that point, but I had never seen Lettice at evening service before.

Gladys Cram was there, looking rather blatantly young and healthy against a background of wizened spinsters, and I fancied that a dim figure at the end of the church who had slipped in late, was Mrs. Lestrange.

I need hardly say that Mrs. Price Ridley, Miss Hartnell, Miss Wetherby, and Miss Marple were there in full force. All the village people were there, with hardly a single exception. I don't know when we have had such a crowded congregation.

Crowds are queer things. There was a magnetic atmosphere that night, and the first person to feel its influence was myself.

As a rule, I prepare my sermons beforehand. I am careful and conscientious over them, but no one is better aware than myself of their deficiencies.

To-night I was of necessity preaching *extempore*, and as I looked down on the sea of upturned faces, a sudden madness entered my brain. I ceased to be in any sense a Minister of God. I became an actor. I had an audience before me and I wanted to move that audience —and more, I felt the power to move it.

I am not proud of what I did that night. I am an utter disbeliever in the emotional Revivalist spirit. Yet that night I acted the part of a raving, ranting evangelist.

I gave out my text slowly.

*I came not to call the righteous, but sinners to repentance.*

I repeated it twice, and I heard my own voice, a resonant, ringing voice unlike the voice of the every-day Leonard Clement.

I saw Griselda from her front pew look up in surprise and Dennis follow her example.

I held my breath for a moment or two, and then I let myself rip.

The congregation in that church were in a state of pent-up emotion, ripe to be played upon. I played upon them. I exhorted sinners to repentance. I lashed myself into a kind of emotional frenzy. Again and again I threw out a denouncing hand and reiterated the phrase.

" I am speaking to *you* . . ."

And each time, from different parts of the church, a kind of sighing gasp went up.

Mass emotion is a strange and terrible thing.

I finished up with those beautiful and poignant words—perhaps the most poignant words in the whole Bible :

" *This night thy soul shall be required of thee.* . . ."

It was a strange, brief possession. When I got back to the Vicarage I was my usual faded, indeterminate self.

I found Griselda rather pale. She slipped her arm through mine.

"Len," she said, "you were rather terrible to-night. I—I didn't like it. I've never heard you preach like that before."

"I don't suppose you ever will again," I said, sinking down wearily on the sofa. I was tired.

"What made you do it?"

"A sudden madness came over me."

"Oh! it—it wasn't something special?"

"What do you mean—something special?"

"I wondered—that was all. You're very unexpected, Len. I never feel I really know you."

We sat down to cold supper, Mary being out.

"There's a note for you in the hall," said Griselda. "Get it, will you, Dennis?"

Dennis, who had been very silent, obeyed.

I took it and groaned. Across the top left-hand corner was written: *By hand—Urgent.*

"This," I said, "must be from Miss Marple. There's no one else left."

I had been perfectly correct in my assumption.

"DEAR MR. CLEMENT,—I should so much like to have a little chat with you about one or two things that have occurred to me. I feel we should all try and help in elucidating this sad mystery. I will come over about half-past nine, if I may, and tap on your study window. Perhaps dear Griselda would be so very kind as to run over here and cheer up my nephew. And Mr. Dennis too, of course, if he cares to come. If I do not hear, I will expect them and will come over myself at the time I have stated.

"Yours very sincerely,
"JANE MARPLE."

I handed the note to Griselda.

"Oh! we'll go," she said cheerfully. "A glass or two of home-made liqueur is just what one needs on

Sunday evening. I think it's Mary's blanc mange that is so frightfully depressing. It's like something out of a mortuary."

Dennis seemed less charmed at the prospect.

"It's all very well for you," he grumbled. "You can talk all this highbrow stuff about art and books. I always feel a perfect fool sitting and listening to you."

"That's good for you," said Griselda serenely. "It puts you in your place. Anyway, I don't think Mr. Raymond West is so frightfully clever as he pretends to be."

"Very few of us are," I said.

I wondered very much what exactly it was that Miss Marple wished to talk over. Of all the ladies in my congregation, I consider her by far the shrewdest. Not only does she see and hear practically everything that goes on, but she draws amazingly neat and apposite deductions from the facts that come under her notice.

If I were at any time to set out on a career of deceit, it would be of Miss Marple that I should be afraid.

What Griselda called the Nephew Amusing Party started off at a little after nine, and whilst I was waiting for Miss Marple to arrive I amused myself by drawing up a kind of schedule of the facts connected with the crime. I arranged them so far as possible in chronological order. I am not a punctual person, but I am a neat one, and I like things jotted down in a methodical fashion.

At half-past nine punctually, there was a little tap on the window, and I rose and admitted Miss Marple.

She had a very fine Shetland shawl thrown over her head and shoulders and was looking rather old and frail. She came in full of little fluttering remarks.

"So good of you to let me come—and so good of dear Griselda—Raymond admires her so much—the perfect Greuze he always calls her . . . Shall I sit here? I am not taking your chair? Oh! thank you. . . . No, I won't have a footstool."

I deposited the Shetland shawl on a chair and returned

to take a chair facing my guest. We looked at each other, and a little deprecating smile broke out on her face.

" I feel that you must be wondering why—why I am so interested in all this. You may possibly think it's very unwomanly. No—please—I should like to explain if I may."

She paused a moment, a pink colour suffusing her cheeks.

" You see," she began at last, " living alone, as I do, in a rather out-of-the-way part of the world, one has to have a hobby. There is, of course, woolwork, and Guides, and Welfare, and sketching, but my hobby is —and always has been—Human Nature. So varied— and so very fascinating. And of course, in a small village, with nothing to distract one, one has such ample opportunity for becoming what I might call proficient in one's study. One begins to class people, quite definitely, just as though they were birds or flowers, group so-and-so, genus this, species that. Sometimes, of course, one makes mistakes, but less and less as time goes on. And then, too, one tests one- self. One takes a little problem—for instance, the gill of picked shrimps that amused dear Griselda so much —a quite unimportant mystery but absolutely incom- prehensible unless one solves it right. And then there was that matter of the changed cough drops, and the butcher's wife's umbrella—the last absolutely meaning- less unless on the assumption that the greengrocer was not behaving at all nicely with the chemist's wife—which, of course, turned out to be the case. It is so fascinating, you know, to apply one's judgment and find that one is right."

" You usually are, I believe," I said, smiling.

" That, I am afraid, is what has made me a little conceited," confessed Miss Marple. " But I have always wondered whether, if some day a really big mystery came along, I should be able to do the same thing. I mean—just solve it correctly. Logically, it ought to be exactly the same thing. After all, a tiny working model of a torpedo is just the same as a real torpedo."

"You mean it's all a question of relativity," I said slowly. "It should be—logically, I admit. But I don't know whether it really is."

"Surely it must be the same," said Miss Marple. "The—what one used to call the factors at school—are the same. There's money, and mutual attraction between people of an—er—opposite sex—and there's queerness, of course—so many people are a little queer, aren't they?—in fact, most people are when you know them well. And normal people do such astonishing things sometimes, and abnormal people are sometimes so very sane and ordinary. In fact, the only way is to compare people with other people you have known or come across. You'd be surprised if you knew how very few distinct types there are in all."

"You frighten me," I said. "I feel I'm being put under the microscope."

"Of course, I wouldn't dream of saying any of this to Colonel Melchett—such an autocratic man, isn't he? —and poor Inspector Slack—well, he's exactly like the young lady in the boot shop who wants to sell you patent leather because she's got it in your size, and doesn't take any notice of the fact that you want brown calf."

That, really, is a very good description of Slack.

"But you, Mr. Clement, know, I'm sure, quite as much about the crime as Inspector Slack. I thought, if we could work together——"

"I wonder," I said. "I think each one of us in his secret heart fancies himself as Sherlock Holmes."

Then I told her of the three summonses I had received that afternoon. I told her of Anne's discovery of the picture with the slashed face. I also told her of Miss Cram's attitude at the police station, and I described Haydock's identification of the crystal I had picked up.

"Having found that myself," I finished up, "I

should like it to be important. But it's probably got nothing to do with the case."

" I have been reading a lot of American detective stories from the library lately," said Miss Marple, " hoping to find them helpful."

" Was there anything in them about picric acid ? "

" I'm afraid not. I do remember reading a story once, though, in which a man was poisoned by picric acid and lanoline being rubbed on him as an ointment."

" But as nobody has been poisoned here, that doesn't seem to enter into the question," I said.

Then I took up my schedule and handed it to her.

" I've tried," I said, " to recapitulate the facts of the case as clearly as possible.'

### MY SCHEDULE

*Thursday, 21st inst.*

12.30 a.m.—Colonel Protheroe alters his appointment from six to six-fifteen. Overheard by half village very probably.

12.45—Pistol last seen in its proper place. (But this is doubtful, as Mrs. Archer had previously said she could not remember.)

5.30 (approx.)—Colonel and Mrs. Protheroe leave Old Hall for village in car.

5.30—Fake call put through to me from the North Lodge, Old Hall.

6.15 (or a minute or two earlier)—Colonel Protheroe arrives at Vicarage. Is shown into study by Mary.

6.20—Mrs. Protheroe comes along back lane and across garden to study window. Colonel Protheroe not visible.

6.29—Call from Lawrence Redding's cottage put through to Mrs. Price Ridley (according to Exchange.)

6.30–6.35—Shot heard. (Accepting telephone call time as correct.) Lawrence Redding, Anne Protheroe and Dr. Stone's evidence seem to point to its being earlier, but Mrs. P. R. probably right.

6.45—Lawrence Redding arrives Vicarage and finds the body.
6.48—I meet Lawrence Redding.
6.49—Body discovered by me.
6.55—Haydock examines body.

NOTE.—The only two people who have no kind of alibi for 6.30–6.35 are Miss Cram and Mrs. Lestrange. Miss Cram says she was at the barrow, but no confirmation. It seems reasonable, however, to dismiss her from case as there seems nothing to connect her with it. Mrs. Lestrange left Dr. Haydock's house some time after six to keep an appointment. Where was the appointment, and with whom ? It could hardly have been with Colonel Protheroe, as he expected to be engaged with me. It is true that Mrs. Lestrange was near the spot at the time the crime was committed, but it seems doubtful what motive she could have had for murdering him. She did not gain by his death, and the inspector's theory of blackmail I cannot accept. Mrs. Lestrange is not that kind of woman. Also it seems unlikely that she should have got hold of Lawrence Redding's pistol.

" Very clear," said Miss Marple, nodding her head in approval. " Very clear indeed. Gentlemen always make such excellent memoranda."

" You agree with what I have written ? " I asked.

" Oh, yes—you have put it all beautifully."

I asked her the question then that I had been meaning to put all along.

" Miss Marple," I said. " Who do you suspect ? You once said that there were seven people."

" Quite that, I should think," said Miss Marple absently. " I expect every one of us suspects some one different. In fact, one can see they do."

She didn't ask me who I suspected.

" The point is," she said, " that one must provide an

explanation for everything. Each thing has got to be explained away satisfactorily. If you have a theory that fits every fact—well, then, it must be the right one. But that's extremely difficult. If it wasn't for that note——"

"The note ?" I said, surprised.

"Yes, you remember, I told you. That note has worried me all along. It's wrong, somehow."

"Surely," I said, "that is explained now. It was written at six thirty-five and another hand—the murderer's—put the misleading 6.20 at the top. I think that is clearly established."

"But even then," said Miss Marple, "it's all wrong."

"But why ?"

"Listen." Miss Marple leant forward eagerly. "Mrs. Protheroe passed my garden, as I told you, and she went as far as the study window and she looked in and she didn't see Colonel Protheroe."

"Because he was writing at the desk," I said.

"And that's what's all wrong. That was at twenty past six. We agreed that he wouldn't sit down to say he couldn't wait any longer until after half-past six —so, why was he sitting at the writing-table then ?"

"I never thought of that," I said slowly.

"Let us, dear Mr. Clement, just go over it again. Mrs. Protheroe comes to the window and she thinks the room is empty—she must have thought so, because otherwise she would never have gone down to the studio to meet Mr. Redding. It wouldn't have been safe. The room must have been absolutely silent if she thought it was empty. And that leaves us three alternatives, doesn't it ?"

"You mean——"

"Well, the first alternative would be that Colonel Protheroe was dead already—but I don't think that's the most likely one. To begin with he'd only been there about five minutes and she or I would have heard the shot, and secondly, the same difficulty remains about his being at the writing-table. The second alternative is, of course, that he was sitting at the writing-table writing a note, but in that case it must have been a different note altogether. It can't have been to say he couldn't wait. And the third——"

" Yes ? " I said.

" Well, the third is, of course, that Mrs. Protheroe was right, and that the room was actually empty."

" You mean that, after he had been shown in, he went out again and came back later ? "

" Yes."

" But why should he have done that ? "

Miss Marple spread out her hands in a little gesture of bewilderment.

" That would mean looking at the case from an entirely different angle," I said.

" One so often has to do that—about everything. Don't you think so ? "

I did not reply. I was going over carefully in my mind the three alternatives that Miss Marple had suggested.

With a slight sigh the old lady rose to her feet.

" I must be getting back. I am very glad to have had this little chat—though we haven't got very far, have we ? "

" To tell you the truth," I said, as I fetched her shawl, " the whole thing seems to me a bewildering maze."

" Oh ! I wouldn't say that. I think, on the whole, one theory fits nearly everything. That is, if you admit one coincidence—and I think one coincidence is allow-able. More than one, of course, is unlikely."

" Do you really think that ? About the theory, I mean ? " I asked, looking at her.

" I admit that there is one flaw in my theory—one fact that I can't get over. Oh ! if only that note had been something quite different——"

She sighed and shook her head. She moved towards the window and absent-mindedly reached up her hand and felt the rather depressed-looking plant that stood in a stand.

" You know, dear Mr. Clement, this should be watered oftener. Poor thing, it needs it badly. Your maid should water it every day. I suppose it is she who attends to it ? "

" As much," I said, " as she attends to anything."

" A little raw at present," suggested Miss Marple.

" Yes," I said. " And Griselda steadily refuses to attempt to cook her. Her idea is that only a thoroughly undesirable maid will remain with us. However, Mary herself gave us notice the other day."

" Indeed. I always imagined she was very fond of you both."

" I haven't noticed it," I said. " But, as a matter of fact, it was Lettice Protheroe who upset her. Mary came back from the inquest in rather a temperamental state and found Lettice here and—well, they had words."

" Oh ! " said Miss Marple. She was just about to step through the window when she stopped suddenly, and a bewildering series of changes passed over her face.

" Oh ! dear," she muttered to herself. " I *have* been stupid. So that was it. Perfectly possible all the time."

" I beg your pardon ? "

She turned a worried face upon me.

" Nothing. An idea that has just occurred to me. I must go home and think things out thoroughly. Do you know, I believe I have been extremely stupid— almost incredibly so."

" I find that hard to believe," I said gallantly.

I escorted her through the window and across the lawn.

" Can you tell me what it is that has occurred to you so suddenly ? " I asked.

" I would rather not—just at present. You see, there is still a possibility that I may be mistaken. But I do not think so. Here we are at my garden gate. Thank you so much. Please do not come any farther."

" Is the note still a stumbling block ? " I asked, as

she passed through the gate and latched it behind her.
She looked at me abstractedly.

"The note ? Oh ! of course that wasn't the real note.
I never thought it was. Good-night, Mr. Clement."

She went rapidly up the path to the house, leaving
me staring after her.

I didn't know what to think.

## CHAPTER XXVII

GRISELDA and Dennis had not yet returned. I realised that the most natural thing would have been for me to go up to the house with Miss Marple and fetch them home. Both she and I had been so entirely taken up with our preoccupation over the mystery that we had forgotten anybody existed in the world except ourselves.

I was just standing in the hall, wondering whether I would not even now go over and join them, when the door bell rang.

I crossed over to it. I saw there was a letter in the box, and presuming that this was the cause of the ring, I took it out.

As I did so, however, the bell rang again, and I shoved the letter hastily into my pocket and opened the front door.

It was Colonel Melchett.

" Hullo, Clement. I'm on my way home from town in the car. Thought I'd just look in and see if you could give me a drink."

" Delighted," I said. " Come into the study."

He pulled off the leather coat that he was wearing and followed me into the study. I fetched the whisky and soda and two glasses. Melchett was standing in front of the fireplace, legs wide apart, stroking his closely-cropped moustache.

" I've got one bit of news for you, Clement. Most astounding thing you've ever heard. But let that go for the minute. How are things going down here ? Any more old ladies hot on the scent ? "

" They're not doing so badly," I said. " One of them, at all events, thinks she's got there."

" Our friend, Miss Marple, eh ? "

" Our friend, Miss Marple."

"Women like that always think they know every-thing," said Colonel Melchett.

He sipped his whisky and soda appreciatively.

"It's probably unnecessary interference on my part, asking," I said. "But I suppose somebody has questioned the fish boy. I mean, if the murderer left by the front door, there's a chance the boy may have seen him."

"Slack questioned him right enough," said Melchett. "But the boy says he didn't meet anybody. Hardly likely he would. The murderer wouldn't be exactly courting observation. Lots of cover by your front gate. He would have taken a look to see if the road was clear. The boy had to call at the Vicarage, at Haydock's, and at Mrs. Price Ridley's. Easy enough to dodge him."

"Yes," I said, "I suppose it would be."

"On the other hand," went on Melchett, "if by any chance that rascal Archer did the job, and young Fred Jackson saw him about the place, I doubt very much whether he'd let on. Archer is a cousin of his."

"Do you seriously suspect Archer?"

"Well, you know, old Protheroe had his knife into Archer pretty badly. Lots of bad blood between them. Leniency wasn't Protheroe's strong point."

"No," I said. "He was a very ruthless man."

"What I say is," said Melchett, "Live and let live. Of course, the law's the law, but it never hurts to give a man the benefit of the doubt. That's what Protheroe never did."

"He prided himself on it," I said.

There was a pause, and then I asked:

"What is this 'astounding bit of news' you promised me?"

"Well, it *is* astounding. You know that unfinished letter that Protheroe was writing when he was killed?"

"Yes."

"We got an expert on it—to say whether the 6.20 was added by a different hand. Naturally we sent up samples of Protheroe's handwriting. And do you know the verdict ? *That letter was never written by Protheroe at all."*

" You mean a forgery ? "

" It's a forgery. The 6.20 they think is written in a different hand again—but they're not sure about that. The heading is in a different ink, but the letter itself is a forgery. Protheroe never wrote it."

" Are they certain ? "

" Well, they're as certain as experts ever are. You know what an expert is ! Oh ! but they're sure enough."

" Amazing," I said.

Then a memory assailed me.

" Why," I said, " I remember at the time Mrs. Protheroe said it wasn't like her husband's handwriting at all, and I took no notice."

" Really ? "

" I thought it one of those silly remarks women will make. If there seemed one thing sure on earth it was that Protheroe had written that note."

We looked at each other.

" It's curious," I said slowly. " Miss Marple was saying this evening that that note was all wrong."

" Confound the woman, she couldn't know more about it if she had committed the murder herself."

At that moment the telephone bell rang. There is a queer kind of psychology about a telephone bell. It rang now persistently and with a kind of sinister significance.

I went over and took up the receiver.

" This is the Vicarage," I said. " Who's speaking ? "

A strange, high-pitched hysterical voice came over the wire :

" *I want to confess,*" it said. " *My God, I want to confess.*"

" Hullo," I said, " hullo. Look here, you've cut me off. What number was that ? "

A languid voice said it didn't know. It added that it was sorry I had been troubled.

I put down the receiver, and turned to Melchett.

"You once said," I remarked, "that you would go mad if any one else accused themselves of the crime."

"What about it ? "

"That was some one who wanted to confess. . . . And the Exchange has cut us off."

Melchett dashed over and took up the receiver.

"I'll speak to them."

"Do," I said. "You may have some effect. I'll leave you to it. I'm going out. I've a fancy I recognised that voice."

# CHAPTER XXVIII

I HURRIED down the village street. It was eleven o'clock and at eleven o'clock on a Sunday night the whole village of St. Mary Mead might be dead. I saw, however, a light in a first floor window as I passed, and realising that Hawes was still up, I stopped and rang the door bell.

After what seemed a long time, Hawes' landlady, Mrs. Sadler, laboriously unfastened two bolts, a chain, and turned a key, and peered out at me suspiciously.

"Why, it's Vicar!" she exclaimed.

"Good-evening," I said. "I want to see Mr. Hawes. I see there's a light in the window, so he's up still."

"That may be. I've not seen him since I took up his supper. He's had a quiet evening—no one to see him, and he's not been out."

I nodded, and passing her, went quickly up the stairs. Hawes has a bedroom and sitting room on the first floor.

I passed into the latter. Hawes was lying back in a long chair asleep. My entrance did not wake him. An empty cachet box and a glass of water, half-full, stood beside him.

On the floor, by his left foot, was a crumpled sheet of paper with writing on is. I picked it up and straightened it out.

It began : "*My dear Clement——*"

I read it through, uttered an exclamation and shoved it into my pocket. Then I bent over Hawes and studied him attentively.

Next, reaching for the telephone which stood by his elbow, I gave the number of the Vicarage. Melchett must have been still trying to trace the call, for I was told that the number was engaged. Asking them to call me, I put the instrument down again.

I put my hand into my pocket to look at the paper I had picked up once more. With it, I drew out the note that I had found in the letter box and which was still unopened.

Its appearance was horribly familiar. It was the same handwriting as the anonymous letter that had come that afternoon.

I tore it open.

I read it once—twice—unable to realise its contents.

I was beginning to read it a third time when the telephone rang. Like a man in a dream I picked up the receiver and spoke.

" Hullo ? "

" Hullo."

" Is that you, Melchett ? "

" Yes, where are you ? I've traced that call. The number is——"

" I know the number."

" Oh ! good. Is that where you are speaking from ? "

" Yes."

" What about that confession ? "

" I've got the confession all right."

" You mean you've got the murderer ? "

I had then the strongest temptation of my life. I looked at Hawes. I looked at the crumpled letter. I looked at the anonymous scrawl. I looked at the empty cachet box with the name of Cherubim on it. I remembered a certain casual conversation.

I made an immense effort.

" I—don't know," I said. " You'd better come round."

And I gave him the address.

Then I sat down in the chair opposite Hawes to think. I had two clear minutes in which to do so.

In two minutes time, Melchett would have arrived.

I took up the anonymous letter and read it through again for the third time.

Then I closed my eyes and thought. . . .

# CHAPTER XXIX

I DON'T know how long I sat there—only a few minutes in reality, I suppose. Yet it seemed as though an eternity had passed when I heard the door open and, turning my head, looked up to see Melchett entering the room.

He stared at Hawes asleep in his chair, then turned to me.

" What's this, Clement ? What does it all mean ? "

Of the two letters in my hand I selected one and passed it to him. He read it aloud in a low voice.

" MY DEAR CLEMENT,—It is a peculiarly unpleasant thing that I have to say. After all, I think I prefer writing it. We can discuss it at a later date. It concerns the recent peculations. I am sorry to say that I have satisfied myself beyond any possible doubt as to the identity of the culprit. Painful as it is for me to have to accuse an ordained priest of the church, my duty is only too painfully clear. An example must be made and——"

He looked at me questioningly. At this point the writing tailed off in an undistinguishable scrawl where death had overtaken the writer's hand.

Melchett drew a deep breath, then look at Hawes.

" So that's the solution ! The one man we never even considered. And remorse drove him to confess ! "

" He's been very queer lately," I said.

Suddenly Melchett strode across to the sleeping man with a sharp exclamation. He seized him by the shoulder and shook him, at first gently, then with increasing violence.

" He's not asleep ! He's drugged ! What's the meaning of this ? "

His eye went to the empty cachet box. He picked it up.

" Has he—— ? "

" I think so," I said. " He showed me these the other
day. Told me he'd been warned against an overdose.
It's his way out, poor chap. Perhaps the best way. It's
not for us to judge him."

But Melchett was Chief Constable of the County before
anything else. The arguments that appealed to me had
no weight with him. He had caught a murderer and he
wanted his murderer hanged.

In one second he was at the telephone, jerking the
receiver up and down impatiently until he got a reply.
He asked for Haydock's number. Then there was a
further pause during which he stood, his ear to the
telephone and his eyes on the limp figure in the chair.

" Hullo—hullo—hullo—is that Dr. Haydock's ? Will
the doctor come round at once to High Street ? Mr.
Hawes'. It's urgent . . . what's that ? . . . Well, what
number is it then ? . . . Oh, sorry."

He rang off, fuming.

" Wrong number, wrong number—always wrong
numbers ! And a man's life hanging on it. HULLO—
you gave me the wrong number. . . . Yes—don't waste
time—give me three nine—*nine*, not five."

Another period of impatience—shorter this time.

" Hullo—is that you, Haydock ? Melchett speaking.
Come to 19 High Street at once, will you ? Hawes has
taken some kind of overdose. At once, man, it's vital."

He rang off, strode impatiently up and down the room.

" Why on earth you didn't get hold of the doctor at
once, Clement, I cannot think. Your wits must have all
gone wool gathering."

Fortunately it never occurs to Melchett that any one
can possibly have any different ideas on conduct to those
he holds himself. I said nothing, and he went on :

" Where did you find this letter ? "

" Crumpled on the floor—where it had fallen from his
hand."

" Extraordinary business—that old maid was right
about its being the wrong note we found. Wonder how
she tumbled to that. But what an ass the fellow was

not to destroy this one. Fancy keeping it—the most damaging evidence you can imagine!"

"Human nature is full of inconsistencies."

"If it weren't, I doubt if we should ever catch a murderer! Sooner or later they always do some fool thing. You're looking very under the weather, Clement. I suppose this has been the most awful shock to you?"

"It has. As I say, Hawes has been queer in his manner for some time, but I never dreamed——"

"Who would? Hullo, that sounds like a car." He went across to the window, pushing up the sash and leaning out. "Yes," it's Haydock all right."

A moment later the doctor entered the room.

In a few succinct words, Melchett explained the situation.

Haydock is not a man who ever shows his feelings. He merely raised his eyebrows, nodded, and strode across to his patient. He felt his pulse, raised the eyelid and looked intently at the eye.

Then he turned to Melchett.

"Want me to save him for the gallows?" he asked. "He's pretty far gone, you know. It will be touch and go anyway. I doubt if I can bring him round."

"Do everything possible."

"Right."

He busied himself with the case he had brought with him, preparing a hypodermic injection which he injected into Hawes' arm. Then he stood up.

"Best thing is to run him into Much Benham—to the hospital there. Give me a hand to get him down to the car."

We both lent our assistance. As Haydock climbed into the driving seat, he threw a parting remark over his shoulder.

"You won't be able to hang him, you know, Melchett."

"You mean he won't recover?"

"May or may not. I didn't mean that. I mean that even if he does recover—well, the poor devil wasn't responsible for his actions. I shall give evidence to that effect."

"What did he mean by that ? " asked Melchett as we went upstairs again.

I explained that Hawes had been a victim of encephalitis lethargica.

"Sleepy sickness, eh ? Always some good reason nowadays for every dirty action that's done. Don't you agree ? "

"Science is teaching us a lot."

"Science be damned—I beg your pardon, Clement ; but all this namby pambyism annoys me. I'm a plain man. Well, I suppose we'd better have a look round here."

But at this moment there was an interruption—and a most amazing one. The door opened and Miss Marple walked into the room.

She was pink and somewhat flustered, and seemed to realise our condition of bewilderment.

"So sorry—so very sorry—to intrude—good-evening, Colonel Melchett. As I say, I am so sorry, but hearing that Mr. Hawes was taken ill, I felt I must come round and see if I couldn't do something."

She paused. Colonel Melchett was regarding her in a somewhat disgusted fashion.

"Very kind of you, Miss Marple," he said drily. "But no need to trouble. How did you know, by the way ? "

It was the question I had been yearning to ask !

"The telephone," explained Miss Marple. "So careless with their wrong numbers, aren't they ? You spoke to me first, thinking I was Dr. Haydock. My number is three five."

"So that was it ! " I exclaimed.

"There is always some perfectly good and reasonable explanation for Miss Marple's omniscience.

"And so," she continued. "I just came round to see if I could be of any use."

"Very kind of you," said Melchett again, even more

drily this time. " But nothing to be done. Haydock's taken him off to hospital."

" Actually to hospital ? Oh, that's a great relief ! I am so very glad to hear it. He'll be quite safe there. When you say 'nothing to be done,' you don't mean that there's nothing to be done for him, do you ? You don't mean that he won't recover ? "

" It's very doubtful," I said.

Miss Marple's eyes had gone to the cachet box.

" I suppose he took an overdose ? " she said.

Melchett, I think, was in favour of being reticent. Perhaps I might have been under other circumstances. But my discussion of the case with Miss Marple was too fresh in my mind for me to have the same view, though I must admit that her rapid appearance on the scene and eager curiosity repelled me slightly.

" You had better look at this," I said, and handed. her Protheroe's unfinished letter.

She took it and read it without any appearance of surprise.

" You had already deduced something of the kind, had you not ? " I asked.

" Yes—yes, indeed. May I ask you, Mr. Clement, what made you come here this evening ? That is a point which puzzles me. You and Colonel Melchett— not at all what I should have expected."

I explained the telephone call and that I believed I had recognised Hawes' voice. Miss Marple nodded thoughtfully.

" Very interesting. Very providential—if I may use the term. Yes, it brought you here in the nick of time."

" In the nick of time for what ? " I said bitterly.

Miss Marple looked surprised.

" To save Mr. Hawes' life, of course."

" Don't you think," I said, " that it might be better if Hawes didn't recover ? Better for him—better for every one. We know the truth now and——"

I stopped—for Miss Marple was nodding her head

with such a peculiar vehemence that it made me lose the thread of what I was saying.

" Of course," she said. " Of course ! That's what he wants you to think ! That you know the truth—and that it's best for every one as it is. Oh, yes, it all fits in —the letter, and the overdose, and poor Mr. Hawes' state of mind and his confession. It all fits in—*but it's wrong.* . . ."

We stared at her.

" That's why I am so glad Mr. Hawes is safe—in hospital—where no one can get at him. If he recovers, he'll tell you the truth."

" The truth ? "

" Yes—that he never touched a hair of Colonel Protheroe's head."

" But the telephone call," I said. " The letter—the overdose. It's all so clear."

" That's what he wants you to think. Oh, he's very clever ! Keeping the letter and using it this way was very clever indeed."

" Who do you mean," I said, " by ' he ? ' "

" I mean the murderer," said Miss Marple.

She added very quietly :

" I mean Mr. Lawrence Redding. . . ."

# CHAPTER XXX

WE stared at her. I really think that for a moment or two we really believed she was out of her mind. The accusation seemed so utterly preposterous.

Colonel Melchett was the first to speak. He spoke kindly and with a kind of pitying tolerance.

" That is absurd, Miss Marple," he said " Young Redding has been completely cleared."

" Naturally," said Miss Marple. " He saw to that."

" On the contrary," said Colonel Melchett drily. " He did his best to get himself accused of the murder."

" Yes," said Miss Marple. " He took us all in that way—myself as much as any one else. You will remember, dear Mr. Clement, that I was quite taken aback when I heard Mr. Redding had confessed to the crime. It upset all my ideas and made me think him innocent—when up to then I had felt convinced that he was guilty."

" Then it was Lawrence Redding you suspected ? "

" I know that in books it is always the most unlikely person. But I never find that rule applies in real life. There it is so often the obvious that is true. Much as I have always liked Mrs. Protheroe, I could not avoid coming to the conclusion that she was completely under Mr. Redding's thumb and would do anything he told her, and, of course, he is not the kind of young man who would dream of running away with a penniless woman. From his point of view it was necessary that Colonel Protheroe should be removed—and so he removed him. One of those charming young men who have *no* moral sense."

Colonel Melchett had been snorting impatiently for some time. Now he broke out.

" Absolute nonsense—the whole thing ! Redding's

time is fully accounted for up to 6.45 and Haydock says positively Protheroe couldn't have been shot then. I suppose you think you know better than a doctor. Or do you suggest that Haydock is deliberately lying—the Lord knows why ? "

" I think Dr. Haydock's evidence was absolutely truthful. He is a very upright man. And, of course, it was Mrs. Protheroe who actually shot Colonel Protheroe —not Mr. Redding."

Again we stared at her. Miss Marple arranged her lace fichu, pushed back the fleecy shawl that draped her shoulders, and began to deliver a gentle old maidish lecture comprising the most astounding statements in the most natural way in the world.

" I have not thought it right to speak until now. One's own belief—even so strong as to amount to know-ledge—is not the same as proof. And unless one has an explanation that will fit all the facts (as I was saying to dear Mr. Clement this evening) one cannot advance it with any real conviction. And my own explanation was not quite complete—it lacked just one thing—but suddenly, just as I was leaving Mr. Clement's study, I noticed the palm in the pot by the window—and—well, there the whole thing was ! Clear as daylight ! "

" Mad—quite mad," murmured Melchett to me.

But Miss Marple beamed on us serenely and went on in her gentle lady-like voice.

" I was very sorry to believe what I did—very sorry. Because I liked them both. But you know what human nature is. And to begin with, when first he and then she both confessed in the most foolish way—well, I was more relieved than I could say. I had been wrong. And I began to think of other people who had a possible motive for wishing Colonel Protheroe out of the way."

" The seven suspects ! " I murmured.

She smiled at me.

" Yes, indeed. There was that man Archer—not likely, but primed with drink (so inflaming) you never know. And, of course, there was your Mary. She's been walking out with Archer a long time, and she's a queer tempered girl. Motive *and* opportunity—why, she was alone in the house ! Old Mrs. Archer could easily have got the pistol from Mr. Redding's house for either of those two. And then, of course, there was Lettice— wanting freedom and money to do as she liked. I've known many cases where the most beautiful and ethereal girls have shown next to no moral scruple— though, of course, gentlemen never wish to believe it of them."

I winced.

" And then there was the tennis racquet," continued Miss Marple.

" The tennis racquet ? "

" Yes, the one Mrs. Price Ridley's Clara saw lying on the grass by the Vicarage gate. That looked as though Mr. Dennis had got back earlier from his tennis party than he said. Boys of sixteen are so very susceptible and so very unbalanced. Whatever the motive—for Lettice's sake or for yours, it was a possibility. And then, of course, there was poor Mr. Hawes and you—not both of you naturally— but alternatively, as the lawyers say."

" Me ? " I exclaimed in lively astonishment.

" Well, yes. I do apologise—and indeed I never really thought—but there was the question of these disappearing sums of money. Either you or Mr. Hawes must be guilty, and Mrs. Price Ridley was going about everywhere hinting that you were the person in fault— principally because you objected so vigorously to any kind of inquiry into the matter. Of course, I myself was always convinced it was Mr. Hawes—he reminded me so much of that unfortunate organist I mentioned ; but all the same one couldn't be absolutely *sure*——"

" Human nature being what it is," I ended grimly.

" Exactly. And then, of course, there was dear Griselda."

" But Mrs. Clement was completely out of it," interrupted Melchett. " She returned by the 6.50 train."

" That's what she *said*," retorted Miss Marple. " One

should never go by what people say. The 6.50 was half an hour late that night. But at a quarter-past seven I saw her with my own eyes starting for Old Hall. So it followed that she must have come by the earlier train. Indeed she was seen ; but perhaps you know that ? "

She looked at me inquiringly.

Some magnetism in her glance impelled me to hold out the last anonymous letter, the one I had opened so short a time ago. It set out in detail that Griselda had been seen leaving Lawrence Redding's cottage by the back window at twenty-past six on the fatal day.

I said nothing then or at any time of the dreadful suspicion that had for one moment assailed my mind. I had seen it in nightmare terms—a past intrigue between Lawrence and Griselda, the knowledge of it coming to Protheroe's ears, his decision to make me acquainted with the facts—and Griselda, desperate, stealing the pistol and silencing Protheroe. As I say—a nightmare only—but invested for a few long minutes with a dreadful appearance of reality.

I don't know whether Miss Marple had any inkling of all this. Very probably she had. Few things are hidden from her.

She handed me back the note with a little nod.

" That's been all over the village," she said. " And it did look rather suspicious, didn't it ? Especially with Mrs. Archer swearing at the inquest that the pistol was still in the cottage when she left at midday."

She paused a minute and then went on.

" But I'm wandering terribly from the point. What I want to say—and I believe it my duty—is to put my own explanation of the mystery before you. If you don't believe it—well, I shall have done my best. Even as it is, my wish to be quite sure before I spoke may have cost poor Mr. Hawes his life."

Again she paused, and when she resumed, her voice held a different note. It was less apologetic, more decided.

" This is my own explanation of the facts. By

Thursday afternoon the crime had been fully planned down to the smallest detail. Lawrence Redding first called on the vicar, knowing him to be out. He had with him the pistol which he concealed in that pot in the stand by the window. When the vicar came in, Lawrence explained his visit by a statement that he had made up his mind to go away. At five-thirty, Lawrence Redding telephoned from the North Lodge to the vicar, adopting a woman's voice (you remember what a good amateur actor he was).

" Mrs. Protheroe and her husband had just started for the village. And—a very curious thing (though no one happened to think of it that way)—Mrs. Protheroe took no hand-bag with her. Really a *most* unusual thing for a woman to do. Just before twenty-past six she passes my garden and stops and speaks, so as to give me every opportunity of noticing that she has no weapon with her and also that is quite her normal self. They realised, you see, that I am a noticing kind of person. She disappears round the corner of the house to the study window. The poor colonel is sitting at the desk writing his letter to you. He is deaf as we all know. She takes the pistol from the bowl where it is waiting for her, comes up behind him and shoots him through the head, throws down the pistol and is out again like a flash, and going down the garden to the studio. Nearly any one would swear that there couldn't have been time ! "

" But the shot ? " objected the colonel. " You didn't hear the shot ? "

" There is, I believe, an invention called a Maxim silencer. So I gather from detective stories. I wonder if, possibly, the sneeze that the maid, Clara, heard might have actually been the shot ? But no matter. Mrs. Protheroe is met at the studio by Mr. Redding. They go in together—and, human nature being what is is, I'm afraid they realise that I shan't leave the garden till they come out again ! "

I had never liked Miss Marple better than at this

moment, with her humorous perception of her own weakness.

"When they do come out, their demeanour is gay and natural. And there, in reality, they make a mistake. Because if they had really said good-bye to each other, as they pretended, they would have looked very different. But you see, that was their weak point. They simply *dare* not appear upset in any way. For the next ten minutes they are careful to provide themselves with what is called an alibi, I believe. Finally Mr. Redding goes to the Vicarage, leaving it as late as he dares. He probably saw you on the footpath from far away and was able to time matters nicely. He picks up the pistol and the silencer, leaves the forged letter with the time on it written in a different ink and apparently in a different handwriting. When the forgery is discovered it will look like a clumsy attempt to incriminate Anne Protheroe.

"But when he leaves the letter, he finds the one actually written by Colonel Protheroe—something quite unexpected. And being a very intelligent young man, and seeing that this letter may come in very useful to him, he takes it away with him. He alters the hands of the clock to the same time as the letter—knowing that it is always kept a quarter of an hour fast. The same idea—attempt to throw suspicion on Mrs. Protheroe. Then he leaves, meeting you outside the gate, and acting the part of some one nearly distraught. As I say, he is really most intelligent. What would a murderer who had committed a crime try to do ? Behave naturally, of course. So that is just what Mr. Redding does not do. He gets rid of the silencer, but marches into the police station with the pistol and makes a perfectly ridiculous self-accusation which takes everybody in."

There was something fascinating in Miss Marple's resumé of the case. She spoke with such certainty that we both felt that in this way and in no other could the crime have been committed.

"What about the shot heard in the wood ? " I asked

" Was that the coincidence to which you were referring earlier this evening ? "

" Oh ! dear, no." Miss Marple shook her head briskly. " *That* wasn't a coincidence—very far from it. It was absolutely necessary that a shot should be heard—otherwise suspicion of Mrs. Protheroe might have continued. How Mr. Redding arranged it, I don't quite know. But I understand that picric acid explodes if you drop a weight on it, and you will remember, dear vicar, that you met Mr. Redding carrying a large stone just in the part of the wood where you picked up that crystal later. Gentlemen are so clever at arranging things—the stone suspended above the crystals and then a time fuse—or do I mean a slow match ? Something that would take about twenty minutes to burn through—so that the explosion would come about 6.30 when he and Mrs. Protheroe had come out of the studio and were in full view. A very safe device because what would there be to find afterwards—only a big stone ! But even that he tried to remove—when you came upon him."

" I believe you are right," I exclaimed, remembering the start of surprise Lawrence had given on seeing me that day. It had seemed natural enough at the time, but now. . . .

Miss Marple seemed to read my thoughts, for she nodded her head shrewdly.

" Yes," she said, " it must have been a very nasty shock for him to come across you just then. But he turned it off very well—pretending he was bringing it to me for my rock gardens. Only——" Miss Marple became suddenly very emphatic. " *It was the wrong sort of stone for my rock gardens!* And that put me on the right track ! "

All this time Colonel Melchett had sat like a man in a trance. Now he showed signs of coming to. He snorted once or twice, blew his nose in a bewildered fashion, and said :

" Upon my word ! Well, upon my word ! "

Beyond that, he did not commit himself. I think

that he, like myself, was impressed with the logical certainty of Miss Marple's conclusions. But for the moment he was not willing to admit it.

Instead, he stretched out a hand, picked up the crumpled letter and barked out :

" All very well. But how do you account for this fellow Hawes ! Why, he actually rang up and confessed."

" Yes, that was what was so providential. The vicar's sermon, doubtless. You know, dear Mr. Clement, you really preached a most remarkable sermon. It must have affected Mr. Hawes deeply. He could bear it no longer, and felt he must confess—about the misappropriations of the church funds."

" What ? "

" Yes—and that, under Providence, is what has saved his life. (For I hope and trust it *is* saved. Dr. Haydock is so clever.) As I see the matter, Mr. Redding kept this letter (a risky thing to do, but I expect he hid it in some safe place) and waited till he found out for certain to whom it referred. He soon made quite sure that it was Mr. Hawes. I understand he came back here with Mr. Hawes last night and spent a long time with him. I suspect that he then substituted a cachet of his own for one of Mr. Hawes, and slipped this letter in the pocket of Mr. Hawes' dressing gown. The poor young man would swallow the fatal cachet in all innocence—after his death his things would be gone through and the letter found and every one would jump to the conclusion that he had shot Colonel Protheroe and taken his own life out of remorse. I rather fancy Mr. Hawes must have found that letter to-night just after taking the fatal cachet. In his disordered state, it must have seemed like some thing supernatural, and, coming on top of the vicar's sermon, it must have impelled him to confess the whole thing."

" Upon my word," said Colonel Melchett. " Upon my word ! *Most* extraordinary ! I—I—don't believe a word of it."

He had never made a statement that sounded more

unconvincing. It must have sounded so in his own ears for he went on :

" And can you explain the other telephone call—the one from Mr. Redding's cottage to Mrs. Price Ridley ? "

" Ah ! " said Miss Marple. " That is what I call the coincidence. Dear Griselda sent that call—she and Mr. Dennis between them, I fancy. They had heard the rumours Mrs. Price Ridley was circulating about the vicar, and they thought of this (perhaps rather childish) way of silencing her. The coincidence lies in the fact that the call should have been put through at exactly the same time as the fake shot from the wood. It led one to believe that the two must be connected."

I suddenly remembered how every one who spoke of that shot had described it as " different " from the usual shot. They had been right. Yet how hard to explain just in what way the " difference " of the shot consisted.

Colonel Melchett cleared his throat.

" Your solution is a very plausible one, Miss Marple," he said. " But you will allow me to point out that there is not a shadow of proof."

" I know," said Miss Marple. " But you believe it to be true, don't you ? "

There was a pause, then the colonel said almost reluctantly :

" Yes, I do. Dash it all, it's the only way the thing could have happened. But there's no proof—not an atom."

Miss Marple coughed.

" That is why I thought perhaps—under the cir- cumstances——"

" Yes ? "

" A little trap might be permissible."

# CHAPTER XXXI

COLONEL MELCHETT and I both stared at her.

"A trap? What kind of a trap?"

Miss Marple was a little diffident, but it was clear that she had a plan fully outlined.

"Supposing Mr. Redding were to be rung up on the telephone and warned."

Colonel Melchett smiled.

"'All is discovered. Fly!' That's an old wheeze, Miss Marple. Not that it isn't often successful! But I think in this case young Redding is too downy a bird to be caught that way."

"It would have to be something specific. I quite realise that," said Miss Marple. "I would suggest— this is just a mere suggestion—that the warning should come from somebody who is known to have rather unusual views on these matters. Dr. Haydock's conversation would lead any one to suppose that he might view such a thing as murder from an unusual angle. If he were to hint that somebody—Mrs. Sadler—or one of her children—had actually happened to see the transposing of the cachets—well, of course, if Mr. Redding is an innocent man, that statement will mean nothing to him, but if he isn't——"

"If he isn't?"

"Well, he might just possibly do something foolish."

"And deliver himself into our hands. It's possible. Very ingenious, Miss Marple. But will Haydock stand for it? As you say his views——"

Miss Marple interrupted him brightly.

"Oh! but that's theory! So very different from practice, isn't it? But anyway here he is, so we can ask him."

247

Haydock was, I think, rather astonished to find Miss Marple with us. He looked tired and haggard.

" It's been a near thing," he said. " A very near thing. But he's going to pull through. It's a doctor's business to save his patient and I've saved him, but I'd have been just as glad if I hadn't pulled it off."

" You may think differently," said Melchett, " when you have heard what we have to tell you."

And briefly and succinctly, he put Miss Marple's theory of the crime before the doctor, ending up with her final suggestion.

We were then privileged to see exactly what Miss Marple meant by the difference between theory and practice.

Haydock's views appeared to have undergone complete transformation. He would, I think, have liked Lawrence Redding's head on a charger. It was not, I imagine, the murder of Colonel Protheroe that so stirred his rancour. It was the assault on the unlucky Hawes.

" The damned scoundrel," said Haydock. " The damned scoundrel ! That poor devil Hawes. He's got a mother and a sister too. The stigma of being the mother and sister of a murderer would have rested on them for life, and think of their mental anguish. Of all the cowardly dastardly tricks ! "

For sheer primitive rage, commend me to a thorough-going humanitarian when you get him well roused.

" If this thing's true," he said, " you can count on me. The fellow's not fit to live. A defenceless chap like Hawes."

A lame dog of any kind can always count on Haydock's sympathy.

He was eagerly arranging details with Melchett when Miss Marple rose and I insisted on seeing her home.

" It is most kind of you, Mr. Clement," said Miss Marple, as we walked down the deserted street. " Dear me, past twelve o'clock. I hope Raymond has gone to bed and not waited up."

" He should have accompanied you," I said.

" I didn't let him know I was going," said Miss Marple.

I smiled suddenly as I remembered Raymond West's subtle phsychological analysis of the crime.

" If your theory turns out to be the truth—which I for one do not doubt for a minute," I said, " you will have a very good score over your nephew."

Miss Marple smiled also—an indulgent smile.

" I remember a saying of my Great Aunt Fanny's. I was sixteen at the time and thought it particularly foolish."

" Yes ? " I inquired.

" She used to say : ' The young people think the old people are fools ; but the old people *know* the young people are fools ! ' "

# CHAPTER XXXII

THERE is little more to be told. Miss Marple's plan succeeded. Lawrence Redding was not an innocent man, and the hint of a witness of the change of capsule did indeed cause him to do " something foolish." Such is the power of an evil conscience.

He was, of course, peculiarly placed. His first impulse, I imagine, must have been to cut and run. But there was his accomplice to consider. He could not leave without getting word to her, and he dared not wait till morning. So he went up to Old Hall that night—and two of Colonel Melchett's most efficient officers followed him. He threw gravel at Anne Protheroe's window, aroused her, and an urgent whisper brought her down to speak with him. Doubtless they felt safer outside than in— with the possibility of Lettice waking. But as it happened, the two police officers were able to overhear their conversation in full. It left the matter in no doubt. Miss Marple had been right on every count.

The trial of Lawrence Redding and Anne Protheroe is a matter of public knowledge. I do not propose to go into it. I will only mention that great credit was reflected upon Inspector Slack, whose zeal and intelligence had resulted in the criminals being brought to justice. Naturally, nothing was said of Miss Marple's share in the business. She herself would have been horrified at the thought of such a thing.

Lettice came to see me just before the trial took place She drifted through my study window, wraith-like as ever. She told me then that she had all along been convinced of her stepmother's complicity. The loss of the yellow beret had been a mere excuse for searching the study. She hoped against hope that she might find something the police had overlooked.

" You see," she said in her dreamy voice, " they didn't hate her like I did. And hate makes things easier for you."

Disappointed in the result of her search, she had deliberately dropped Anne's ear-ring by the desk.

" Since I *knew* she had done it, what did it matter ? One way was as good as another. She *had* killed him."

I sighed a little. There are always some things that Lettice will never see. In some respects she is morally colour blind.

" What are you going to do, Lettice ? " I asked.

" When—when it's all over, I am going abroad." She hesitated and then went on. " I am going abroad with my mother."

I looked up, startled.

She nodded.

" Didn't you ever guess ? Mrs Lestrange is my mother. She is—is dying, you know. She wanted to see me and so she came down here under an assumed name. Dr. Haydock helped her. He's a very old friend of hers— he was keen about her once—you can see that ! In a way, he still is. Men always went batty about mother, I believe. She's awfully attractive even now. Anyway, Dr. Haydock did everything he could to help her. She didn't come down here under her own name because of the disgusting way people talk and gossip. She went to see father that night and told him she was dying and had a great longing to see something of me. Father was a beast. He said she'd forfeited all claim, and that I thought she was dead—as though I had ever swallowed that story ! Men like father never see an inch before their noses ! "

" But mother is not the sort to give in. She thought it only decent to go to father first, but when he turned her down so brutally she sent a note to me, and I arranged to leave the tennis party early and meet her at the end of the footpath at a quarter-past six. We just had a hurried meeting and arranged when to meet again. We left each other before half-past six. After-

wards I was terrified that she would be suspected of
having killed father. After all, she *had* got a grudge
against him. That's why I got hold of that old picture
of her up in the attic and slashed it about. I was afraid
the police might go nosing about and get hold of it and
recognise it. Dr. Haydock was frightened too. Sometimes, I believe, he really thought she had done it !
Mother is rather a—desperate kind of person. She doesn't
count consequences."

She paused.

" It's queer. She and I belong to each other. Father
and I didn't. But mother—well, anyway, I'm going
abroad with her. I shall be with her till—till the
end. . . ."

She got up and I took her hand.

" God bless you both," I said. " Some day, I hope,
there is a lot of happiness coming to you, Lettice."

" There should be," she said, with an attempt at a
laugh. " There hasn't been much so far—has there ?
Oh, well, I don't suppose it matters. Good-bye, Mr.
Clement. You've been frightfully decent to me always—
you and Griselda."

Griselda !

I had to own to her how terribly the anonymous letter
had upset me, and first she laughed, and then solemnly
read me a lecture.

" However," she added, " I'm going to be very sober
and God-fearing in future—quite like the Pilgrim
fathers."

I did not see Griselda in the rôle of a Pilgrim father.

She went on :

" You see, Len, I have a steadying influence coming
into my life. It's coming into your life, too, but in your
case it will be a kind of—of rejuvenating one—at least,
I hope so ! You can't call me a dear child half so much
when we have a real child of our own. And, Len, I've
decided that now I'm going to be a real ' wife and
mother ' (as they say in books), I must be a housekeeper too. I've bought two books on Household

Management and one on Mother Love, and if that doesn't turn me out a pattern I don't know what will! They are all simply screamingly funny—not intentionally, you know. Especially the one about bringing up children."

"You haven't bought a book on How to Treat a Husband, have you?" I asked, with sudden apprehension as I drew her to me.

"I don't need to," said Griselda. "I'm a very good wife. I love you dearly. What more do you want?"

"Nothing," I said.

"Could you say, just for once, that you love me madly?"

"Griselda," I said— "I adore you! I worship you! I am wildly, hopelessly and quite unclerically crazy about you!"

My wife gave a deep and contented sigh.

Then she drew away suddenly.

"Bother! Here's Miss Marple coming. Don't let her suspect, will you? I don't want every one offering me cushions and urging me to put my feet up. Tell her I've gone down to the golf links. That will put her off the scent—and it's quite true because I left my yellow pullover there and I want it."

Miss Marple came to the window, halted apologetically, and asked for Griselda.

"Griselda," I said, "has gone to the golf links."

An expression of concern leaped into Miss Marple's eyes.

"Oh, but surely," she said, "that is most unwise—just now."

And then in a nice, old-fashioned, lady-like, maiden-lady way, she blushed.

And to cover the moment's confusion, we talked hurriedly of the Protheroe case, and of "Dr. Stone," who had turned out to be a well-known cracksman with several different aliases. Miss Cram, by the way, had been cleared of all complicity. She had at last admitted taking the suit-case to the wood, but had done so in all

good faith, Dr. Stone having told her that he feared the
rivalry of other archæologists who would not stick at
burglarly to gain their object of discrediting his theories.
The girl apparently swallowed this not very plausible
story. She is now, according to the village, looking out
for a more genuine article in the line of an elderly
bachelor requiring a secretary.

As we talked, I wondered very much how Miss Marple
had discovered our latest secret. But presently, in a
discreet fashion, Miss Marple herself supplied me with
a clue.

" I hope dear Griselda is not overdoing it," she
murmured, and after a discreet pause. " I was in the
bookshop in Much Benham yesterday——"

Poor Griselda—that book on Mother Love has been
her undoing !

" I wonder, Miss Marple," I said suddenly, " if you
were to commit a murder whether you would ever be
found out."

" What a terrible idea," said Miss Marple, shocked.
" I hope I could never do such a wicked thing."

" But human nature being what it is," I murmured.

Miss Marple acknowledged the hit with a pretty old
ladyish laugh.

" How naughty of you, Mr. Clement." She rose.
" But naturally you are in good spirits."

She paused by the window.

" My love to dear Griselda—and tell her—that any
little secret is quite safe with me."

Really Miss Marple is rather a dear. . . .

LONDON AND GLASGOW : COLLINS' CLEAR-TYPE PRESS.

## FREEMAN WILLS CROFTS

# SIR JOHN MAGILL'S LAST JOURNEY

SIR JOHN MAGILL, a well-known figure in the public life of Ulster, is coming to Ireland via the Stranraer-Larne route. He never reaches his destination. No trace of the missing man can be discovered. What strange fate has befallen Sir John Magill? Inspector French is called in, and admits that it is his most baffling case. With that admission we feel sure all admirers of Inspector French will agree, and they will agree, and they will follow eagerly the various stages in the unravelling of this the greatest of Inspector French mysteries.

## NANCY BARR MAVITY

# THE BODY ON THE FLOOR

" SUICIDE," said the Chief of Police, and the Coroner agreed with him. So did the great criminological expert engaged by the defence. But Peter Piper, the whistling reporter whose psychological hunches had solved the Tule Marsh murder case, thought differently. The woman who lay dead on the floor could have killed herself —according to the evidence she probably did—but would a woman planning suicide send her dress to the cleaner's? The answer revealed one of the strangest scandals and most amazing crimes of the century.

## A. FIELDING
Author of *The Craig Poisoning Case*, etc.

# THE
# WEDDING CHEST MYSTERY

WHAT purports to be a Chinese wedding chest is given by Major Hardy to a Mr. and Mrs. Armstrong for their Chinese suite. A private inquiry agent has been requested to meet Mr. Armstrong at his house at an afternoon reception given the day on which the chest arrives, and the place where the latter stands has been appointed for the rendezvous. When opened, the chest contains, instead of some dwarf trees which were to be distributed among the guests, the dead body of Mr. Armstrong. How it came to be there, what really happened to Armstrong, and why it happened, form the puzzle which Chief Inspector Pointer of Scotland Yard and the private inquiry agent solve together.

## G. D. H. & M. COLE
Author of *Burglars in Bucks*, etc.

# THE
# CORPSE IN CANONICALS

SUPERINTENDENT WILSON thought he was in a cul de sac! Having been called to Middlebury to investigate the disappearance of Elinor Symonds' necklace, he arrives only to find that it has been returned as mysteriously as it went. He goes back to Scotland Yard, but in a few days he sees that his cul de sac is rather an avenue leading to one of the most amazing murders in his career. The body of a clergyman is found in the garden of the chief constable's house, and the police are faced not with the problem of finding a clue, so much as with finding the right clue out of the many provided— a revolver with all its chambers full, a small bottle of poison, a chloroform-soaked handkerchief, a cigar stump and a visiting card! *The Corpse in Canonicals* is a most ingenious piece of crime fiction with that grip on the reader that ingenuity of plot alone cannot produce. G. D. H. and M. Cole are adding to that power which made successes of *Poison in the Garden Suburb* and *Burglars in Bucks*.